LIE
DOWN WITH THE
DEVIL

**Center Point
Large Print**

**This Large Print Book carries the
Seal of Approval of N.A.V.H.**

LIE
DOWN WITH THE
DEVIL

Linda Barnes

CENTER POINT PUBLISHING
THORNDIKE, MAINE

This Center Point Large Print edition
is published in the year 2008 by arrangement with
St. Martin's Press.

Copyright © 2008 by Linda Appelblatt Barnes.

The text of this Large Print edition is unabridged. In other
aspects, this book may vary from the original edition.
Printed in the United States of America.
Set in 16-point Times New Roman type.

ISBN: 978-1-60285-263-1

Library of Congress Cataloging-in-Publication Data

Barnes, Linda.
    Lie down with the devil / Linda Barnes.--Center Point large print ed.
        p. cm.
    ISBN: 978-1-60285-263-1 (lib. bdg. : alk. paper)
        1. Carlyle, Carlotta (Fictitious character)--Fiction.
    2. Women private investigators--Massachusetts--Boston--Fiction. 3. Boston (Mass.)--Fiction.
    4. Murder--Investigation--Fiction. 5. Large type books. I. Title.

PS3552.A682L54 2008b
813'.54--dc22

2008019826

For Luis Gabriel

Acknowledgments

The author would like to thank many of the usual suspects, including Richard Barnes, Sam Barnes, Gina Maccoby, Kelley Ragland, Matt Martz, and Sarah Smith. She would also like to thank Kate Mattes for book signings, Christmas parties, and moral support.

PART ONE

CHAPTER 1

When my fare hauled himself out of the cab near Uphams Corner, I took it as a sign, but face it, even if the fat man's destination had been fifty miles from my goal, I'd have found another convenient omen. I'd made the decision late last night. I needed to have it out with Mooney.

The rump end of a minor hangover beat a tattoo in my left temple, and I knew that if I didn't take action, I'd stay home tonight, sprawled on the sofa like a deadbeat, watching old movie reruns, pouring too many Rolling Rocks down my throat. Again. Since it's my considered opinion that it's better to do anything than nothing, I was determined to find out why Mooney wasn't answering his phone, why he hadn't replied to my increasingly urgent messages. Mooney's a guy you can count on, reliable as taxes, so his unresponsiveness was alarming.

I buttoned my sweater closer to my chin and tried for more warmth from the heater. It gave a gasp and a shudder. Tepid air trickled out near my icy feet.

I didn't want to track Moon down at Headquarters. I had mixed feelings about my former place of employment, plus there was the parking. Fact: Parking at the new Crosstown site is laughable, nonexistent and maddening, the subject of lawsuits by irritated officers. Nor did I relish the thought of hanging out at Moon's apartment building, spooking his neighbors. So I took advantage of my drop-off point to head farther south, swerving over the Neponset River Bridge to Quincy Shore Drive. Stopped at a traffic light, I squinted into the rearview mirror, ran a hand through my disheveled hair, then cupped it over my mouth and smelled my breath. I hadn't had a drink in hours, but it seemed like the smell of beer was seeping from my pores.

I popped the center armrest console, hoping for breath mints, and found nothing but crumpled gas receipts and wadded tissues. If it had been my car, instead of one of Gloria's crummy Fords, breath mints would have nested sweetly among the tapes, CDs, tampons, and apple cores, but my vintage red Toyota was dead at the bottom of a New Hampshire ravine and I still hadn't purchased a replacement. I'd planned to do it, made a list of possibilities, but a mad dash out of the country had put it and everything else in my life on hold.

Gloria's voice chimed over the two-way, asking any available cab to do a pickup in Maverick Square. I switched her off with barely a flicker of guilt. East Squantum Street changed its name to Dorchester Street without so much as a by-your-leave, and then the Long Island Causeway stretched its skinny neck out to Moon Island, home of the Boston Police Department Firing Range.

When I drive, I listen to music. Maybe it was

because the cab didn't have a working radio that my thoughts strayed, replaying the conversation I'd had last night just before the six-pack beckoned from the refrigerator.

Sam Gianelli, phoning from who knows where. When I'd asked his location, I got silence, meaningful silence, a warning silence I resented.

"You think I wouldn't know if my line was tapped?" I'd said.

I'd heard him sigh, but he hadn't answered. And yes, it had been a stupid thing to say. Maybe they've got some new gizmo I can't test for; maybe they're one step ahead. So I didn't press for his location, but I'd tried to press on other things, like when he was coming back to the States, like what I could do to unravel the mess that was keeping him out of the country.

That had gotten a response, a quick one.

"Nothing, Carlotta. That's exactly why I called. I mean, I called to see how you're doing, how Paolina's doing, too, but I want it clear. Don't get involved. Don't mess with this."

Hell with that, I'd thought; I was involved.

"So what are you saying, Sam? Good-bye? Are we going to limit the relationship to phone sex from now on?"

"Don't do anything."

"But, Sam—"

"I'll call again."

A click. A hang-up. A dead end. So I'd drunk my

11

beers and decided that nothing was harder than doing nothing. Remembering, I steered one-handed through heavy traffic, brooding and yanking at a strand of hair. Wherever Sam was, I decided, it was probably warmer than Boston. Most likely piles of snow hadn't turned brown and muddy, with a top layer of dingy gray. I was only planning to ask Mooney a few questions, and asking wasn't doing. If Sam inquired, I could still say I'd done nothing, respected his wishes, foolish as they were.

Mooney was my old boss at the BPD. I'd worked for him—with him—for six years before I turned in the badge and went private. I was the restless one, the woman in a hurry, the one who needed change to survive. He was the creature of habit and I was counting on that habit now: The last Thursday of the month, first thing in the morning, Mooney shot at the Moon Island range.

In the 1700s, Boston's Harbor Islands served as military outposts to protect the then-bustling seaport. Today, most of them form a chain of national parks. Some, like Bumpkin, Hangman, Snake, Nixes Mate, and Worlds End, in addition to the more mundanely named Thompson and Spectacle, are open to the public. Moon Island, a bump connecting Long Island to the mainland, is more a peninsula than an island, thanks to the causeway. There's a firefighter training facility at the eastern end, right before the Long Island Bridge, and a nineteenth-century wastewater treatment plant. The firing range is tucked in between the two.

Pulling into a space in the level gravel lot, I opened the cab door and sniffed an unexpectedly salty breeze. Living in Cambridge, the way I do, you can almost forget the proximity of the Atlantic. I inhaled the sea air gratefully. There's something cleansing about the ocean, all that green water licking the shore, endless and timeless, soothing and hypnotizing. It would be here forever. It didn't care.

I sucked in a deep breath, trying to summon some of the Atlantic's cool indifference for my upcoming encounter, attempting to submerge my feelings, keep them hidden like the secret reefs and rocks beneath the surface of the sea. I suspected that my ex-boss had gotten every single one of my messages, that he'd decided to ignore them because he didn't want to part with information. I needed to make him understand that he needed to answer my questions. I needed to stay calm in spite of emotion that roiled like the great white waves breaking near the shore.

I slammed the car door harder than I intended to, and the noise reverberated. My parka, too heavy to drive in, was stowed in the trunk. I pulled it on and zipped it shut against the wind.

Since I was no longer a member of the force, I technically had no right to pass through the small white bungalow and visit the range. I didn't think anyone would bother to stop me since members of the general public, while not welcome to shoot at will, are required to make the occasional appearance. The Moon Island range is where citizens go to get their gun licenses renewed. I could always lie and give that as my purpose, but I didn't think I'd need deception. A smile, a wave, a confident walk, they fool even cops.

My luck was in; I didn't need a cover story because I knew the guy on the desk.

"Mooney," I said, coming in the front door, continuing out the rear.

He was in the third lane, wearing dark glasses and ear protectors, firing, spent cartridges flying from his Glock. He didn't notice me and that was fine.

For half a second I was sorry I hadn't brought my Smith. I like to shoot; I like the smell of the range. I'm not crazy about target shooting; I don't get off on it the way some of the guys used to—I am the best and all that competitive malarkey. I'm good. I've got a good eye for spotting a volleyball on a court, a good eye for a target, but I know target is just a sport, like volleyball. It's not street.

I watched Mooney out of the corner of one eye. I took his wardrobe for granted, the navy pants and light blue shirt that might as well be a uniform. I knew his routine: 120 rounds, three times the limit carried on the street, fourteen in the gun and two thirteen-round clips. Moon's not a street cop anymore, but he talks about going back, says he'd rather be moved down the ranks than up. Lots of guys say that, talk about the good old days, but I believe Mooney. He's good at working the streets, better at streets than bureaucracy, and he excels at bureaucracy. When the suits bring pressure to bear, he tells the uncomfortable truth, ready to step down to the detective bureau or walk a beat and wear the uniform again. So far he's kept his position as head of Homicide, but he walks a fine line. I thought I saw him notice me, and I wondered what my presence would do for his numbers.

"Hey, I figured that was you."

The instructor approached; what was his name? Harry, right, Harry something. A nice broad-beamed guy who'd lost his partner in a shootout and decided to teach other cops how and, more important, when to use their weapons. I smiled and nodded. What are you supposed to say when someone says, "I figured that was you"?

"Look what I got," he said with a face-splitting grin, displaying a gun case big enough to house a major hunk of artillery. "H-K MK23. Special Ops gun. Wanna give it a try?"

I gave a less-than-enthusiastic shrug.

"Well, okay, then. Forget it. Navy SEAL buddy of mine dropped it off. Guys say it's got too much kick for a woman."

"Stop prodding, Harry." His smile got even broader when I said his name.

"You're just waiting, right?"

"Right."

"You need to reup for anything?"

"No." I don't have to keep my numbers up the way Mooney does.

"Got more women now. Had to put in another bath-room."

When I used to go to the range, the toilet was for the guys, and the women made do. That's the way it was when I was in the force and that's usually the way it is now, except everybody talks about how times have changed.

Harry removed the pistol from the case. "Pretty thing, isn't it? A lot of the SEALs want something smaller and lighter, but this is a stopper for sure. Forty-five ACPs and those'll sure drop a target faster than a nine. Double action. You can use the JHP bullets, too, the expandables."

I have about as much patience for gun talk as I do for wine talk. I like to shoot and I like to drink, but I don't practice either vocabulary.

"Pretty heavy, though."

He handed it to me, and I thought why the hell not? Mooney wouldn't duck out on me, now that he'd seen me. Harry handed over ear protectors and goggles.

Just like threading a needle, a cop friend named Jo Triola once told me, and we'd joyfully shared the secret giggles of the girly metaphor. You couldn't say that to any of the guys, that shooting a gun was like threading a needle. If it wasn't a sports metaphor, Jo and I had learned early on, better not say it at all. The concentration required to shoot well, to fire efficiently and effectively, shuts out the rest of the world. If I could continually manufacture tasks that required the same level of concentration as shooting, I wouldn't have to question Mooney, wouldn't need to talk to anyone, wouldn't have to face up to . . .

I got lost in the sound and the smell and the immediacy of the task at hand, and suddenly it was as clear as if it were happening all over again. Muscle memory can do that to you, I suppose, because the last time I'd fired a gun, not this gun, but a similarly heavy gun, an unfamiliar gun, and smelled the pungent tang of cordite, I'd heard the reports unfiltered by earmuffs. I'd been in South America, in Colombia, in Cartagena, and the scene had had nothing to do with orderly lanes and motionless paper targets. It had to do with revenge and hatred, with ensuring that my little sister walked out of the room alive. The sweat trickled down my back in spite of the cold and I could have shot forever, slapping magazine after magazine into the well, imagining the people I'd have liked to kill, trying not to imagine those I wished I could bring back from the dead. As fast as I could pump bullets into the target wasn't fast enough. I rammed another magazine home and repositioned my body and I wasn't standing in the lane at Moon Island anymore. I was in an airless second-floor room with thick whitewashed walls, smelling sweet florals and spring rain and cordite.

"Hey, what the hell? You okay?"

"What?"

"Keep it pointed downrange," Harry was yelling in my ear. "He's dead. You fucking shredded him."

"Sorry."

"What the hell!"

Eventually you run out of ammunition; that's what it comes down to. You're forced to go back to the daily routine, the one-foot-ahead-of-the-other stuff, the get-up-in-the-morning stuff. The confronting-your-old-boss-at-the-firing-range stuff.

Mooney was suddenly there, the way he is, solid and as unassuming as a man the size of a linebacker can be, his face concerned but wary. I caught a glint of gray in the brown hair near his right temple.

"I'll take care of this, Harry," he said.

The instructor glanced at him and then at me, turned and walked away, carrying the H-K and shaking his head.

"Carlotta."

"You meant to call me back, right?"

"If I'm gonna avoid you, I guess I'll need to change a few habits."

"I can find you anytime."

"You found me now."

"You know what I want."

"Forget about it, Carlotta."

"What do you mean, forget about it?"

"It's a secret indictment. Secret. They're called that for a reason."

"No warrant?"

"Not yet."

"Why? Why is the DA keeping it under wraps? Is it political?"

He shrugged.

"Mooney, it's murder."

"That's right."

"*Which* murder? Whose? Who the hell died? You can at least tell me that."

"Look, I can't talk to you. I can't be seen with you."

"You can't be seen with me? Why?"

He lowered his voice. "You know a fed named Dailey?"

"No."

"Gianelli know him?"

"How would I know?"

"You haven't told anybody that I gave Gianelli the heads-up?"

"I would never do that."

"Has anybody been following you around? You know, in an American-made sedan, gray or brown? You know the deal."

"No. What the—?"

"Just answer the question."

"I should answer your questions, but you won't answer mine? Look, Moon, if I don't even know what crime he's supposed to have committed, I can't do anything. I can't help—"

"Ask Gianelli."

"Sam doesn't want my help."

"Right, Carlotta. He doesn't want your help. You ever wonder why?"

"What's that supposed to mean?"

He licked his lower lip and for a moment I thought he was going to turn away without another word. He stared at the ground as he spoke, kept his voice even and uninflected. "I don't know, but it occurs to me that maybe Gianelli doesn't want you to find out what really happened. He may not want your help because there's no way you *can* help. He may say he didn't do it, but what I don't understand is why the hell you believe him. You know who he is, right? What he is? You know where he comes from. A man lives with that kind of shit since he's a boy—You tell me: How do you live with shit all around you and not get dirty?"

I stared at him, all the rational and convincing words I'd meant to use forgotten. I could hear the waves against the rocks and the *pom-pom-pom* of a silenced .22

"Look, I have to go," he said quickly. "I can't tell you anything. I never could."

"Mooney, I—"

"Don't ask me again. You know what I'm talking about, Carlotta. Isn't it time to admit it to yourself?"

I didn't say anything. I pressed my lips together and stared at the gravel until the individual stones melted into a solid band of gray.

"Hey, how's Paolina? Jeez, I'm sorry, Carlotta, I should have asked right off. I should have called you back, just to ask."

"Yeah," I said, swallowing an unexpected lump in my throat. "You should have."

CHAPTER 2

Az me lebt mit a teivel, vert men a teivel. Translated freely from my grandmother's native Yiddish: "He who lives with a devil becomes a devil."

Mooney's tirade struck home in more ways than he knew. It's not that I don't think about what Sam does for a living; it's that I *try* not to think about it. Because when I do think about Sam's line of work, when I ponder the Gianelli family's generations-long involvement in organized crime, I find myself recalling my grandmother and her proverbs, and wondering not only about Sam, but also about myself and the person I might become. If I do marry him, will I come to take his work for granted? Slough it off, forget about it, live with the devil and become the devil?

Wasn't there another saying, not a Yiddish one, but an English standard, that began "Lie down with the devil"? Lie down with the devil and what? I couldn't recall the tag end of the slogan. Maybe I just didn't want to.

When I flew to Bogotá to search for my little sister, I left clients in the lurch. Oh, I phoned them—or rather, I had Roz, my quasi-assistant, phone them to apologize, commiserate, and recommend other local investigators—but those clients were gone and they weren't coming back. When you ditch clients, word gets around: I was out of the loop and at least two of the lawyers who routinely shuttled clients my way were going to require major acts of contrition before they sent anyone again.

I drove a full shift—picking up fares in Southie and dropping them in Eastie, ferrying businessmen from the Four Seasons to Logan—because no matter how screwed up your life might be, bills manage to arrive on time, property tax payments fall due, and super-market checkout clerks want cash in exchange for the groceries. That's why I keep my hackney license up to date. Driving tides me over the tough times; if I drive, I don't have to accept ugly divorce cases or take on clients who strike me as con men at first glance. But the problem with cabbing—aside from meager pay, lousy hours, expensive gas, crummy traffic, and bad tips—is that it takes your time, not your concentration. You can drive and let your thoughts roam, let them idle and sink into crevices of anxiety. No doubt about it: Other people's problems are better than your own, which was why I was nowhere near as irritated at Roz for setting up an unauthorized appointment with a prospective client as I might have been.

Roz used to be my tenant, pure and simple. Then she became my housekeeper. Now she functions as a sort of all-purpose assistant, although not the kind who reliably does as she is told. What with the fallout from Colombia, I had told her I wasn't yet ready to get back on the job. This morning, when she'd sprung her friend-of-a-friend, please-do-it routine on me, I hadn't been eager, but who knows, maybe it was the fact that

I had a solid shot with a client tonight that had given me the momentum to face Mooney this morning.

What had I expected? From Mooney, I don't know, but something more than the nothing I got. From the client? If I could have ordered off a fantasy menu, I'd have picked a Brioni-clad corporate client offering reliable, well-paid work. Maybe a low-level manager was trying to pull off a little financial embezzlement. I could investigate him and his methods, or possibly find out how the prototype of some new product wound up in a competitor's showroom.

Instead, at 7:37 on Thursday evening, I got Jessica Franklin.

She was young. She was pretty, with a sweet round face and dark glossy hair so straight it could have been scalped off an Asian girl. Her shoes were cheap teetery heels, and we'd barely gotten past the initial formalities—name, address, and occupation—when she burst into tears.

When people say "burst into tears," they usually mean she started to cry or a tear trickled down her cheek, but that's not what I mean at all. This was bursting, the way a balloon bursts: one second there, next second *pop.* One second sunshine, next second downpour, cloudburst. Jessica Franklin's sweet face screwed up into a mask of tragedy and she started crying with the desperate abandon of a baby, with unselfconscious sobs and snot and a reckless wail.

"Hey," I said, "it can't be that bad."

Jessica wailed.

"Why don't you tell me about it?"

She wailed harder, picking up her purse and rummaging in its deep interior. I passed her some tissues, thanking God there were tissues, a whole box of them right where they should be on my desk, but she ignored them and kept rummaging and then, with the waterworks at flood level, she lost her grip on the handbag. I reached out to grab it, but the handle eluded my grasp, and I succeeded only in speeding its cartwheel descent.

Loose change, keys, and jewelry clanged to the floor. A deck of cards plopped onto a pile of Kleenex along with a small stapler, a cell phone, a bottle of scarlet nail polish, a makeup brush, a hairbrush, a pack of cigarettes, matchbooks, a toothbrush, a cascade of Band-Aids, pens and pencils, rubber bands, and a red bandanna.

"God," the woman said, jumping to her feet and squatting, then kneeling awkwardly on the bare floorboards. "I'm so damned clumsy." Her hands scrabbled at the pile of junk and fanned the playing cards across the floor. "Oh, shit. Hell, no, please, don't help me. Please. We'll start over in a minute. I'll shake hands and stop crying, really. Don't help me, please, it's bad enough already. I feel like some kind of animal—out of control, like a puppy dog crawling on the floor."

She was heavier than I'd thought at first glance, her knees dimpled and soft. She wore a short dark skirt and a tweedy heather-colored sweater. Her face was heart-shaped and her gentle eyes a deep soft brown.

24

She looked too young to have the kind of troubles that would lead her to hire a private investigator, but the tears said otherwise.

She worked quickly and methodically, dumping things back in the purse, scooping the cards with skillful fingers, giving them an expert shuffle before securing them with a rubber band. While she worked she tried to regain control, and she seemed to be calming down until she came across a large envelope. As she touched it, her eyes welled, and the moaning sobs began anew.

Wordlessly, she passed me the envelope. At her nod, I opened it, then blinked in surprise: a wedding invitation.

The pale unaddressed envelope was lined with silver moiré paper; the enclosed card featured modern script. When I read the names, I glanced quickly at my appointment calendar, and yes, the young woman crouched on the floor, holding a wad of tissues to her streaming eyes, was none other than the bride-to-be. A thin silver band circled the ring finger of her left hand.

"Come on," I said, helping her off the floor. "Sit down. Talk to me." I didn't think she'd handed over the invitation so I could congratulate her on the upcoming nuptials.

She collapsed in the chair. Speech still beyond her power, she picked up her purse and started rummaging again. I thought we were in for a repeat performance and braced myself for a second shower of personal items. She made a noise somewhere between a croak and a sob, then gave up and yanked a slip of paper from either a well-concealed pocket or the waistband of her skirt.

This one was cheap copy paper, folded roughly in eighths. I unfolded it.

HE WON'T BE SLEEPING HOME FRIDAY NIGHT. HE'LL BE SLEEPING WITH HER.

A fresh paroxysm of weeping accompanied my reading. I doled out more tissues, hoping she'd eventually be able to form words and sentences.

"This is really embarrassing," she mumbled, ducking her head.

"Everybody makes mistakes," I said.

"Yeah, right."

"Some bigger than others." When it comes to mistakes, I know what I'm talking about. Maybe she heard it in my voice, because she stopped sniffling.

"I mean, what do you think of a girl who gets totally involved with a guy, just swept right off her feet, and she doesn't even know who he is?"

What did I think? When I'd met Sam Gianelli, I'd assumed he was simply a businessman, owner of the cab company I drove for part-time. His mob connections, which—had I been a local, Boston born and bred—I might have inferred from his last name, were far less apparent than his physical charms.

I said, "I'd think she had a lot of company, Miss Franklin."

"Call me Jessie. Please."

Jessie Franklin had a killer dimple that dotted the

right side of her face. She must have been an adorable child. Not quite as adorable as my adopted little sister, Paolina, but close.

"So congratulations," I said, checking the date on the invitation. "At least you haven't married him yet."

She stared at her shoes. "I don't know what to do. Time's running out."

I glanced at the card again. The wedding was less than two weeks away.

"You have no idea how much fuss there's been."

Modern weddings being what they are, I probably didn't. Me, I got married for the first and only time when I was nineteen in a simpler world. Me and the groom, a couple of witnesses, and my dying father to walk me down the aisle.

"I don't know what to do." Jessie Franklin's words came out in gulps, in fits and starts broken by sniffs and nose-blowing. "Everything's all arranged. My mother—my mother will absolutely die if this doesn't go exactly the way she wants it to go. I mean, my dress, it's gorgeous; it's finally perfect. My mother made them change the hem three times. Three times! Everything has to be so perfect. I mean, she had a fit, arranging everything."

I held up the accusatory note. "Do you have any idea who sent this?"

"No. Of course not. Absolutely not."

"How did you get it?"

She stared at me blankly.

"In the mail? Shoved under a door?"

"I found it. In my purse."

"When?"

"What's today? Thursday? Oh my God, it's Thursday night. Two days ago, and I still don't know what to do."

I've shadowed bank presidents and suspected thieves. I've worked for defense lawyers and district attorneys. This was the first time I'd been approached by a bride-to-be.

I sat back in my chair and toyed with a pencil. I have warm fuzzy feelings about brides. How can you not? Girls are raised to it, the big day, the ultimate dress, the dream-come-true event. Paolina talks about it: *happily ever after.*

I was a bride once. More to the point, I had been well on the way to becoming a bride again until Sam had learned he couldn't reenter the country without being charged with murder. Although she was younger and a stranger, I felt an immediate bond with Jessica Franklin, a forged link. Here she was: another woman engaged to a man she wasn't sure she could trust.

I bit my lip. "You haven't said anything to your mother?"

"Like what? Like first of all, I'm living with my fiancé, which she doesn't know at all, thinks I'm a virgin who's never been kissed. Like— I wouldn't know where to start. My mom and dad, they're old-fashioned big-time and they think I'm living with a girlfriend and working hard every minute and no fooling around. If anybody found out, I'd die. I mean, I'd never hear the end of it, what a no-good dummy I am and what a mess I've made of my life. And if I don't go through with the wedding, what then? No decent man will want me now, that's what they'll say, and all that crap, like it was the 1950s and people still went on dates and held hands in the moonlight. My mom, especially, she'd hit the roof."

"Would she cancel the wedding?"

"If I asked her to, I suppose, but I'd never hear the end of it."

"Do you want her to cancel the wedding?"

I watched Jessica Franklin closely. I'd heard of brides having last-minute regrets, wanting to call the whole thing off, but not having the nerve. Some catch the last-minute flu; a few make a run for it. I wondered if the note had been folded and placed in her handbag by none other than the bride herself. It was such a personal way of delivering bad news. If she hadn't placed the accusation of infidelity in her own bag, I wondered whether she'd considered what the method of delivery meant: an enemy close enough to touch.

What kind of person was Jessica Franklin? It's hard to make any kind of judgment about a person in crisis. Jessica at work—she was in the billing department at St. Elizabeth's hospital—might have been clever and competent, but the Jessica in my office was an emotional mess, and that was the only snapshot I had to go on. I wasn't sure which she needed more, a psychiatrist or a PI, but there she was, sitting in my client chair, and I don't do therapy.

"You want me to find out who sent it?"

I hoped she didn't think I'd be able to lift finger-prints off the document, wave a magic wand, and reveal the name of the miscreant in five seconds flat. Fingerprints were out. The thing had been handled and the paper wasn't the sort I could deal with at home. If I'd still been working Homicide, I could have sent it to the state crime lab and waited a year for results.

"I—I don't care who sent it. I just want to know it isn't true."

"Have you asked?"

"Asked Ken?" She spoke as though it was absolutely out of the question, an impossibility, as though the man in the moon or the prime minister of Canada would have been a more logical choice to ask instead of Kenneth L. Harrison, the groom listed on the invitation.

Probably, I thought, she should just call off the wed-ding, no matter how much money had been spent, no matter the shame and humiliation. If she couldn't ask her intended a simple question, how would they be able to stay married when the questions came thick and fast later on?

When I nodded, she hung her head. "I can't."

"But you think he's unfaithful?"

"Unfaithful. That sounds so clean. You mean, why do I think he's fucking around? Why do I think he's been using me for a cheap place to rent and a good place to eat?"

I didn't respond; she didn't want a response.

She said, "Could you follow him, watch him, see what he does?"

"You can't follow a guy around all the time, not if you want the marriage to work."

"No, no, I mean just on Friday, this Friday night, tomorrow night."

"You won't be here?"

"I travel sometimes—business seminars—and tomorrow night I'll be in New York."

"Don't go."

"I can't get out of it; I left it too late."

"Take Ken with you."

"Oh, I couldn't."

"You think the letter writer's telling the truth?"

"I don't know. I mean, I've thought about it. God, that's all I've thought about. It's not like I call Ken and he's not there or I've seen lipstick on his shirts. He's the only man—He's the only man I've ever loved, and if—I don't know. I thought that was what a private investigator would do, and I wanted a woman, somebody who'd—It's just an overnight trip, you know, and I can't ask anybody I know. I can't ask my dad; he'd just go out and kill Ken, or he'd kill me, if he found out we were living together. I don't know which. I couldn't stand either one. You know, the whole lecture about what men are and how women have to bear up and get over it, or else a full-out cry against marrying Ken, who never was good enough for me anyway. I don't want my family or friends ever to know about this, not ever."

I raised an eyebrow. A member of her family or one of her friends had set the whole thing up.

She said, "This is what I've told myself; this is what I've decided. If he stays home tomorrow night, I'll go with it. I'll marry him. If he doesn't, if he doesn't sleep at home, I'll call it off."

She blew her nose, glanced briefly around the room, and stuffed the used tissues in her handbag. "You live here?"

I nodded. My office does double duty. It's also the living room of the big Cambridge Victorian my aunt Bea left me in her will.

"Are you married?"

"No."

Her face was alive with interest, but I wasn't eager to answer any more questions. I might have been reading into the situation, but it seemed to me that she was interested only because she was looking for an alternative, an answer to a question: *What do women do if they don't get married? How do they live?*

I don't consider myself a role model, just somebody who does what she can.

Jessica said, "I'll pay. I'll pay for your time and for gas and whatever else you charge for—and a bonus because I've left it so late. I have the money. Don't you see, I have to know."

"Let me get this straight: You want me to wait on

your doorstep and tell you when Ken comes home, and whether he leaves again?"

She bit her lip. "Well, no."

"What then?

"I guess I want to know where he goes." She swallowed and sniffed and I thought, *Oh, no, she's going to start wailing again.* "I want to know who."

I held up the anonymous note. "You think you know who sent this?"

"No. I just don't want to be unfair! What if it's nothing? I mean, what if he's visiting a sister or—"

"Does he have a sister? Locally?"

"No. But what if he's crashing at a friend's, a male friend's?"

That, I thought, could be worse. But I didn't even want to bring up the possibility. The girl was upset enough.

I said, "So you think he might go to a party without you, or visit an old friend?"

"He doesn't have family around here. He might go out, to a bar or something, watch a game, but there's nobody I know who'd want him to stay overnight, so if he did, I'd know. I mean, could you follow him, write down where he goes, who he sees?"

Following, tailing, is a skill at which I excel, requiring good eyes, patience, and sheer cussed doggedness. I could do it and feel competent, more than competent. The offer was tempting. I don't do divorce work, but I do handle due diligence cases, preventive work. Jessie's dilemma was somewhere between the two, in a hazy new area.

"You really don't want to ask the guy?"

"I love him," she said. "Whatever he said, I'd believe him."

"If you love him—"

"No," she said. "I love him, but I'm not like that." Her expression altered, grew even graver. "I won't share him. I mean, either what we have is special and separate or it's nothing. I don't want to be with somebody I can't trust."

If she trusted him, she wouldn't be hiring me, I thought.

"Okay," I said. "Where does Ken work?"

She answered more questions, filled out the usual forms, paid half up front, offering cash. Now I like cash as much as the next person, but it always makes me a little nervous. I signaled as much by raising an eyebrow.

"It's not that I don't want your name on a check or anything," she said. "It's just that I've got more cash on hand than usual. I hit it big at Foxwoods."

I'd noticed matchbooks from Foxwoods, the Connecticut casino, when she'd dropped her handbag.

"Would you rather have a check?"

Her offer soothed my suspicious nature. I took the cash and we made arrangements to meet Monday afternoon when she got back from New York.

"I might call sooner," she said. "If that's okay."

Poor baby, I thought. She wants to know, but she doesn't want to know.

"Sure," I said. "No problem."

34

She wants to know, but she doesn't want to know.

The words echoed long after Jessica Franklin departed. They described me as well as my new client. I wanted to know about Sam, but I didn't want to know.

I went to the fridge, yanked out a Rolling Rock, downed it standing at the counter, staring at nothing. Beer fueled my way upstairs, gave me the guts to walk past my little sister's empty room.

A week ago today. A week ago tonight. Late. Past midnight, I'd climbed the same steps, noticed the crack of light beneath her door, opened it to the tableau of Paolina's mask-like face and the knife and the thin line of blood tracing the cut on the inside of her left arm.

Tomorrow I'd meet her new doctor, the long-term therapist. I'd find out how badly those weeks in Colombia had damaged my little girl.

I wanted to know. I didn't want to know.

CHAPTER 3

Friday morning, much too early. Dry mouth. Headache. The clock ticked loudly in the small room. On the corner table, a plant arced upward, searching for light. The corner was dark, but the plant was lush and glossy. Maybe it was a plastic replica, but I doubted it. Everything in the office was as perfect as the plant: dustless, orderly bookshelves, shining mahogany desktop, cool blue walls, flickering fireplace. The reclining couch in the corner gave a hint that this was more than a waiting room. But I was waiting. The clock kept ticking and I kept waiting.

The doctor's shoes whispered on the carpet as he entered and settled himself behind the desk. He was perfect, too, aside from being eighteen minutes late for our appointment. A central-casting shrink, not old, simply mature, with graying temples and crow's feet at the corners of eyes that matched the walls. His name was Eisner, Aaron Eisner, and he spoke slowly, weighing each word as it left his mouth.

"I'm recommending residential placement, given the brief contact I've had with the patient. Considering what I know about the immediate cause of her distress, a time of continuous evaluation and monitoring seems indicated."

"You think she might—?"

"Harm herself?"

"She did harm herself," I said.

Harm. That was a good word. Better than the word that wouldn't cross my lips. Better than *kill. Do you think my little sister is planning to kill herself?*

His voice was calm and reassuring. "We know a great deal more about these self-inflicted injuries than we used to, a good thing and a bad thing. If it weren't endemic, we wouldn't know so much."

"Like what?" I said. "Like why would she do it?"

"I could try to explain her behavior—the cutting— as an attempt to alter her mood state. To improve it."

"You're saying she tried to change the way she felt

by slicing her arm with a kitchen knife? How would that make her feel better?"

"It's counterintuitive, you mean?"

"I don't want to play word games. How?"

"Among those who self-injure, the act of self-harm tends to bring their levels of psychological and physiological tension down to a tolerable level. The relief is almost immediate."

"How? Why?"

He clasped his hands, interweaving long, tapered fingers. "Let's say that your sister feels a strong uncomfortable emotion—"

How would you feel if you'd watched your father die? I thought.

"And she doesn't know how to handle it; she may not even know how to name it. But she has discovered that hurting herself reduces the emotional discomfort quickly. She may still feel terrible, but she doesn't feel panicky or jittery or trapped, the way she did before."

I pressed my lips into a thin line. Paolina had been tied up for hours at a time by the kidnappers. Maybe she'd bitten the inside of her lip or dug her nails deep into her palms, learned about self-inflicted pain then.

"But not all people react that way," I said.

"No. One factor common to people who self-injure is abuse."

As far as I knew, the last time my little sister was physically abused—prior to the kidnapping—was as a child of seven, when her mother brought her to the Area D station, her face cut and bruised. Marta had turned in her own boyfriend, insisted he be jailed.

In some ways she'd been a decent mother. I had to keep reminding myself of that.

"Another factor," Eisner said, "is a sort of invalidation. Many of these people were taught at an early age that their interpretations of—and feelings about—the things around them were wrong or bad. They may have learned that certain feelings weren't allowed."

Marta had been a child herself when Paolina was born. Who knows what she taught her daughter?

"And then there's the serotonin imbalance. We're learning a lot about neurotransmitters, things that may one day make treatment far more effective."

One day, I thought. *What about now?* What about a girl who ought to be in high school, catching up on her classwork, a girl who should be choosing a dress for the junior prom?

I'd called in every favor, yanked every string I could pull, to get Paolina admitted here, to East House at McLean, the psychiatric hospital affiliated with Harvard. It hadn't been easy, and if I couldn't figure out how to play the insurance game, it would be incredibly costly. Everyone I knew in mental health, cops and civilians both, assured me that this was the best place, the very best place.

"Then there's PTSD," Eisner said.

"Posttraumatic stress, yeah, I know about that."

"She's been through the wars, this girl. Is there anything else you can tell me about her captivity? Any other details?"

"I wasn't with her most of the time. I know she was kept in the trunk of a car. I know she was tied to a chair. And she was forced to make a phone call, to get her father to come, to set up her father."

"A tethered goat."

Maybe that's why she won't talk, I thought. Because when she did talk, it led to Roldan's death.

Eisner glanced at the clock. "One thing you should remember is that this was not a suicide attempt. Cutting is a coping mechanism."

His voice was kind and my head suddenly felt too heavy for my neck. I planted my elbows on my knees and rested my head in my hands.

"Are you okay?"

"Me? Sure." I tried out a smile. It felt like my face would crack with the effort, my skin shatter like a mirror and fall to the ground.

"Really?" he said mildly.

I nodded.

"You must have gone through quite a lot yourself. To bring Paolina home."

I sat silently, thinking.

"How do you cope?" he said.

I don't talk about it. I fix it. I do things. I move. I make it okay.

"Do you have any idea how long this will take?" I said. "Paolina's already missed a lot of school. I don't know how long Rindge and Latin will wait before they make her repeat the year."

"Excuse me for mentioning it, but I can't help

39

noticing that you pull your hair. I wondered if you were aware that—"

"Trichotillomania. I know what that is, too." I know because an-other shrink told me when I was forced to see him because I'd shot a man, killed him, on one of my last days as a cop. I dropped my right hand to my side. Most of the time I'm not even aware that I do it, that I grab a single strand of copper hair and loop it around my finger, fondling it, tugging it.

"I was going to say that hair-pulling is sometimes another way of controlling or altering one's mood state. Self-harm is not that rare; it affects roughly the same amount of people as the number affected by eating disorders."

Right, I thought. *People who yank their hair out or overeat don't bleed on the floor.*

"Does she talk to you?" I asked.

His eyebrows went up.

"Look, I know you're not supposed to—"

"She hums," he said. "She taps out rhythms."

"Can I see her?"

"I'm sorry."

"What do you mean?"

"She doesn't want visitors."

"I'm not a visitor. I'm here for her. Whenever she wants to see me, whenever she's ready to talk."

"I understand." He got to his feet, not hastily, not rudely. He'd had practice putting an end to interviews.

40

CHAPTER 4

The icy air in the parking lot felt bracing after the overheated room. I fumbled for my car keys and wondered if I'd always remind Paolina of the terror she'd felt when gunfire erupted in the dimly lit room, if my presence would unfailingly bring back memories of the father she'd found only to lose. I considered the possibility that she would never want to see me again, then shut my mind to it, as firmly as if I were closing a heavy door.

Driving home, I pondered an early lunch, wondered why I'd skipped breakfast, when mealtimes would get back to normal, and whether they'd ever been normal in the first place. The trip to Colombia hadn't messed with my internal clock, since Bogotá and Boston share the same time zone. But meals there hadn't arrived at regular intervals. Time had passed in a disorderly progression, alternating between chunks that sped by faster than lightning and moments that inched as slowly as growing grass.

Soup, I thought; homey, thick, and soothing, a pale imitation of something my grandmother might have spent a whole day concocting, adding a pinch of this, a pinch of that as the spirit moved her. Alas, no homemade stuff for me, but I might get lucky and find a forgotten can of Campbell's at the back of a kitchen cupboard.

That's what I was dreaming of—soup—until I saw

the rumpus on my doorstep: Roz, my tenant, house cleaner, and assistant, hanging halfway out the door, yanking a muscular tough by the arm and shrieking. Just the sort of tranquil domestic scene I longed to come home to.

Given my neighborhood, the guy could have been anything from a violent PETA activist to a struggling burglar caught mid-crime, but whenever I see Roz and a young man tussling, the first thing I think is: There she goes again. From what I could see, this guy had a good body, which increased my level of suspicion. Yes, I was thinking sex, and the infinite opportunity for things to go wrong within the context of the act. Roz goes for variety in men. By variety I mean numbers rather than variations in type. She falls for hard, well-muscled bodies every time, exults in afternoon quickies and one-night stands, and is no fan of making gradual acquaintance through the fine art of conversation.

She has a high entertainment level. Maybe that's why I keep her.

Why do I keep her? The idea froze me behind the wheel. Sometimes you step out of your life for a while and when you step back in, nothing seems to make sense. I'd gone to Colombia to retrieve my little sister, and ever since I'd returned I had felt like a visitor in my own life, wondering how I'd come to live in my aunt Bea's old house and rent a room to a strange person like Roz.

No time for reflection now, not with curses flying

and neighbors starting to peer out the windows. I left the cab at the curb and approached cautiously. I wasn't sure what the hell was going on, so I didn't want to get too close.

"Hey," I bellowed at the top of my lungs when I got tired of being ignored.

Both combatants shot me glances. Roz's had a shade of relief; the guy's held nothing but anger. He seemed vaguely familiar, which rein-forced the idea that I'd seen him with Roz before.

"Trouble?" I asked mildly.

The man let out a string of obscenities. Roz punctuated it with, "Fucking thief!"

"Why don't we take it inside?" I said.

"I'm like fucking doing you a favor, and this bitch—"

Roz did something with her foot, something quick and karate-flavored that made an impact.

"Doing *me* a favor?" I said over his howl. "Do I know you?"

"Christ, it's me, Jonathan. Jonno San Giordino. Katharine is my mother. She's married to—"

She was married to Sam Gianelli's father, his third trophy wife. Or was it his fourth?

"I brought your things. I should have fucking dumped them in an alley."

"He was going through your files. I saw him!" That from Roz.

I thought my head might burst. I needed a bowl of soup. I needed a beer. I'd never heard a good word about Sam's rotten stepbrother, Jonno, and Roz was

43

wearing a too-tight fuchsia T-shirt that said, FOUR OUT OF THREE PEOPLE HAVE TROUBLE WITH FRACTIONS. If I'd been carrying the pistol I'd emptied yesterday on the firing range, the neighbors would have had a real show.

"Inside," I said, using my crowd-control cop voice. "Both of you."

Roz registered triumph—the bastard wasn't getting away—and Jonno looked like he wanted to spit in my eye. When Roz let go of his wrist, he thought about fleeing. I took a step closer. Feet shuffled; the door opened and closed. The window curtains next door stopped bulging and I prayed the snoop would put the phone down without dialing 911. My stomach growled.

"Roz," I said, "what was he doing in—?"

"Where in hell is Sam?" the man interrupted.

I shrugged. "Roz—"

"I'm not saying a fucking word with that bitch around." Jonno didn't want me to give her a chance to tell her story.

Roz didn't look keen to tell the tale either. I wondered if it involved not only letting Jonno into the house, but also giving a handsome man free rein in my office while she went to change into something more comfortable.

"Roz," I said gently.

"Take a fucking hike," Jonno said.

"Shut up," I said firmly, followed by, "Roz, why don't you give us a minute?"

"Holler if you need me. I'll be happy to kick his ass down the stoop." She ceded ground ungraciously, flying up the stairs and banging the door at the top.

The sense of familiarity I'd felt on first seeing Jonno wasn't because we'd met before, but because he reminded me so vividly of his mother. Her ice blue eyes stared out from above his high cheekbones. His eyebrows were heavier, his hair shorter, but both had the same tawny caramel coloring, possibly from the same exclusive salon. When he smiled at me, a flash of dental perfection, I felt as though my clothes came off the wrong rack in the wrong shop, the same way I felt when Katharine gave me the once-over.

I took the single step down to the living room, leaving him to follow in my wake. Three cardboard boxes, each larger than a wine carton, were stacked in the corner near the sofa.

Jonno sank into my client chair with a sigh. His blue sweater made clouds look prickly. He wore it over a pale shirt and khakis that were definitely not wash and wear. His shoes glowed.

He gazed at me thoughtfully for a moment before saying, "So he didn't even give you a ring."

A ring? I thought. *A phone call?* Then I realized he was staring pointedly at my left hand; he meant an engagement ring.

"And how is that your business?" I decided to remain standing. I wanted whatever advantage I could get.

"I heard you got engaged."

45

"And that's why you wanted to paw through my files?"

"That bitch—"

"What were you looking for?"

"She's crazy."

I'd always considered it a possibility, but the more he protested, the more I thought Roz had caught him in the act.

He said, "Look, I brought your things from Charles River Park. The boxes? I could have tossed your stuff. Or put it in storage. Like his."

"You don't think it's a little soon to be doing that?"

"I want your key. To the apartment."

"I don't keep it in the file cabinet."

"I need it."

"Bulletin: Sam gave it to me. When he asks me to return it, I'll give it back."

"So you're going to be difficult."

I shrugged. What, me? Difficult?

"We'll change the locks."

"We?"

The change from singular to plural was not unexpected. I'd met Mama, the very expensive Katharine, on several occasions. I'd heard she kept a close eye on her only son.

"Yeah, Eddie Nardo says Sam's a fool, you know that? And Nardo's an up-front guy, says what he thinks. Nardo says Sam's a real asshole, what he did. All his life brought up to the business. All his life, one lesson drilled into his head: Don't let it get personal.

Man, it's the total stupidity of the whole thing. It'll probably kill the old man."

Nardo, not Katharine. The name gave me pause. Eddie Nardo was a lawyer, an advisor, a man Sam spoke of with respect. The "old man" was Sam's father, and whether he was really alive was a matter of whom you asked on which day. He'd had so many strokes and was attached to so much medical equipment that some people thought Katharine was calling the shots. Some thought Nardo.

"Personal?" I repeated. "Stupid?" Suddenly I wanted Jonno to keep talking. I sat behind the desk and fastened a look of rapt attention on my face.

"Yeah, and it all comes back to you."

"Me?" I did everything but bat my eyelashes.

"Man says he wants to marry you, but I guess the other woman didn't think he should walk out on her. Who knows? Maybe she got pregnant? Maybe he'd already married her? Poor little bitch should have just let him go."

"You don't know what you're—"

"Then again, maybe she had something on him."

"She? Who?"

Jonno let me see his dental work again, a wide slow smile. "If Sam didn't mention her, I don't see why I should. Didn't give you a ring, didn't tell you about the girlfriend. Maybe all the panties at the apartment were yours, but maybe not."

He wanted a reaction, so I was careful not to give him one.

He said, "You probably don't know where he is, do you? You probably don't know a goddamn thing."

He walked out before I could call Roz to kick him out. I took a quick look at my desktop, wanting to toss something after him. A paperweight. A brick. A bomb.

His cologne lingered in the air.

CHAPTER 5

I sat motionless at my desk, thinking furiously. The closest Sam had come to an explanation of his inability to return to the States was a quickly muttered, "Something happened in Las Vegas." Now, thanks to Jonno, I had two legs of the stool. Or possibly two legs of the spider. The location of the crime: Las Vegas. And according to Jonno, the alleged victim was a woman.

Roz pounded downstairs. Before she could open her mouth, I said, "I need you to get me a list of DBs in Vegas."

"Huh? Deadbeats in Vegas? That's gonna take some time."

"Dead bodies," I corrected. "Female."

"Wait a minute. Hang on. What about that guy? You let him go?" Her jaw was set. She seemed to think that making a list of women who'd turned up dead in Las Vegas wouldn't be half as much fun as kicking Jonno down the front stoop would have been.

"Yeah, I let him go," I said. Then I gave her parameters for the DB search, using Sam's age and taste to speculate on the age of the victim and the date of his last trip to Vegas to guess the possible date of the crime.

"Is this for the new client? Jessica?"

I shook my head no.

"You're not taking the case? But we—"

"We?"

"You need the work."

"I'm taking it."

"Oh. Okay."

"And you're doing this other stuff. In addition to background on Jessica. Okay?"

It seemed like the best thing I could do at the moment, hand the research off to Roz and prep for the upcoming tail job, even though part of me wished we could trade. Trading places was out of the question: Roz is a whiz at computers, but she doesn't drive.

I do drive. I love to drive, but at the moment I had no car. I sat at my desk and pulled my hair. Gloria's cabs are good tail vehicles up to a point, and that point was the Boston city limits. A Boston cab sticks out in the suburbs. I was considering rentals when the boxes Jonno had left in the corner caught my eye.

Could it be that easy?

I would have sworn I hadn't stored much at Sam's apartment, but there in box number one, mashed rather than folded, were two of my favorite sweaters and the bathrobe that usually hung in my upstairs closet. Yes, there was underwear, but I didn't take time to root for alien undergarments.

The next carton was stuffed with paperback Civil War histories, *C.C.* scrawled on the inside cover in Sam's handwriting. He's got a thing about books, writes his name in all his volumes to make sure that if he lends them, he gets them back. I hadn't realized he'd initialed my books, but I was grateful; at least they wouldn't languish in some prefab storage bunker. The idea of Sam's soft wool suits bundled and shoved into an anonymous shed made me swallow. The idea of Jonno handling my underwear made my forehead feel too tight and my eyes burn.

I turned to the third carton. Heavy corrugated cardboard like the rest, it looked new, purchased, not a grocery store throwaway. I turned it on its axis, searching for a logo that might identify a moving company, thinking maybe the moving company would give me the name of the storage facility, thinking I could rescue Sam's cashmere sweaters and silk ties.

The sides of the container were unmarked. Maybe the bottom would give a clue. I'd check it later, when I had time to unpack the boxes.

Label the third carton miscellaneous. Ropes of lacy ribbon, crinkled wrapping paper, two copper-colored bangle bracelets, a photo of Sam, thinner and younger, posing with his feet up on his old desk at the Green and White Cab Company. No gray in his hair, no lines at the corners of his eyes.

Was all that eye shadow mine? I buried the thought, provoked more by Jonno's observation about panties than by my own insecurity. What was a little infidelity after all, compared to murder, the murder of a woman, a personal, face-to-face murder?

When my on-again, off-again lover, my fiancé, a man I'd come to know when he was the boss and I was young and almost a virgin, first told me he couldn't return to the United States, I'd flat-out assumed it had to do with gaming or racketeering or conspiracy because the Gianelli name is so entwined with the history of the Boston mob that no one bothers to separate the two. I'd further assumed it had to do with Sam's current quest to move mob assets into legitimate businesses, a quest made tougher by the current anti-terrorism laws. I'd been stunned to learn that Sam had been named in a murder indictment, but still I'd assumed it had to do with the family business, with a long-ago murder, some rival crook found stuffed in a submerged trunk, a death two or three times removed from the man I slept with, the man I'd agreed to marry.

Something happened in Las Vegas.

I bit my lip. Yanked my hair and wondered how Paolina's shrink would interpret the impulse. A woman . . . Someone Sam had slept with during one of the many gaps in our togetherness? I'd never expected him to practice abstinence while we were apart. I certainly hadn't been any plaster saint. And whenever we renewed the relationship it was without any awkward confessions; neither of us felt the need to discuss extracurricular flings.

Dammit, where was it? The miscellany box had

summer clothes wedged at the bottom, a pair of san-
dals, a single flattened house slipper, a pamphlet
issued by a consumer group on new methods of identity theft. Aha! Two purses, small date-night purses
rather than serious handbags for carrying daily essentials like flashlights and lock-picks. I opened the first,
found tickets to a Huntington Theater production of
Ma Rainey's Black Bottom, tissues, lipstick. The
second purse jingled promisingly and opened to reveal
not money, but the object of my quest: Sam's spare car
key. The key to an indigo Jaguar XK.

Driving in Boston is basically a contact sport, and
because it's a contact sport and because I have a native
Detroiter's love of glossy high-powered automobiles,
I made the decision long ago to drive a "sensible" car
in this city. When my serviceable Toyota got its first
scratch, I left it as a talisman, hoping it would ward off
the dings, dents, and bumps to follow. If you're going
to drive in the Commonwealth, your car's going to get
salt on it every winter and suffer from potholes and
acid rain and crazy drivers. It's going to spend time in
the shop, getting retouched and repainted. I'd always
shaken my head at Sam's expensive vehicles, but I'd
driven them eagerly whenever he offered, enjoying
the speed, the handling, the quick acceleration, racing
cheerfully along Route 2 or speeding through the Big
Dig tunnels, foot hard on the gas, eyes peeled for state
troopers.

If Jonno hadn't changed the locks at Charles River
Park yet, what were the chances he'd gotten around to

moving the Jag? Sam had his key with him wherever he was now. I'd noticed it on the nightstand in Cartagena. And I had the spare key, borrowed and forgotten in my little tan purse.

Sam's Jaguar was fast and agile, a hell of a ride. I could lie way back on the highway, trust the engine to make up time in a hurry. An indigo Jag was a better tail car than a creaky Ford cab any day of the week.

CHAPTER 6

In the summer of 1960, Boston's West End was bulldozed to rubble. Some called it urban renewal and some called it slum clearance, but when the dust cleared, there was Charles River Park, an eight-building complex that would have looked great in Miami Beach. The tall pale buildings had no ties to New England, so to grab some local flavor, they named the towers after Hawthorne, Whittier, Emerson, Lowell, and Longfellow. I like to imagine those old dead white guys rolling in their graves. Not to mention stogie-smoking Amy Lowell.

The only thing most Bostonians know about CRP is the sign. If you're stuck in traffic—or should I say, *when* you're stuck in traffic—on Storrow Drive, there it is, a taunting IF YOU LIVED HERE, YOU'D BE HOME NOW. The complex occupies almost as much space as Boston Common, but few outsiders enter the grounds. It's deliberately unwelcoming, cut off, isolated, and fearful, with its own grocery store and its own security patrol. Those who live at CRP use the city, but the city does not use CRP. Visitors are not encouraged.

Charles River Park has barbed wire and fences and twenty-four-hour security guards. They're looking for trouble from the outside. Armed gangs, hooded thugs, burglars, car thieves, not a lone white woman like me.

I strolled into the Pace Market and purchased two boxes of Kleenex. Jessie Franklin had been hard on my tissue supplies. I got a couple bottles of water, two bananas, a few other essentials. The clerk may have thought it odd when I asked him to bag the stuff lightly, each tissue box in a separate paper sack, but he did as I asked.

Burdened with my shopping, I walked past the basketball courts, the tennis courts, and the pool. I circled the pool, lingering in the shadows, waiting for the right company. Two women, nurses by their sensible shoes, passed by. Then a teenager, hunched into a hooded jacket. I didn't have to wait long.

Business suit, overcoat, no briefcase, maybe heading out for a night on the town. Keys jingled in his gloved left hand and he was making a beeline for the back entrance of the Longfellow garage.

"Cold, huh?" I said, swinging into step beside him.

"You bet. Wind whistles between the buildings. Not as bad as Chicago, I suppose."

"Windy city," I agreed. I've heard that Chicago's reputed windiness refers to its politicians, but who knows? "You work downtown?"

"Copley Square. Wind around the Pru, that's bad."

He was a gent. He didn't wait for me to use my key on the door. He used his key, then held the door wide for me and my grocery bags. As I always say, why break and enter when you can get a guy to hold the door?

So far so good. Perfect.

Except the Jaguar wasn't there.

I glanced around the garage, eyeballing dark corners and empty alcoves, just to make sure Sam hadn't parked in a spot other than his own, but my first take was the right take: no indigo XK. To say I was disappointed is to understate. I was dressed warmly for the bitter evening, but my backside had counted on a cushy leather seat for a quick ride home before the evening's assignment. Jonno San Giordino had been more efficient than I'd bargained for.

I got back in the elevator cube, dropped the grocery bags, and hesitated over the buttons. Did I want to press the penthouse floor, go up to Sam's place, see Jonno's handiwork? Did I have time? I consulted my watch, determining the latest time I could leave, beg a cab, and make the rendezvous with Jessie and her fiancé.

Where the hell was the Jaguar? The last time I'd seen Sam, he'd dropped me at Logan. Then, I'd learned later, he'd left town as well, flying to Vegas. No way would Sam have left his car at Logan. The long-term lot at Logan is more like a used car showroom for auto thieves than a parking lot.

I hit the lobby button and hefted the bags.

"Hey, babe, wuzzup?" Raoul, the doorman, glanced up with a wolfish grin. His eyes were sleepy and unfocused. He took note of me only because I'd cleared my throat and made him lose count of his reps. He was using the small weights, the ten-pounders he kept stashed under the desk. Maybe someone had complained about the fifties.

"How are you?" I replied cheerfully.

"Doin' fine, doin' fine."

Raoul, the night doorman, was notorious for paying no attention. That's not quite true. He paid attention, a great deal of attention, but only to his muscular development. As far as he was concerned, as long as his pecs and abs were in great shape, the lobby could disappear in a puff of smoke. He put on a good act; he was more than capable of shining on the management company that employed him, but most of the tenants knew. And he was so damned pleasant all the time, greeting everybody with a wide smile and happily carrying heavy packages upstairs for all and sundry, that the tenants didn't really care that he paid no attention at all. At least he'd smile and say good evening. To anyone and everyone, whether they had any business being in the building or not.

"Mr. Gianelli leave a message for me?" I asked.

Sam had done so in the past. Lubricated with a couple of bills, Raoul's memory was excellent.

"Uh, Mr. G. Right. Uh, no. Nothing like that, ma'am. Uh, miss."

Raoul gave me his full attention as I crossed to the

elevator. Before the doors had closed, his hand was reaching for the phone.

Had Jonno hired him as a spy: "Anybody goes up to the Gianelli apartment, you give me a buzz and I'll make it worth your while"?

I took the elevator up to Sam's floor. My key still fit the lock, but I didn't venture inside. I knew the place too well. There was no safe concealed behind a picture frame, no secret compartment under the floor. Those improvements were confined to the family's North End enclave.

When Sam moved into Charles River Park, he'd had two smaller condos knocked into one, making his apartment the sole dwelling on the floor. The outside corridor stretched from the elevator to well beyond the stairwell, ending in a small alcove. I shoved a potted palm slightly to the right and concealed myself and my groceries behind it. Raoul had most likely called Jonno, but I figured I might as well find out if anyone else had an interest in the goings and comings at Sam's place.

It took only six minutes.

The man was built like a door, broad through the shoulders and hips, not so much tall as solid. He had a florid face and a drinker's red-veined nose. Late forties, maybe fifty. His baggy suit jacket made me think cop.

He used a key on Sam's door. As he entered, I departed, groceries in hand, flying down all twelve flights to the garage, where I exited by the same door

I'd entered. Then I circled around to the front of the building to find a late-model Ford Taurus parked in the turnabout. Light brown. An American-made sedan, just like the car Mooney had asked about.

I memorized the license plate. Roz can work wonders with a license plate. I don't know if she mesmerizes the clerks at the DMV or what. I've never asked her to sleep with anybody to gather information, but she may regard it as part of the job.

What was the name of the federal agent Mooney had mentioned? Dailey, I thought. Reilley? Too bad I couldn't run the description by my old friend.

I took a deep breath and plunged down the path into the cold. The ten-minute trudge to the Science Park T stop seemed to take forever. Honestly, at one point, I thought about stealing a damned car. This city, seems like everybody else does.

CHAPTER 7

The Jag would have been a lousy tail car. Too conspicuous, I told myself, scrunched behind the wheel of another aged Ford cab. The bucket seat in Sam's car would have put me instantly to sleep, and the heating unit that kept it toasty under your butt, who needed it? The musky smell would have made me nostalgic and I didn't need that either. The Spartan chill of Gloria's cab would keep me alert. If I kept the roof lights off outside the city limits, the cab, in the dark of night, would look like any other car.

Right.

Tailing a citizen does not require the same virtuosity as playing the violin, but if it did, I flatter myself I'd be the Isaac Stern of tailing, or at least a concertmaster in a decent orchestra. I'm good at waiting. I can amuse myself for hours, tuning my mind to a guitar riff I want to master, wandering through an intricacy of fingering possibilities while my eyes search for movement in the darkness.

There was the possibility I'd lose him: a one-person tail is always risky, but Jessica Franklin hadn't let my warning deflect her determination to hire me. If I lost him, she'd insisted, I'd have a place, her place on Pomeroy Street in Allston, to wait and pick him up again. And if he didn't show at her place, didn't sleep in the right bed, then she'd know.

So the job was a simple tail, period, full stop, finish. She didn't want even a cursory background check done on her Ken. I'd recommended one, the whole megillah, tracing the prospective groom back to the day of his birth, making sure he'd done what he said he'd done, lived where he'd said he'd lived, worked where he'd said he'd worked. But no, if the man didn't commit adultery tonight, my client was willing to spend the rest of her life with him.

How trusting. How quaint.

I'd run through the arguments: This isn't small-town America anymore and many less-than-decent people have figured that out. The anonymity of cities lets the cons start over, recreate themselves from scratch.

They're not saddled with their father's reputation or their mother's; nobody knows who their family is, so it's easy as pie to be whoever somebody believes them to be. Private investigators fill the role the family used to take in matchmaking, and why not? Somebody ought to do it. We're nosy Aunt Bessie with a nephew at Amherst who never met your Ken on campus all those years he said he was there. So, does Ken really have that master's degree? Was he really born in North Dakota in 1985? Is his dad a big shot in import/export or doing time at Walpole? Most folks are honest, but alas, crooks don't come with FDA warning labels tattooed across their foreheads.

I glanced for the twenty-seventh time at the photo the bride-to-be had reluctantly parted with, a five-by-seven that told me some of what she saw in the guy. He was a handsome devil, maybe a little too handsome for his own good. Sandy hair, wide eyes, well-shaped freckled nose, nice smile. Good-looking guys; I don't know, do they really tell more lies? Is there scientific proof? Did my client's desire to have him tailed imply that she felt insecure in the relationship, suspected that, behind her back, people were wondering what a guy like that saw in her, asking why he hadn't hooked up with some supermodel-type instead? I decided to have Roz run the basics on the man, no matter whether Kenny-boy slept at home or not.

The rain started at 7:38. Just what I needed. Jessica had guaranteed that she and the boyfriend would exit the restaurant by the front door at a quarter to eight. The attendant would bring up Ken's Volvo, which he'd have previously left with valet parking. The Volvo S60 was a plus, a distinctive silhouette with oddly shaped taillights, a relatively easy car to track.

I'd filled up on gas, checked the oil and the wiper blades. The cab was old, but the engine was sound; it didn't snort or stall. I'd be paid more than cabbie wages. Nothing to beef about, just rain-slicked roadway and no idea where the man might be headed. Maybe he'd head straight to Jessica's like a homing pigeon and sleep peacefully in his own bed. Maybe the printed message was a lie delivered by a jealous coworker of Jessica's or a spiteful ex-girlfriend of Ken's.

I'd tried to get the names and addresses of Ken's former gal pals, but Jessica wasn't having any. She'd behaved as if naming her suspicions would make them real. Just tail the man and tell her where he goes, write down any addresses.

Maybe he had a whole harem. His looks, it was possible.

The door to Mamma Vincenza's opened, a slice of yellow light in the dark. My client led the way out. I watched her closely, but she didn't glance around. I'd warned her about that. Don't look for me; don't give the show away. She smiled and chatted with Ken like a good little actress.

He wore a camel-colored overcoat that had set him back several hundred, a maroon scarf neatly twisted at his throat. He didn't touch her as they got into the car. The Volvo was silver, with a moonroof.

Hello, luck. A gift, an absolute gift: His left taillight was busted. An irregular sliver of red plastic had slipped its mooring, and the Volvo was unique on the highway. I wondered if Jessica had broken it to help me out. If she'd done it, I owed her a tip of my hat for enterprising behavior.

Speaking of hats, I had a couple of different ones in the car, plus a raincoat, a shawl, my bottles of water, a bottle for other purposes, bananas, a stash of Fig Newtons, and a plastic bag of hard candies to suck on. I was wearing layers and running shoes, ready for a long haul and looking forward to it. Tailing and surveillance are my meat; I like to do what I do well, and my fellow officers used to claim I had an infinite capacity for watching and waiting for something to happen.

In my work, it's a strength. In my life . . . How long could I watch and wait for Sam to return? I'd waited a long time already, for him to make up his mind, for me to make up my mind. And now that we had come to an agreement, now that the proposal had been made and accepted, where was the payoff?

I'm too old to believe in happily-ever-after transformations, but for a minute, I'd let my guard down and bought into the fantasy. We hadn't gone so far as to have invitations printed as Jessica's mother had, but there had been a sense of anticipation. Now I had to peel it away, dismiss the scent of orange blossoms and the whole irrational mystique that's grown up around weddings, the perfect culmination, the perfect day, as though one day could alter the future, as though the right ceremony could forge a bond beyond the bond already created.

Legality, that's what it was, a simple legal procedure that could be countered and later reversed by another civil procedure.

Marriage was what you made it. And so many made a mockery of it. My client was wary, and why not?

I followed the Volvo with the broken taillight, three cars back, northeast on North Square toward Sun Court Street. North Square turned into Moon Street and I hung a right onto Lewis, lots of rights and lefts till we hit the Surface Road and slid onto Summer. This was the easy part, the warm-up, because I knew where the Volvo was headed: South Station for the train to New York, the 8:20 Acela Express. Ken let Jessica off on Atlantic Avenue, leaving her on the wrong side of the street with lanes of busy traffic to cross. I didn't see them kiss. Not a good sign. I wondered if she'd been able to carry off the dinner with aplomb, without asking him what his plans were for the evening or doing anything else to stoke suspicion.

As he drove away, I saw him lift a cell phone to his ear.

Ah, cell phones. They've made deception so much easier. When I'd asked whether she'd ever called home and found him unexpectedly absent, she'd replied that they had no landline, just cells. You call someone on his cell, ask whether he's home, and he says, "Sure, honey, just kicking back here on the sofa watching the Celtics. How's your day been?" You can't exactly ask him to hold up the camera phone and shoot a picture to your phone so you can check his veracity. Not without inviting trouble.

He drove while he talked, but unlike so many other Bostonians, he drove well, holding his speed and position on the busy streets. If I was going to lose him, I'd lose him in the downtown swirl, I thought, so I edged closer, only one car behind, and tagged along through a yellow, then another one. Not suspicious behavior. Hell, there's practically nothing you can do in a cab that's suspicious in this city. The way Boston cabbies drive is truly awful, encompassing everything from abrupt U-turns in heavy traffic to wrong-way jaunts down one-way streets. And the cops usually wink. The way cops drive, well, that's another story.

We took a quick right-left combo, my shadowlike behavior less than notable because that's the way most of the traffic was heading. The man had just eaten, so we weren't heading into the South End for a restaurant stop.

I was abruptly aware of a pulsing beat, heavy thumping bass coming from the Volvo. Yes, Ken had put his phone away and was jerking his head rhythmically. Maybe loud party music was his way of consoling himself for the departure of his fiancée. Or maybe the man was getting in a party mood and the anonymous letter was right on the button.

CHAPTER 8

The Volvo reversed course, scooted over to Kneeland Street, and darted through Chinatown. Ken cut a right onto Washington Street without signaling and headed into the financial district. The shortcuts the man knew, he would have made a good cabbie. Fortunately, he didn't seem to keep a keen eye on the rearview mirror. The god of traffic lights stayed with me; the red lights didn't part us. The music blared so loudly that I could have followed him by ear.

I almost lost him near Winthrop Square, but there he was turning the corner. A little speed and I was on him as he made his way through the concrete canyons. Rain blurred the windshield and I prayed it would calm back into a drizzle. If it hadn't been for the broken taillight, I'd have lost him twice.

He pulled over and parked abruptly. I rolled past; nothing else I could do, and circled the block at breakneck speed, a maneuver any cabbie in search of a fare learns to execute quickly.

The parking space was empty, the Volvo gone. Damn. He hadn't parked. Had he pulled over to answer a phone call? To see if he was being tailed? The roads here were twisty one-way streets. I made a set of widening turns, reluctant to admit I'd lost him. There! I caught a flash of a white zigzag taillight and screeched a left from the right-hand lane to a chorus of indignant honks.

I stayed well back as the Volvo led the way to Government Center, turned onto Cambridge Street, and sailed over the Longfellow Bridge into East Cambridge. Through Kendall Square, right on Broadway, right again. Just past a knot of high-rises, he pulled in to park at the curb.

Another phone call? Another ruse? Again, unless I wanted to advertise my presence, there was nothing I could do but circle the block.

The Volvo, to my surprise, was still there, parked. I caught a glimpse of a silhouette entering the lobby of one of the tall buildings nearby. The shadow carried something in hand, not a briefcase, more the shape of a woman's tote bag. Right height, right weight, right coat.

I pulled in at a fireplug, puzzled. Killed the lights.

It didn't look like the sort of building for an assignation, more like lab space for one of the many MIT offshoot start-ups in the area. Possibly legal offices or stockbrokers. It was after hours, Friday night, hardly time for a business meeting. Who knew? Maybe he was playing sex games on a desktop with a willing paralegal. I made a note of the time and the address and settled back to wait, proud of myself for tracking him thus far.

I thought about calling Paolina, safe, physically safe, at McLean. No. Even if she agreed to talk, I couldn't risk any activity that might split my concentration.

I regretted—well, almost regretted—not bringing a

partner, someone who'd casually enter the building foyer, determine whether there was a guard, read the billboard listing the various offices. Someone who'd help while the time away, someone who'd talk, who'd help me decode Ken's driving habits.

Mooney used to do that. Mooney always talked. It was one of the reasons we'd never dated; I'd enjoyed talking to the man too much to risk our professional relationship. God knows, I've had my troubles with romantic relationships. I despise the very word *relationship.*

I put on a pair of lensless spectacles, removed my hat, and fluffed up my hair. If Ken, the groom, happened to change his habits and check the rearview, the cab itself would be unremarkable in the darkness, without the roof lights little more than a pair of well-lit circles. Some people, when they stop at traffic lights, glance at the drivers behind them, and if he did, I wanted him to see a different look, even if only a different misty outline.

I was tempted to race in and write down the names of the offices myself, but I'd have an awkward situation on my hands if he suddenly emerged, so I settled in to keep an eye on the door. I didn't think there was much risk of missing his return to the Volvo. The place might have a back exit, but why bother with his car out front? I didn't think he'd stay indoors long. It wasn't intuition; he was parked in a no-parking zone.

He emerged twenty-two minutes later and stuffed the tote in the trunk. I logged the time, gave him a half-block head start, and we were off to the races.

Twenty-two minutes might be time enough for a quickie on an office desk, but it didn't seem an attractive option. Okay, so maybe he had a little business to finish up after dinner. Now was the time for a playboy to head to a bar or to the unknown girlfriend's bed. Or maybe he'd go back to the Allston digs he shared with his devoted fiancée, drink the lonely night away, watch the Celtics win. That would keep my costs down; Gloria expected me to return the cab with a full tank.

He drove faster. I stopped thinking about where he might be going and concentrated on keeping up, following the silver zigzag as it slid through the river of red taillights. Back into Boston, the traffic lighter now, the workers all gone home, curled up contentedly by the fire or the flickering television. At a stoplight, I grinned at myself in the rearview. Tailing the guy felt good. If Allston was our destination, we'd head west soon.

He turned south. I kept the tail loose, followed him onto 93, the Central Artery, into the underground network of tunnels that locals call the Dig or the death-trap depending on the daily news, headed toward Route 3. I scrunched my eyes, then opened them wide. The Dig is like one of those kids' toys, a marble run. If you pick the correct lane, it shunts you out to your destination; if you have the misfortune to get in the wrong lane, you go to the wrong place. Often only one lane goes where you're headed and at the moment I didn't have any idea where I was bound. The silver zigzag raced on, flashing in and out of traffic. Was he on to me, or just having fun, enjoying the night drive?

Whew. I'd guessed right, gotten lucky, going with the majority as we zipped under downtown, emerging from the claustrophobic tunnel alive, no heavy concrete panels crashing on my head tonight, escaping onto Route 3, dashing toward the South Shore. I tried to convince myself this was a good thing for my client. Aunt Ruthie in Hingham, sweet old Aunt Ruthie had invited our bridegroom over for a cup of chamomile tea.

There were strip joints on the South Shore. Maybe I'd spend most of the night in the Foxy Lady parking lot while Ken threw himself a little solo bachelor party. What would my client think of that?

I kept to the right lane, primed for the Volvo's exit. We passed Quincy and Braintree. We passed Hingham. Marshfield. Plymouth. Where the hell was the man going? On vacation?

Vacation is what I think of when I cross the Sagamore Bridge over the Cape Cod Canal. Escape. Turning off the clock, turning back the clock to a simpler quieter time. I don't go to the Cape—or "down the Cape," as the natives say—in summer; too many tourists. I prefer it in the fall when the weather's still fine and the ocean warm, preheated by the August sun. There's a sense of relief on the Cape in the fall, all the summer people with their bustle and desperation gone. Sam and I once rented a cabin in Orleans and never woke before noon.

Mooney and I drove down to interview a witness in Falmouth. We stopped at a clam shack, walked along a white sand beach. I kept my distance, unwilling to be accused of playing up to the boss. Hadn't done any good; the guys hooted when we returned and I had to take a lot of crap about sunburns.

The bridge shoved us onto Route 6, the Cape Highway, a straight shot to Provincetown, the end of the world.

It was just past ten o'clock. In downtown Boston, the streets would be packed with restaurant- and moviegoers, with fans emptying out of the Garden, long since renamed but never called anything else. Here, traffic was sparse. I slowed down, settled in behind a plumber's van, and soothed myself with the thought that Route 6 had few exits and those carefully marked. I could lie back a few cars, watch for the silver zigzag to leave the roadway.

The downside: If I missed him, I couldn't double back on the divided highway. I shifted my butt in the seat, made myself deliberately uncomfortable to keep alert.

He didn't take the first exit or the second. Not the third. The fourth was the charm, and I was momentarily relieved; I didn't think my kidneys could make the trip to Provincetown.

Exit 4. Route 149. As a cabbie, I carry a mental map of the Boston area, but it grows sketchier the farther I

70

get from town. The surroundings seemed vaguely familiar. Where had I driven heading south on 149? The old Barnstable Fairgrounds? Yes. The fairgrounds were to the west and Cotuit Bay must be at the end of the dimly lit, narrow two-lane road. Ken must be nearing his destination. No reason to leave Route 6 if he intended to continue east on 28, its southern low-speed parallel. I edged the cab a little closer. Sam and I had visited a restaurant down this way, close to the tiny town of Marstons Mills. Wasn't there a small rotary, a traffic circus, a place where I might lose the magic taillight?

The Volvo stayed on the main drag, doing a 180 around the small circle before continuing to the south as though the rotary had been nothing but a stop sign. I wondered if there was ever enough traffic to make cars stop and wait at the rotary, whether there would ever be popular demand for a traffic light. Didn't look like it, with wide open spaces all around.

Much of this part of the Cape is devoted to golf courses, but some of the low flat land is a military reservation. There are small towns dotted here and there, clumps of weather-beaten houses, wildlife sanctuaries. I wondered about Indian reservations. The town of Mashpee is nearby and that's the center of the Wampanoag tribe, along with Aquinnah on Martha's Vineyard. The Nausett tribe, smaller than the Wampanoag, shares its name with the small town west of Mashpee. The taillights vanished over a rise and I sped up.

Lighting was minimal, but I didn't want to risk my brights. Damn. Just as my hand moved off the steering wheel to find them, the wheel wrenched hard to the right and then I was fighting with the cab, hanging on as a loud thump, thump, thump announced trouble and the tires locked and skidded.

Instinct took over. One minute the car was out of control and the next minute it was slowing and stopping, sliding but stopping, not quite on the road, but not quite in the ditch, and my hands were clenched so tightly on the steering wheel that I thought I might need help to pry them off.

Quiet. It was absolutely still, like church, except no one coughed or rustled in the pews. Dark and quiet and still. No cars, no streetlights, scudding clouds across the faint hint of a moon.

Damn again. I knew that sound. I knew what made a car behave like that. A blowout, a flat, and while I'd checked the oil and gas, I hadn't cracked the trunk and checked for a spare. *Oh, please,* I prayed silently. *There's got to be a spare.* I got my flashlight out of my bag and flicked it on, pointing the beam out the side window.

I couldn't see grass; I couldn't see ground. I knew there were no cliffs on the Cape, just dunes overlooking the ocean still far to the south, but who wants to take chances, so I slid to the passenger side, closer to the center of the road, and got out. I didn't slam the car door. The silence was so profound, it didn't seem right to break it.

As I edged around the car to inspect the tires, I kicked something that skittered across the road. My lowered flashlight caught a gleam of silver. I bent and studied the pavement.

Carpet tacks. Too many of them. In fact, a whole box of carpet tacks.

The rain started again, pockmarking the gravel at the side of the road, its faint patter the only sound on the planet. The metallic barrage of a jackhammer or the wail of a siren would have been a welcome intervention. I won't say that the worst parts of Dorchester and Mattapan hold no terrors for me, but they hold familiar fears. I'm a city kid. The dark rural silence sent shivers up my spine.

Mooney used to get on my case whenever I'd make an intuitive leap, make use of what he used to call unwarranted imagination. Hey, I'd respond, most cops have no imagination, period. Now I gave mine free rein.

Had the man in the Volvo tossed the tacks, or had they been lying here for hours, days? If they'd been here even ten minutes ago, why had the Volvo passed with no problem? Luck of the draw? Karma?

I decided to hold Ken responsible for the tacks.

Okay. Had he simply been trying to stop me? Was the man insane or just reckless and impulsive? Had injury been his deliberate goal? Had he assumed I was someone else, some unknown—to me, at least—enemy? Would he U-turn the Volvo, return to demand why I'd been tailing him? Come back to finish me off? Would I hear a car approaching on the roadway with the sputtering rain? See a car if it traveled with no headlights?

Every cheesy horror flick I'd ever seen took place at night in the deserted woods. Woods exactly like those that kissed the margins of Route 149. After fifteen minutes spent crouched in the wet, leafy underbrush, I decided imagination might be running rampant. I decided Ken wasn't coming back.

By then my hair was plastered to my head and my clothing soaked through. I was also shivering uncontrollably. And the rain kept pelting down.

PART TWO

CHAPTER 9

I threw myself into the air, timing the leap to meet the opposing center, smashing the ball at a wicked downward angle for the kill. Tie game: 10–10. Our point, our serve, the rhythm of the game speeding up, the momentum changing, slowly turning in our favor. I could feel the surge of energy around me, a corresponding ebb across the net. A teammate smacked my upraised palm.

"Let's do it," Marlena, our co-captain, yelled.

When everything else in my life turns ugly, I have a place to go. Some people find succor in the warmth of their family, but I find what I need in the smell of the locker room, in the warped wooden floorboards of the old Cambridge Y in Central Square. I find it in the thwack of skin on a volleyball, the community of players who show up three times a week for no glory or pay, to test their skills and keep their edge. I find it in Loretta, who cares for her elderly mother in the Cambridge projects and is always the first to offer a hand up after a fall, and in Jody, who alternates between cursing and apologizing for her foul mouth. I find it in focusing so narrowly and moving so quickly that there's no chance to dwell on the disastrous past.

I leapt again, but by this time, my counterpart across the net had grown tired of my routine. She leapt, too, straight-arming the net instead of the ball. I should have seen it coming, but I didn't. My nose hit the butt of her palm, that hard place near the base of the thumb, and I went down fast, blood oozing from my nostrils.

Tears welled unbidden and I pressed both forefingers against the bridge of my nose, prodding both sides, squeezing and thinking, *Please, not again.* Loretta had a bag of ice on my face so fast, I don't remember waiting for it. My nose has been broken three times, so I used my diagnostic skills. I didn't think this was break number four. I hadn't heard that awful grinding noise. The cartilage along the bridge seemed stable. I could breathe.

Sitting out the next game with a towel staunching the scarlet flow, I had way too much time to reconstruct and deconstruct, to think about Friday night and replay the long lost weekend.

Only one flat tire, and thank God and Leroy, Gloria's car mechanic brother, there had been a functional spare in the trunk. So much for the good news. With no cell service out in the back of beyond, I couldn't call 911 to tell the cops to clean up the tacks, much less call Roz to order her to sit on Jessica's apartment. It had taken way too much time to change the tire, the barely accessible front right tire, poised over a ditch, in icy pouring rain, with a crappy tire iron and a rickety jack.

A car had come around the rotary within minutes once I'd started the repair. I'd had visions of a helper, a trucker with a two-way radio, a Good Samaritan, a cop. The sedan had given me a wide berth, driving by without hesitation. Angrily, I'd watched it out of sight, almost hoping it would pick up a stray tack or two. Then I'd found myself considering Mooney's comment about the American-made sedan, wondering whether someone might have been trailing me while I was trailing Ken. Then I'd decided I was getting more than borderline paranoid. The driver was simply tired, eager to hit the sheets, uninterested in prolonging his evening to help a sopping wet six-foot damsel wielding a tire iron.

I'd finished tightening the lug nuts, swept the tacks into the ditch with the aid of the flashlight and a plastic snow sweeper. I'd even made a few passes through Marstons Mills, up and down the rainy side streets, searching for the Volvo.

No luck at all.

A cheer went up from the Y-Birds' side of the net. One more game for the match. I yelled encouragement, wiped my nose with a fresh tissue, pinched it, and leaned back, wincing. My nose was still sore from blowing it practically nonstop Saturday, Sunday, and Monday. Oh, I know, you catch cold from germs, not from rain and chill, but the rain and the chill had gotten to me nonetheless. The Y was my first post-Cape, post-cold venture out of the house.

The bride-to-be, Jessica Franklin, hadn't called Sunday, so I hadn't had to confess my abject failure over the phone. It hadn't surprised me, her decision to wait till Monday, but it had surprised me when she didn't show for our Monday meeting. Didn't come, didn't call, wasn't answering her cell. I was planning to stop by her apartment after the game. I wasn't looking forward to the conversation, and now I'd get to conduct it through a swollen red nose.

And speaking of failure, consider my latest conversation with Sam. Just when my cold was at its fruitiest, head pounding, nose dripping, guess who called, waking me, sweating and shivery, at an ungodly hour? Still phoning from nowhere. I'd unburdened myself about Paolina, about the cutting, and McLean.

"Don't worry about money. You need money, go to Eddie Nardo."

"This the same Eddie Nardo who's putting your stuff in storage?"

Silence.

I'd told him that I didn't need his money right now. Paolina's late father hadn't planned on his stash being used for therapy instead of college, but therapy was what my sister needed now if college was ever going to be an option.

I wasn't planning to say anything about Jonno's revelation, about the dead woman in Sam's recent past. I really wasn't, but I was exhausted and sick, and I guess I got angry when he asked me again. Meet him, please. Run away, marry him in Italy. And this right after we'd talked about Paolina. He knows I'd never leave her.

"I told you to leave the legal stuff alone," he'd responded, voice tight. "I'm taking care of it."

"How? Long distance?"

"I'll get back to you," he'd said, and like our last phone call, this one ended when he hung up.

"How's it going?" Loretta called. "Can you play yet?"

I focused on the game. We were down by two. Movement seemed sluggish, listless; both teams were running on fumes.

"Soon," I said. "Give me five."

I shifted the icy towel on my nose. I hadn't linked Sam to Anthony "Big Tony" Gianelli until I'd already fallen for him. Then, when I became a cop, I'd made the choice to avoid information about anyone named Gianelli. Not for me a special assignment to Organized Crime, not for me a precinct in the North End. I'd stayed far from OC, tried not to think about OC, and now OC was being pushed in my face. How do you do monstrous things and not become a monster?

Mooney thought Sam was guilty, and why not?

My nose hurt and I felt mean. I tossed the bloody towel on the bench, went in and played erratically, making the hard shots, missing the easy stuff.

Two men marched into the gym near the end of the match. They drew my eyes like a magnet; both wore suits and had a thickness across their shoulders and upper bodies that spoke to me of underarm holsters. They stood for a moment, framed by a shaft of sunshine, then made their way to the bleachers and sat heavily.

Just when you think it can't get any worse, my grandmother allegedly used to say, *it always does.*

We fought back to a tie, but wound up blowing the lead and losing by two lousy points.

CHAPTER 10

"Cops." Loretta edged close to me in the locker room and spoke in a stage whisper. "Outside. For you."

A couple of players stopped, shirts over their heads, shorts halfway down their thighs, and stared. They know I used to be a cop, but on the whole we keep our outside worlds outside the game. I know Annie's a lawyer. I know Margie works for Blue Cross and Deirdre has an autistic kid, but we keep our volleyball games about volleyball. I showered quickly, which I always do because the Cambridge Y is not some fancy spa where you want to luxuriate in the ambience. Believe me, you just want to get the sweat off and exit before you have a chance to notice the mold on the plastic shower curtain or the silverfish scuttling into the dark corners.

I got dressed on autopilot. *This is about Sam,* I thought. At last; about time; no more dancing around. Someone was finally going to fill in the blanks, tell me exactly what Sam was accused of doing. Cops were going to try to make me alibi him or betray him; maybe they would demand that I reveal his location. I don't know what I'd expected to feel, but one major component was relief. I toweled off, took the scrunchie off my ponytail, shook out my hair.

They were Boston cops, not federal agents. That was the first surprise.

"Nasty shot, that last one. Nice. Ya play college ball?" The bigger cop spoke first. He was built like a tackle, his neck the size of a bull's.

My alma mater, UMass Boston, a commuter school, hardly had any teams, just students too busy holding down jobs to provide much in the way of rah-rah spirit. I shook my head no.

"Ya totally deeked 'em. One minute, you're goin' right and then, wham, ya shift midair."

There's nothing worse than a cop trying to flatter you.

"Carlyle, right?" the big guy went on. "I'm McHenry and this here is McDonough. We both answer to Mac, so guess what? They teamed us up."

He waited. I nodded.

"We're outa Area A." The second Mac was short, lean, and black, not what you'd expect from the surname.

"What's this about?" I wanted to head to Dunkin' Donuts in Central Square. I was hungry. Maybe they'd buy me a glazed and a cup of coffee.

"Got a car?"

I shook my head. I'd returned the maimed cab to Gloria. Today was my day to rent or buy.

The Big Mac said, "Something we want to show you."

The Little Mac said, "We'll drive."

I should have said no right then, told them I was busy and under no obligation to accompany them anywhere. But I wanted to know about Sam, and curiosity—well, curiosity left me open to error.

The backseat of their unit wasn't caged, but the door-openers were nonoperational. I settled in uneasily. Little Mac drove.

Big Mac turned his torso and leaned over the seat. "So, lotta dykes on the team?"

"Mostly just us pagan cannibals," I said flatly.

Little Mac snorted.

I spent most of the drive wondering how I could fool the Macs into giving me more information than I intended to give them. I had nothing to say about Sam, and once they figured that out, they weren't exactly going to open up. The challenge was to make them want to tell me stuff, make them think that if they painted Sam's crime in sufficiently lurid colors, I'd be overwhelmed and offer him up, maybe reveal other crimes as yet unknown.

They hadn't served me with a grand jury subpoena. Nothing says you have to tell the truth when cops ask questions. Nothing says you even have to answer. It's just that I grew up with the cheerful banter of my dad's cop buddies in my ears, practically the mascot of his Detroit precinct, left on their doorstep while my mother marched for social justice. Not that I blamed her; they were righteous causes, every one. Not that I blamed anybody. It's just that I understood why Sam, born into the mob the way I was born into the cops, got sucked in. Sam wanted to please his dad, much as I wanted to please mine.

Even now, when he's been dead these many years, I had to remind myself that I didn't have to talk to the cops to please my dad. I didn't have to be a cop.

I thought we were heading to the New Sudbury Street Station. I assumed it, a cardinal error. Remnants of my cold, or more likely, getting whacked in the nose, must have addled my brain.

We stayed straight when we should have turned. We drove to Albany Street.

Albany Street used to mean Chinatown, just another street in Chinatown with the pungent smell of restaurant food and shops with windows that opened on a view of hanging poultry, glistening ducks and fat geese. Now Albany Street means the medical examiner's office, the new building, way better than the old one, but a morgue is a morgue, call it what you will.

My stomach flip-flopped and I thought, *Paolina.* Then I thought, no, she's safe. McLean is safe. I swallowed and wished we'd gone for doughnuts, coffee, anything to counteract the sour taste in my mouth.

"Who?" I demanded as they pulled into a metered parking slot.

"Look, nobody's trying to upset you."

"Right. The chief medical examiner just wants to ask me a few questions about DNA analysis?"

"Nah, he—"

"Who?" I repeated.

"We don't know. That's why—"

"What makes you think I'd know?"

"Relax. You read the papers?"

I nodded.

"Then you know we got a mess here. There's bodies stacked up, and we think we can ID one, we give it a try, you know? You're lucky, the one we got for you is pretty fresh. They got stiffs here probably date back years."

They didn't force me to go inside. They didn't squawk about imminent arrest. If I'd refused, I'm not sure what they'd have done. I didn't refuse; demon curiosity won again.

The place smelled ripe. The stink had been only one of the complaints voiced by a tech who'd walked off the job and into the offices of the *Herald.* The smell, the drain backup in the autopsy rooms, the shortage of body bags, the corpses stacked three to a shelf and three to a gurney, the temporary refrigerated truck pressed into service.

The scandal at the ME's competed for space with the grand opening of Lincoln Park's Twin River expansion, a Rhode Island gambling haven boasting over four thousand slot machines. Massachusetts legislators were watching both stories closely. Millions of dollars of state revenue, money sorely needed to pull the ME's office back from disgrace, might head south if citizens crossed the state line to play the slots instead of giving their spare cash to the Mass State Lottery.

I took out a wad of Kleenex and pressed it to my nose.

Little Mac led the way down a long linoleum hallway. "We thought we'd run this lady by you, see if maybe you can help us out. We get a couple more of these stiffs identified, we can go back out on the street like cops. So we'd appreciate it if you'd take a good look."

"Save it," Big Mac said. "She's a tough guy. She's not gonna pass out."

The news stories seemed to have had a galvanizing effect. The place was chaotic, aides shoving gurneys to and fro, shouting commands. Everything was getting done in a rush, in time for rebuttal on Channel 5 at eleven. I swallowed and steeled myself.

"This lady." A woman. Who was she and why did they think I could make the ID? I considered turning and bolting for the door. I mean, what could they do? Shoot me?

They didn't guide me into any formal viewing room or ask whether I wanted to see a grief counselor. They led me to a corridor that ran perpendicular to the first one, to a gurney lined up with other gurneys along the hall.

"Haven't done the cut yet," Little Mac said.

"Why am I not surprised?" Big Mac checked the tag, glanced at me, and casually flipped the sheet.

Not Marta. I didn't even realize I'd expected it to

be Paolina's mother until I saw who it actually was.

Jessica Franklin, the beautiful, tearful young woman who'd come to me for help. Jessica Franklin, "call me Jessie," bride-never-to-be. Lying on the narrow gurney, half her face smashed to pulp, dried blood matting the smooth dark hair.

"You know her?"

The hallway felt so close, suddenly too warm, suddenly stifling, airless, and still. I must have nodded.

"Bingo." The big cop's voice seemed to come from far away.

"You okay?"

"What happened?" I said. "How—?"

One of the Macs flipped the sheet to cover her, but I couldn't look away.

"Your business card in her pocket. Took a couple days to make it out, blood and stuff, but that's all she had. No wallet, no purse."

"Robbery?"

"Hit and run."

"When?" I managed. My voice sounded hoarse and gravelly.

"Late Friday, early Saturday." Little Mac yanked a notebook out of his pocket, ran a finger down a page. "Found Saturday, four in the morning."

"No," I said.

"Whaddaya mean, no? It's in the report."

"She was in New York."

He checked the notebook again. "Nope. She was in the North End."

It made no sense. Had she forgotten her bag at the restaurant, taken a taxi back? Missed her train? I reached out and touched the rough sheet over Jessie's motionless arm.

Sometimes I stonewall the cops to protect a client. Jessica Franklin didn't need protecting anymore.

I spilled everything.

CHAPTER 11

The rectangular light flashed green. I centered the photo of the groom-to-be facedown on the screen, closed the cover, and pressed SCAN. The cops wanted the entire Jessica Franklin file. I wanted my own copy, a clear record of a truncated case.

The machine hiccuped and I removed the shiny paper, turning it right side up. You see a photo, you make a snap judgment. The first time I'd viewed the five-by-seven of Kenneth L. Harrison, I'd said to myself: handsome, well-off. The features were regular, easy on the eye, the smile self-assured, the teeth too even and white for poverty. Circumstances change and judgment alters. Photos, features, don't change, but now, knowing what I knew, Ken's smile seemed less carefree, more wary. Now, when I looked in his eyes, I saw the wreck of his hopes, the death of his bride.

I sat at my desk and traced circles on a pad of paper. I know how fragile life is: One minute your mom smiling in the living room and the next, relatives talking in hushed tones, saying it's not your fault; heart attacks happen. I know that blips on the hospital machines can seem strong one minute and disappear the next. But Jessica Franklin was so young, and I hadn't expected it, and I'd been relieved when it was Jessie, not Paolina or Marta.

Was that why I felt so sad, so guilty? I'd done nothing wrong, but part of me kept nagging, niggling, insisting I'd made a mistake, chosen incorrectly, followed the wrong person when Jessie and Ken split up at South Station. What was that about? Did I imagine some dark cloud had hovered over the girl, some portent of impending doom I'd failed to notice?

The doorbell rang and I stuffed the photo hurriedly into a folder and stuck it in my top desk drawer. What was this? Police efficiency all of a sudden? I hadn't finished copying my notes and here they were.

Probably Roz had forgotten her key again. I bit back my annoyance. I'd tried phoning Roz so she could, in turn, reach the friend who'd recommended me to the dead girl, warn her before Jessie's name blared across the news. If it was Roz, she could help me copy the file.

The bell sounded again. I hollered, "Coming," and hurried into the foyer, opening the door without checking the peephole, expecting Roz or, failing that, expecting the stolid Macs.

Eddie Nardo, the mob lawyer, always wore a hat. I'd asked Sam about it once, and he'd said it was because Nardo couldn't wear a crown without somebody making a wiseass comment. Now Nardo himself stood on my porch, hat in hand, and I decided the fedora might have something to do with his thinning hair.

I was surprised at how small he was. He projected the power of a larger man, a take-charge guy, a serious person. A lot of little guys play tough, or so I've heard. Nardo was tough; his reputation had penetrated even my shell.

"Mind if I come in?" He offered a disarming smile. His big black Mercedes was parked on the street. He had a driver, but no other obvious bodyguards. "Cold out here."

I said, "Okay, Mr. Nardo, come on in."

"Eddie," he said. "Call me Eddie, like Sam does."

I hated to think of him and Sam together. Nardo's black cashmere topcoat shamed my spindly coatrack, but I didn't offer a coat hanger.

"Hey, you got a nice place here." He took his time crossing the foyer, down the single step to the living room. He sat across from my desk, settling in and crossing his legs, making the small chair look bigger than it was.

"Thanks."

His shoes, supposing he'd paid retail, must have cost eight hundred easy. He sat there, relaxed, at ease, like I'd invited him by for a chat. Maybe he was expecting me to offer him a drink.

"Can I help you?"

He smiled and shifted his weight, leaning back like

he was going to claim the chair for a while. "So, you hear from Sam lately?"

"Why?"

"Just if you're talking to him, you tell him we're keeping his dad out of the loop. No need for Big Tony to fret, ya know? Nothing he can do the way he is."

"Which is?"

"If Sam asks, you say Tony's holding his own."

"*I* asked because I was curious. I don't know that I'll get a chance to pass the information along." I didn't want to become a mob conduit. I thought it was interesting that Eddie would come to me, like a confession that he wasn't in touch with Sam.

"If you were going to tell Tony what happened," I went on, casually, "what would you say to him?"

"Look, I'm sorry. I mean, I hate to keep you in the dark if that's where you are, but Sam, ya know, the boy's like a son to me, and I don't want to say anything might come between the two of you. He's a good man and he loves you. That ought to be enough."

So much for the fishing expedition.

"But, hey, you need money, Sam wants you to have whatever you want. He's worried about the little girl. He said I should just write out a check, or leave you a blank one, if you'd rather."

"Not necessary. Not yet. I'll let you know." So he had been talking to Sam. "Is that all?"

"Well, no." He shot me the smile again. "Really, ya know, I came to beg your pardon."

That surprised me. "What for?"

"I wanted that bum, Jonno, to come with me, but Katharine, she can't see that her little darling should have to do anything he doesn't want to do. Other than that, ya know, she's a hardheaded woman, a business woman, but where Jonno's concerned, she might as well be some ditzy house wife. My baby boy. No matter what crap he does, it's always for the best."

I waited.

"Jonno's got no use for Sam, ya know? Some kind of weird sibling rivalry shit—excuse the language. Like he wanted Tony all for himself. Wants a father, another father, because his own father was a useless SOB. So what I'm saying is he had no business closing up the Charles River place like that, thinking he's gonna take it over. He jumped the gun, ya know? We all think Sam will beat this thing, that it's not going to be long before he's back in town."

I wanted to believe him.

"I'm holding things together till he comes, but Jonno, well, he's a hell of a problem, going off half-cocked like he does. So I wanted to tell you, the apartment is still Sam's. I'll get his stuff moved back, no problem. Jonno doesn't speak for the rest of the family. Understand?"

I nodded.

He regarded the boxes. "He just dumped this stuff here?"

"He did."

"He's got a nerve. I'll be glad to bring it back. He had no business doing it. I don't know, the kid's not exactly under control." Nardo rubbed his hands together, got up, and moved toward the boxes.

"Leave them," I said.

"Hey, it's no trouble. I'll buzz my driver. He'll grab a couple. Whenever you want to come over to the apartment, unpack, put everything the way you want it, you do that. You want to live there, move in full-time, it's okay by me."

"Thanks," I said, "but I kept too much stuff there anyway. I'll take care of it."

"You sure?"

"Sure."

"I meant what I said, about the money, about Sam being like a son. If there's anything I can do for you, you call me."

I wondered what Nardo's story was. How he came to be who he was. I almost asked him about the Jaguar—where it was and would he help me get it back from Jonno. Then I thought about owing a guy like Nardo a favor.

I handed him the cashmere coat. It felt as soft as sin.

CHAPTER 12

Paolina had free time on Tuesdays and Thursdays from two until three, an unscheduled block when a staff member might escort an approved visitor into the common area. Only Paolina's therapist could approve the visitor, and Eisner tended to update the list daily at 1:55, which was inconvenient, to say the least. If I phoned just before two to discover I'd been added to the list, I couldn't make it there till three, when I would no longer be admitted.

After the Macs came by and took the Franklin file, I decided to make the drive on spec. My chances of getting inside were small, but on the whole, I approved of the visitation policy. Without the restrictions, Marta would have hounded my little sister constantly, harping on what a burden she was, how she needed to get home and babysit her brothers.

Even at the tail end of winter, naked branches on the lofty trees, the grounds at McLean looked like the cover of a Christmas card. This is what it will be like when I visit Paolina at Colgate or Swarthmore or Mount Holyoke, picture-perfect campuses I've seen only in books, campuses far removed from the urban Boston universities cut by T rails and busy roads. The fantasy got me up the entrance road and around to the East Building.

It's a storied place, McLean, a veritable condensed history of New England arts and letters. Lowells and Sextons, girls interrupted and bell-jarred. Paolina had been lucky to be admitted, and at least they no longer called it the McLean Asylum for the Insane.

I tried to shake off my somber mood. Must be the gray gloominess of the day, the aftershock of the morgue. Jessica Franklin would forever represent a failure, an unsolved case. She wouldn't send a card someday, thanking me for saving her from a terrible marriage; no cheery holiday greeting containing photos of her sweet-faced kids by another, better man.

Think of something else, I ordered myself. Be grateful to Sam, even to Nardo, for offering money. Be grateful Paolina will be able to stay at McLean as long as she needs to, be grateful you don't need to desperately troll for clients.

When I saw Mooney's car in the lot, I braked, stared, then pulled in alongside.

I would know that car anywhere, that battered Buick, the quintessential Boston beater, a wreck you'd hesitate to challenge on the highway. Didn't look like it had many more miles left, and he still hadn't gotten the banged-up passenger door fixed. It won't open; the passenger has to enter on the driver's side and crawl over the hump, which must restrict the man's dating.

I picked up my cell phone, punched in the McLean number, and the answer was the same. No, I hadn't been elevated to acceptable visitor status.

I should have driven home. Instead I waited till Mooney came out the door, down the flagged path. When he was ten feet from his car, I emerged and blocked his route.

"Did you see her?"

"Christ, Carlyle, what the hell is that you're driving?"

"Coming from you, that's good. Did you see her?"

"You going in?"

"No."

"Talking to her doctor?"

"No."

"I give up."

"You saw her?"

"Hey, I should have come before. You know the excuses, all the busywork, all the paperwork. I'm buried under it, but I should have come. So thanks for reminding me at the range. I mean, I'm sorry about what happened, but if you hadn't come, I wouldn't have . . ." He wound down and took a breath. "Anyway, why are you here if you're not going inside? You tailing me?"

"How is she?"

He hesitated. "Hard to say. We just talked."

"What did she say?"

"Carlotta, we talked."

"That's more than she'll do with me, Moon."

He looked down at his shoes, kicked at a chunk of gravel. "I know."

"She told you? That she won't talk to me?"

He nodded.

"Shit."

"Hey, come on." He gave a quick look around, like he was sure he was being observed. "Let's get a cup of coffee, go someplace warm."

"I don't want to compromise your virtue."

"Look, it's no joke. The feds think I blew their chance to nab Gianelli. My record, all the years I've worked, and they jump on me."

"They can't prove it."

"They may not need to. You know what they're like.

95

And it's not like I haven't tangled with them before."

"Your guy, Dailey, he a big red-faced guy?"

"Get in the car at least," he said. "I'm freezing."

"My car," I said.

"You didn't buy that thing, did you?"

"I borrowed it. And, by the way, all the doors open."

"Ouch," he said.

The rust-and-blue 1986 Honda Civic featured sprung seats and an interior that smelled like cheap pine air freshener. I hadn't really borrowed it. I'd rented it only an hour earlier, because I was still enthralled by the possibility of finding Sam's Jaguar. Hope and procrastination had brought me to a Somerville rent-a-wreck owned by a friend of a friend, to another sad excuse for a car.

"This is cozy," Mooney said.

"Skip it."

"So you ran into Dailey?"

"What's his story?"

"Rufus Dailey, special agent. Da-da. The only reason he wasn't farmed out to North Dakota after Whitey Bulger skipped was that he was the lead guy on the Gianellis. Can't stand the thought of history repeating itself, Gianelli going fugitive, too. Missed the boat on Whitey, but he's damned well gonna get Gianelli. Rabid-dog type, and if he can get his teeth in me, he'll bite."

"Charming," I said.

"You saw him?"

"Hanging around Sam's apartment."

"Sam's not in the States? No, don't tell me. I don't want to know."

"He's not in the States," I said.

"So," Mooney said after an awkward gap, "you working?"

"I was."

"You get fired?"

"I don't get fired all that often, Moon."

"You quit?"

"I don't do that either." Sometimes I think he's never forgiven me for quitting the force. "My client died. Area A, hit and run."

"Christ, drivers around here. Drunk?"

"They haven't nailed anybody. Couldn't even make the ID on the corpse till they found me. You know a couple of cops named Mac?"

"Area A?"

"They rousted me, brought me over to the ME's."

"Mess over there," he said.

"I tried to get them to tell me about it, when and where and what they were doing to find the car that hit my client. Whether they had wits, who was knocking doors—"

"You didn't get far?"

"Nowhere."

"Look, it's a hit and run. You know how that is. Maybe somebody will sober up and turn himself in."

"And maybe he won't."

"Client hire you because he was scared he might catch something fatal?"

"Her. And no."

"But?"

"It doesn't feel right." I told him about Jessica's trip to New York. "She shouldn't have been where she was found."

"Well, if you want me to have a word with these Mac guys . . ." He looked and sounded reluctant. His breath fogged a circle in the windshield.

"Yeah," I said. "Thanks."

"I oughta go," he said.

"How does she look? Paolina. You can at least tell me that."

"Carlotta, it must be hard, that she won't talk to—"

"How does she look?"

"She's fine. She cut her hair. Just a little. Hey, come on. It's her hair."

"Sorry. It's just I'm not sure this is the right thing for her. Everybody says it is, but being shut up here, thinking about what happened to her all the time—"

"She doesn't think about it all the time. They have classes and stuff. Groups. She's trying to keep up with school. And she listens to music a lot. She's got a CD she checked out of the library. Colombian music. She played it for me."

"So why won't she see me?"

He stared out the side window. "I'm not sure."

"Why do you think?"

"Carlotta, I don't know what to say, except you're a pretty tough act to follow."

I shook my head to show him I didn't follow his logic.

"She sees you as so strong, Carlotta, so perfect. And she fell apart. She cried and cried for days, and she thinks she disappointed you somehow."

"She's a kid."

"Right."

"And I'm not perfect, for Christ's sake."

"Yeah, I told her that. Believe me, I did."

"Thanks."

"But you hold yourself to some tough standards, lady. Maybe Paolina thinks you hold her to standards that are just as high."

"What do you mean?"

"You're tough on yourself; that's all I'm saying. Like when you left the force? You were punishing yourself. Because you didn't live up to your own expectations."

"You studying psychology out here? Taking night classes?"

"Look, I better go."

He opened the door and stepped out. I didn't stop him. Didn't look at him.

Instead I drove away so quickly, my tires spun on the gravel, my hands clenched on the steering wheel. I studied them, with their short unvarnished nails and reddened knuckles. Volleyball hands. Guitar hands. Killer's hands.

I didn't need to punish myself this time; Paolina was doing it for me.

CHAPTER 13

I noticed the flasher in the rearview mirror as I squeezed through the yellow, but I figured it was an ambulance since I cut through traffic signals like that all the time and never get stopped for doing it. I switched to the right-hand lane to make way for the emergency vehicle, but instead of getting passed at speed by an ambulance or a fire truck, a light brown sedan with a portable flasher on the roof swerved in behind me. When the sedan blinked its headlights, I coasted to a stop on the grass verge near the ornate metal gates of Mount Auburn Cemetery.

The beefy red-faced man took his time emerging from behind the wheel.

"See your license, miss?"

"This a traffic stop? Sir?"

"I'm a federal agent."

"With credentials?"

He took his time slipping them out of his back pocket. He wore dark wraparound sunglasses, so I couldn't see his eyes; not their color, not their shape.

"A couple of questions for you," he said.

"Then it's not a traffic stop?"

"It could get to be one." He sounded annoyed.

His tone pleased me in a perverse kind of way. Guess I was in the mood to annoy someone. "Don't tell me. It's a Patriot Act stop?"

"Miss, you want me to search your vehicle?"

Suddenly I didn't want him searching the car at all. How did I know what the hell was in the car? I'd just rented it. There could be half a kilo of coke in the trunk. Or Special Agent Dailey could plant a baggie of marijuana in the dash compartment and cause merry hell.

I smiled as sweetly as I could manage. "Hey, no need. Why not just tell me why you pulled me over and we'll take care of it."

"You know a Boston cop named Joseph Mooney?"

"I do."

"How do you know him?"

"Professionally."

"Really?" His voice went up like I'd just confessed to something.

"Through law enforcement. We worked together. Straight shooter. Ask anybody."

"I'm asking you. When was the last time you saw him?"

"Is he under suspicion for something?"

"I'm asking you."

"Well, I just now spoke to the man. We met by chance. While he was visiting a friend of mine."

"In the looney bin?"

"A good friend. You might say a sister." My smile got chillier.

"Did Mr. Nardo give you any message to pass on to Captain Mooney?"

"Nardo? And Mooney?" I almost laughed. "You are barking up one dead tree."

"Just answer the question."

"No, Mr. Nardo did not give me any message to pass on to Captain Mooney," I recited.

"How would you characterize your relationship with Mr. Nardo."

"I have no relationship with Mr. Nardo."

"He came to your house."

"He was selling Girl Scout cookies."

"You may not know what you're messing with here, Miss Carlyle."

"Oh, but I think I do. I think you don't."

"A little advice, miss? Stay away from Nardo."

"Happy to do it."

"And get that left taillight fixed."

I bit. After he pulled away, I got out and circled the car. And, of course, there was nothing wrong with my left taillight.

But wait a minute: There had been something wrong with the Volvo's left taillight, with Ken Harrison's left taillight. And where had Agent Dailey been late Friday night? I wished I'd gotten the license plate of the sedan that zipped around the rotary after I'd hit the tacks.

Since I was so close and the larder was bare, I stopped at the Shaw's across Mount Auburn Street for cold cuts and eggs. Since the liquor store was within walking distance of the Shaw's lot, I picked up a couple of six-packs. I thought about adding a carton or two of cigarettes, but held fast.

Then, as if to redeem myself for the beer, I left

everything in the trunk and marched into Harvard Square. Despite the cold, the Andean street musicians who had been playing in front of Calliope for the past few weeks were holding court. I listened, arms folded for warmth, until they took a break, then asked where I could buy a set of pipes like the ones the frizzy-haired guitarist occasionally played. I thought Paolina might like them. She couldn't have her trap set at McLean because the drumming might upset the other patients, but the pipes were low and sweet.

The street musician wore woolen gloves with the fingers cut off. We conversed in Spanish. He told me he played the pan pipes, seven bamboo reeds of varying lengths fastened together, but a novice might have more success with the *quena*, a single pipe resembling a recorder. He demonstrated both and I put five dollars in the collection jug.

I thought I'd have to drive out to Wood & Strings in Arlington, or maybe to Daddy's Junky Music, but the musician sent me to a basement emporium on a nearby back street. I bought the smallest pan pipes they had. They cost too much and I didn't care. I'd stop buying beer, save my pennies.

I walked home with my purchase clasped tight against my chest.

Dailey wanted me to know he was keeping an eye on me. The question was why.

CHAPTER 14

I was dressed when the bell rang Wednesday morning. Dressed, but in a haze. It was too early for visitors, I hadn't eaten breakfast, and the shrill summons of the doorbell seemed to pierce my skull. Opening my front door takes time under the best of circumstances, since I have more than one lock and a strong chain as well; it's a neighborhood thing. As I fumbled with the locks, I checked the peephole.

Cops. Big Mac leaned on the bell again, and my ears tried to crawl inside my brain.

Both officers stared at me accusingly when I managed to open the door. They'd changed clothes since yesterday. Each wore a slightly different, but equally unattractive, suit.

"You leave your car on the street around here?" Little Mac asked. So much for civilities, good morning, and so on. I hadn't had my morning coffee yet, and I needed it badly.

"You got demoted to parking detail?" I asked pleasantly.

"Just answer the question."

"I don't have a car at the moment."

They both looked at me like I'd confessed to spending my childhood on the moon. Big Mac retreated a couple of steps. I was hoping he'd retreat all the way to his car, but he went only as far as the top step, where he stopped and scraped the sole of his left shoe. Must have picked up some dog poo on his way across the lawn. Another neighborhood hazard. Besides burglars.

"You telling us you don't drive?" Little Mac said.

"I was in an accident," I said. "My car got totaled."

"When did this happen?"

I walked them through it. They didn't seem to understand how I'd been able to cope for months without a car of my own.

"I live in Cambridge." Since that didn't register, I tried, "You can check the New Hampshire police report for a date. I'll can fax you my insurance forms."

"So what are you doing for a car?" Little Mac kept the ball rolling.

"I don't need one that much. I use the T. It's environmentally friendly."

"But you do need one occasionally?"

"I use a rental. Anything else you want to talk about?"

"Can we come in?"

"Do we have anything else to discuss? I gave you the file—"

"Yeah, we heard you had a sense of humor." Big Mac spoke for the first time. He had an angry flush in his cheeks.

"What?" I said, meaning, What did I do?

Little Mac shook his head sorrowfully.

"I think we should just haul her the hell out of there," the big guy muttered. He scuffed his foot on the porch step again, and I thought about asking him to take his smelly shoe off before I let him in the foyer.

Probably not a good idea. I moved back from the doorstep, not graciously, I admit, and they shuffled inside. We gave each other the eyeball for a while.

I said to McHenry, or was it McDonough? Whatever—the big one. "Don't blame me. It's not my dog; I don't even have a dog."

"Why should we believe you?"

"Why shouldn't you believe me? You want to see my cat?"

"Let's sit down somewhere, okay? Maybe this is just some kind of misunderstanding." Little Mac tried to smooth the waters, but I didn't trust him. I didn't trust them.

I took the seat behind my desk because I wanted to keep them at a distance. Neither of the cops seemed to want to lead off the conversation. I wanted my coffee. Finally I decided that if I didn't want to waste the whole day, I'd have to say something.

I tried turning a single word on its head. "Misunderstanding?"

"Who was the girl?" Big Mac said.

"What girl?"

"The dead girl in the morgue. I saw your face. You knew her, all right."

"Hey, I'm the one who told you I knew her."

"The one you called 'Jessica Franklin.'"

I got a cold feeling in my stomach.

"A whole day," the smaller cop said reproachfully.

106

"More than a day wasted, and now we're exactly where we started."

"Jessica Franklin. That's the name she gave me."

"Hey," Big Mac said, "there is no Jessica Franklin. We know all about it."

"Guys," I said, "there is no Santa Claus and I'm not gonna fight you over the Easter Bunny or the Tooth Fairy. But Jessica Franklin, the girl on your slab? She sat right in that chair last Thursday night and cried her eyes out. Used up a whole box of Kleenex."

Little Mac said, "So it would surprise you to know that Jessica Franklin, the Jessica Franklin who lives at the address you gave us, is alive and well."

"Yeah, it would surprise me. Hey, it would delight me. And if my Jessica Franklin is alive and well, she can absolutely name your corpse. Because it would have to be a sister, a twin sister."

Big Mac said, "Wrong. This Jessica Franklin is a nurse's aide, works over at St. Elizabeth's. She's fifty-four years old and a model citizen. Only time the Allston cops ever heard from her was when she got her wallet lifted two weeks ago."

Shit, I thought.

Roz, I screamed silently, *how the hell could you do this to me?*

I said, "You showed her the dead girl's picture?"

"We don't exactly have a great photo of the dead girl. You show that kind of photo around, you get bad reactions."

"But you described her," I said.

"Old Jessica Franklin didn't seem to know her."

"Shit," I said. "Believe me, this girl was good, really good, Academy Award level, a great little actress. Tears, the whole thing." I was trying to take it in as I spoke. No wedding, no fussy mother, no cheating bridegroom. I was thinking fast.

Big Mac took something out of a folder. I recognized it.

"Looks good," he said. "You got any more lying around?"

"Wedding invitations?"

"No, no, just the stationery. Print-it-yourself stuff. It's not embossed, just a good old ink-jet printer. Looks like you've got a new one."

"Look, the woman, the dead woman, whoever she was, gave it to me."

Little Mac said, "I called the place myself, this Fiore place in Saugus. They do a lot of weddings, but they never heard of this couple."

Roz, I thought. *Dammit, Roz.* Roz had been insistent that it was time for me to go back to work. She wouldn't have thought twice about lying for a good cause, saying that a woman who called in out of the blue was "a friend of a friend," a special case. But she was supposed to check out prospective clients.

How could I sit here and blame it all on Roz? I knew her foibles and I'd hired her; I'd trusted her to do the job.

"She wasn't wearing an engagement ring," Little Mac said.

"She was wearing one when I saw her. Alive."

"Yeah?"

"A silver band, not a stone."

"You don't wear an engagement ring, I notice?"

That was Big Mac's way of telling me he knew who I was, that he'd run a background check, that he knew I was engaged to an organized crime figure, that nothing I said was worth believing.

"Oh, yeah." He yanked another item out of the folder, "And 'Jessica' gave you this photo, too?"

"Her fiancé, the man she hired me to follow."

"Yeah, well, listen, after we had our little heart-to-heart over at Albany Street, we go back to the station and I'm feeling pretty good, you know, because we got a solid ID, a place to start, and I'm happy, you know? I've got this photo on my desk and guess who comes along? Lieutenant Terrance. You know him?"

"No."

"Stiff-ass guy, guy I'd like to impress for once. And you know what he says?"

"No."

"He asks me: Am I a fan? I say, 'Excuse me, sir, a fan of what?' thinking he is no way asking me if I'm his fan because that's kind of a stupid thing to say. So he points at this picture, this photo you gave me, and you said was a guy you followed around the other night. You know who this is?"

"I told you his name."

"It's some guy sings with a punk rock band."

"But—I followed him."

"The guy looked like this? Exactly like this?" He tapped the photo with his index finger.

"He wore a scarf. It was cold. It was dark." I stopped because I could hear how lame it sounded. I'd expected the man to look like the photo. Dammit, he'd been with my client. She'd strolled him out of the restaurant, smiling up at her "fiancé."

"And the woman paid you in cash?" Little Mac said.

"I accept cash."

"You didn't think it was odd?"

"She said she'd done some gambling at Foxwoods."

He gave me a look, like how dumb is that? I didn't blame him.

Big Mac said, "Let's go back to the guy. You tailed him in a cab, you said?"

"Hey, I gave you his license plate."

"Guess what? Stolen."

They were landing so many direct hits, I felt boxed into a corner. "Did you run her prints, the dead woman's?" It seemed like my only choice was to go on the offensive.

No response.

"Is an artist doing a sketch? So you can try it out on the real Jessica?"

"We're not here to answer your questions," Big Mac said. "You're supposed to answer ours."

"If we cooperate—"

Little Mac said, "Cooperation? That's what we thought we were getting down at Albany Street."

Big Mac said, "You made us look bad, Carlyle. Why are you lying to us?"

I could have told them I wasn't lying. Again. I could have sworn on my mother's grave and volunteered to take a lie detector test. Hell, I could have banged my head against the wall, but I didn't want to give them the satisfaction.

So I said nothing. And they took me downtown.

PART THREE

CHAPTER 15

My anger level soared with each innuendo-packed question the Macs tossed my way. There was no point to the exercise beyond the naked display of power; they had decided to waste my time because they thought I had wasted theirs. They denied me a cup of coffee simply because I requested one. My head pounded till I thought it might explode, and when I finally demanded that they charge me or let me go, they let me sit for an hour and twenty-two minutes in an empty interrogation room to show me that they were in charge and I wasn't.

No one offered me a ride home either. The Red Line into Harvard Square was crowded and steamy, full of the smell of wet wool and underwashed bodies. It wasn't until the Central Square stop that I realized I was inspecting each boarding passenger, looking for Jessica Franklin.

I knew she was dead. She had lied to me from beginning to end. If she got on the T, if her ghost got on the T, I would grab her and shake her till she told me why she had lied. I tried to fill myself with righteous anger. The woman had lied to me and now I was in trouble with the cops. All because of her.

Every time I managed to stoke the flame of my anger to a righteous burn, it subsided in a rush of sadness followed by a tide of curiosity. Why had she come to me, that sweet-faced child, with her plausible lies? Who was she? Who was Kenneth L. Harrison?

The minute I got home, I made coffee, adding milk till it was cool enough to chug. Then I hollered for Roz. Time for a reckoning. Yelling felt good, a release, a safety valve, and I knew perfectly well she could hear me. The house is old, the walls thin. I hear her plenty, especially when she and her mate du jour go at it hot and heavy on the tumbling mats she calls furniture.

When she didn't respond, I abandoned my caffeine on the counter and raced upstairs. Moving felt almost as good as shouting. When Roz opened the door to her third-floor hideaway, she looked like a punk Cinderella in rags, her head wrapped in a ratty scarf, a shock of blue hair visible on the right side.

"I was just going to clean the house," she announced breathlessly. "Top to bottom. Honest." She pays reduced rent in exchange for house work, but she cleans neither often nor well.

"I know I fucked up," she rushed on, "but really, I was gonna do more than just check that a Jessica Franklin lived where she said she did. I was gonna run all sorts of checks, but then you told me to do that thing with the dead bodies in Vegas, remember? I thought that was more important."

The Macs hadn't been that loud. I wondered whether she eavesdropped on all my conversations. "But you said—"

114

"She wasn't a 'friend of a friend.' A little white lie, you know? I didn't think it would hurt. You needed to get back to work."

"Did you suggest it, or did she?"

"I don't—Is it important?"

"Yes, it's important! Dammit, I don't know what's important. The girl is dead!"

Roz stared at the floor, then stuck her tongue in the corner of her mouth. "I kinda think she suggested it. I put her off, said you weren't taking clients, and then she said something about really needing to see you, and was there any way we could fix it. She sounded so nice, and—Shit! Cleaning the house, I guess I should stick to that, right?"

"I want to know who that woman is. Was. Why she lied." I tugged my hair and concentrated on breathing. The impersonation was so detailed. It had seemed so real, the fussy mother, the prim father, the nasty anonymous note. Now they'd vanished like evening shadows, leaving behind a wild goose chase to the Cape and an unidentified body on a slab.

Roz shifted her feet uncomfortably. "I guess the cops will find out."

"Those cops? Let me tell you, those guys are not exactly going to devote their lives to it."

Oh, they'd do fingerprints. They'd get a police artist to do a sketch, put it in the newspaper. Maybe they'd get a match on the prints; maybe the perp would come forward. If not, they'd move on. I knew what it was like, how many cases they had, how many court appearances, how many hours they clocked. Hit-and-run clears are never a priority unless the mayor's kid gets crushed. Boston cops are realists. They prioritize, go for the big cases, the murders, the high-profile stuff, not the small-paragraph, second-section crimes.

Yelling at Roz felt good, but it was nothing but a dead-end street. I was angry, but Roz didn't deserve the brunt of the attack. I was angry at a dead woman, but more than that I was furious at myself, at my failure to read Jessica Franklin, to detect her massive and creative lies. I pride myself on my ability to tell the difference between chicken salad and chicken shit. My pride had taken a direct hit.

I kept my voice low. "Okay, you saw her? Jessica?"

"Well, yeah. I let her in. I saw her leave."

"Could you draw her?"

Roz brightened. "Sure."

"Okay. Draw her; that's number one."

"Number two?"

"I followed a car Friday night. I want you to run the plate. The cops said it was stolen—"

"If the cops—"

"Roz, they aren't going to follow up on it, because they think I'm lying to them. If I lied about who the girl was, then my whole story is a lie; that's what they think. I want the details: Where the car was stolen, who reported it."

"Okay."

"So you draw the girl and I'll make copies of the

guy's photo. I already scanned it. It's in the computer."

I'd glimpsed "Ken" through fogged car windows, under fleeting streetlamps, a man wearing a heavy coat. But his general appearance had jibed with the photo. If pseudo–Jessica Franklin had picked this photo, she'd picked it because the rocker looked like Ken, like the guy who was supposed to be Ken Harrison. Enough like the man she wanted me to follow that I'd take the bait. Therefore the photo would be good enough to show around.

Somehow I kept thinking that if I'd done my job right, if I hadn't lost him on the Cape, things might have turned out differently. Maybe the phony bride would still be part of the world, pretending to be somebody else today.

"Okay, so that's three." Roz's voice jarred me back to the present.

"Come downstairs," I said. "And lose the turban. The house can stay dirty one more day."

In my office I wrote out the address of the building "Ken" had visited prior to his trip to the Cape. "Number four: Go door to door, every single office in this building. Make a list of every outfit that rents space there, and see if anyone who works in the building recognizes either the drawing or the photo."

"Right."

"If they recognize the guy in the photo as a member of a band, keep on asking."

"Shit," she said. "Omigod, it's like a publicity still.

Crap, I think I've seen that band. I should have gotten that."

"Would have been nice."

She looked down at her tattered clothing and said, "I ought to change, right?"

"First," I said, "draw."

I handed her paper along with a pencil that she rejected, substituting a charcoal stick from a convenient pocket. I took off for the kitchen to retrieve my abandoned cup of coffee. By the time I returned, the image was taking shape.

Sometimes I forget how good she is. It always strikes me as ironic that Roz, who claims to despise all representational drawing, can catch a likeness in a few hastily drawn lines, catch it with the kind of detail a committed representational artist would kill to duplicate. As I watched the sketch grow more like Jessica, as I made the occasional suggestion, I wanted to ask, What is it that makes you despise your own talent?

My ex, a gifted musician who works sporadically at best, used to claim it wasn't talent but will. The talent was the easy part. The ability to handle the inevitable disappointment, to trust the process, to work when no one seemed to care, to play when no one was listening, to practice for yourself, those were the hard things, the things that made the difference. And luck. Always luck, good or bad.

I pressed my lips together and imagined the real woman, the dead woman, walking into my office, cheeks pink from the cold. What kind of luck had brought the phony Jessica Franklin to my door?

"And what about the dead bodies in Vegas?" Roz said while I made copies of her effort.

My stomach lurched. I had a vision of Sam behind the wheel of a car, his face twisted with hatred, running down a young woman who looked vaguely like Jessica. "They'll wait. You can go change."

"Um, do we—do I get paid for this, or—? No, forget I asked. I screwed up, so I guess I owe you."

It's irrational, but that's exactly how I felt, too. Somehow, in some way, I had screwed up and now I owed Jessica Franklin a debt I might never repay.

CHAPTER 16

I circled the block slowly. Allston's Pomeroy Court was a skinny, down-at-the-mouth street lined with houses in various stages of disrepair. A corner market advertised Pakistani and Indian groceries, fresh halal meats, and cut-price beer. The cars were old and rusty with PROUD TO BE AN AMERICAN bumper stickers. When I parked my rented junker on nearby Guildford Street, it fit into the landscape like a piece of a child's puzzle.

Two overturned plastic chairs decorated the weedy yard of a two-family with peeling beige paint. The adjoining house was green with unfortunate yellow trim. The high, narrow structures, too close to the street and too close to each other, had stingy lawns and forbidding chain-link fences. I checked the address against the one I had written: 82 Pomeroy Court, but failed to picture my Jessica Franklin in the faded maroon house with the torn lace curtains.

When I'd called St. Elizabeth's and asked to speak to Ms. Franklin, nurses' aide, a cool alto had informed me that she was not expected in today. Which meant that she might be home, enjoying a day off. I poked my finger at the bell.

"I'm not buying anything, young lady." A woman's voice.

"I'm not selling," I said through the firmly closed door.

"This isn't magazine subscriptions? I tell those people over and over, if I want a magazine, I'm perfectly okay going out and buying it at the store." Her words were slightly slurred, enough to make me speculate about speech defects and alcohol consumption.

"Please," I said, "you can see through the peephole; I'm all alone. I'd like to ask you a few questions. It won't take long."

A moment's silence, then the rattle of a chain and the click of a dead bolt told me that curiosity had won the battle with fear.

She blinked up at me, a short middle-aged woman with carefully arched eyebrows in a heavily made-up face, wearing a dark sweater and a conservative shapeless skirt. A charm bracelet jangled on her right wrist. I wondered whether I'd caught her on her way out.

"Taking some kind of poll?" she said. "That's rotten

work, and you're lucky anybody opens the door, this neighborhood. Used to be nice with the park right down the block, but now there's nobody in the park but hoodlums. Wear those parkas and sweatshirt hoods up over their heads so you can't tell 'em apart. Woman got raped there, must be going on three years ago. And they never caught him. Never. Police, fine lot they are."

I hoped she'd upbraided the Macs for not catching the rapist.

"You're not coming in," she continued briskly, "so say what you want. Nobody gets in here. I'm old enough to remember the Strangler. Those women, they deserved what they got; imagine opening the door to a man. You were a man, I wouldn't open the door, not even if you said you were a policeman. I always thought that's what he did, said police and they opened up like clamshells."

"What if they had credentials?"

"Pooh. Credentials. What are they worth? Counterfeit. Bought in a store."

The Macs must have had their hands full, questioning her.

"Well, if you're not selling, what do you want? I've got friends stopping by, and I don't have all day."

"Is your name Jessica Franklin?"

"You with the government? This the census?"

"I'm a private investigator." In spite of her professed scorn for credentials, she cracked the screen door to take my card. "I understand your purse was stolen?"

121

"You with the Discovery people? I called just the way you're supposed to, and don't you try and hold me responsible for any charges racked up on that card. I know my rights, and don't try telling me I didn't call. I wrote down the name of the person I spoke to on the phone."

"That was an excellent thing to do, but I'm not with a credit card company. I'm working a case that involves identity theft, and the police thought you might be able to help me. Nurses are such observant people. You've probably noticed that." There: I'd promoted her from nurses' aide to full-fledged professional and flattered her to boot.

"Well," she said, with just a hint of a smile, "training does count for something."

I gave a faint cough and tapped my chest with the flat of my hand. "I don't suppose I could trouble you for a glass of water?"

"Oh, you might as well come in for a minute," she said. "It's so cold out, don't you think? I can't wait for the springtime. Everything looks so much better in the spring."

"The crocuses should be up soon."

"Oh, do you garden?"

"Whenever I have time," I said.

"I'll get your water." She disappeared down the hallway.

I have time to garden precisely never, but I'd noted the neat beds under the dusty windows. Now that I'd gotten across the drawbridge, I hastily scanned the walls for photographs. She did needlepoint, or maybe the cross-stitched mottoes were her grandmother's. They were religious sayings, "The Lord is my Shepherd" and the like. Maybe she'd done them as a child.

In the old-fashioned living room to the right of the hall, a small corner table seemed entirely devoted to silver-framed photographs, a sort of family shrine. I scanned the images quickly, but found no one who looked like my Jessie.

This older Jessica was a collector of teacups and tarnished silver spoons, a preserver of hydrangeas. I heard her footsteps in the hall and hastily retreated to a neutral site.

"Thank you so much," I said gratefully as I accepted the cool glass, tall and clean, with ice. She carried a glass of her own, too. I suspected hers had a dollop of vodka in it.

"Identity theft," she said. "They had something on Channel Five just the other night. That woman, the consumer reporter with the blond hair. You can sit for a minute, but that's all."

I thanked her again and moved to a small armchair. She took the hairy-looking sofa, plumping up the pillows before she sat. The charm bracelet jingled. It had small silvery dice, minute playing cards, miniature martini glasses.

"I understand you lost your wallet," I said.

"Purse. A black leather clutch. I don't go for those oversized bags. It wasn't a particularly good bag, just something I bought a long time ago at Filene's."

"How did you lose it?"

"Oh, I filled all that in on the police report." She seemed uneasy. "I really don't want to go into it again."

"There are different techniques that different groups of thieves use, sort of like trademarks. Like some specialize in grabbing bags at restaurants, bags that are looped over chair backs. Some thieves work grocery stores where women leave their handbags in the carts. Some gangs grab and run, right on the street."

"Well, I'm not exactly sure where mine was taken. I was running a lot of errands that day, and then it was just gone."

"Errands around here? In this area?"

"What difference does it make?"

She didn't like my line of questioning. Either she couldn't remember what she'd told the cops or she was lying about the theft.

"Is there anything else?" she said.

I took out my copy of Roz's drawing. I'd worked with her to soften the chin, widen the eyes, and I was pleased with the result. It looked like my client.

"Do you know this woman?"

There was a flicker in the brown eyes. "I don't think so."

"Are you sure?"

"She looks slightly familiar. But no, I don't know her. Who is she?"

"It's possible she might have been involved in the theft of your bag."

"She's so young."

"Did she wait on you in a restaurant? Maybe a sales clerk? Or a patient?"

"Definitely not a patient. I'd recognize a patient."

"Maybe you recognize this man?" I displayed the photo of my punk rocker.

"Good-looking," she said. "That's trouble right there."

"You haven't seen him either? Locally? At the hospital?"

"Sorry."

"Does he look familiar? The way the woman does?"

"No. Her, now, she's sort of average. I could have passed her on the street or in the grocery store, but him, I'd have noticed. And I'm sorry, but I'm going to have to ask you to leave now. My friends should be here any minute and I need a little time to set up."

She glanced over her shoulder. In the dim hallway, I could just make out the square of a card table leaning against the wall.

"I'll help," I said.

"Oh, it's no trouble."

"Poker?" I said.

"Just a friendly game."

"No gambling?"

"Nothing serious. Now, if there's nothing else . . ."

"If you remember where you saw the girl, please call me."

She hurried me out the door and I went without

protest because I was busily recalling the contents of my Jessica's bag, the mound of stuff she'd knocked to the ground when we first met, the bandanna and the Kleenex, the car keys. The deck of playing cards and the casino matches. Foxwoods matches. This Jessica Franklin played cards on her day off. She wore a charm bracelet hung with dice and cards. My Jessica had picked up the deck and shuffled it like a pro. Maybe the nurses' aide had left her bag in the casino at Foxwoods. Maybe she didn't want the police to know that; maybe gambling and drinking didn't jibe with her idea of herself.

I zipped up my parka and pulled on my gloves. It was a possibility, but where did it lead? Suppose she had left her bag at Foxwoods. Suppose my Jessica had picked it up. They were—what?—two of how many hundreds of thousands who fled the strictures of puritan Massachusetts to gamble in Connecticut. It didn't exactly narrow the field.

I made my way back to the rent-a-wreck, confident I'd find it since it wasn't worth stealing. My cell buzzed as I opened the door and I played hunt-through-all-the-pockets till I found it.

"Hey," Mooney said.

"Hey," I replied warily.

"Look, your hit and run; the ME did the cut. Thought you might be interested to know it's going in the books as a homicide."

Either he'd tell me why or he wouldn't. I froze with my hand on the car door.

"Whoever hit her wasn't happy with once. Backed up and rolled over her again. Then again."

"So you're thinking he knew who she was?"

"He or she."

"He," I said. "Statistics."

"Well, then, put it this way: I hope he knew her," Mooney said slowly. "Because otherwise, we got some kinda nasty devil loose on the street."

CHAPTER 17

The parking attendant shoved a cardboard stub in my hand and took off with the beater, tires screaming. I watched it fishtail around a corner. Whenever Sam pulls his Jaguar into a North End lot, the help hops to it and a parking space magically appears front and center. I didn't think I'd ever seen him pay for the privilege, either. Maybe I should be trolling every parking lot in the North End, asking whether Sam had parked the Jag long-term. Someone could have driven him to the airport.

Maybe I would do just that, after I learned Jessica Franklin's real name and rubbed the Macs' noses in it.

In no other place does the Gianelli name carry greater weight than in Boston's insular North End, but that day, that era, is swiftly drawing to a close. I glanced around at the few remaining construction barriers left over from the Big Dig. Attitudes and habits were changing. The generation of immigrants, with their old world alliances and values, was dying off. The new generation had both feet in America. The land-scape had changed, too. From the 1950s to the 1990s, the North End, geographically cut off from the rest of the city, had retained a fortress-like separation. Now, with the old Central Artery buried underground, no physical barrier existed between the North End and downtown. The borders had been breached, the attractive real estate revealed to outsiders.

The ugly barrier had fallen and I found myself regretting it. There had been a solid reality to the old neighborhoods of Boston, to the ethnic divisions that made the North End what it was and Southie what it was; Charlestown and Dorchester, too. Soon, it would all be homogenized, a Disney-esque mainstreet community. Which, on the whole, was probably better than keeping to codes of silence, stoning school buses, spitting on outsiders, and defending organized crime.

I displayed both Roz's drawing and the punk rocker's photo to the maître d' at Mamma Vincenza's. He didn't recognize either, but he recognized me.

"Signore Gianelli, he doesn't eat anymore? He doesn't like our food? There's a problem?"

"No problem," I said, smiling in spite of myself at the public wringing of hands, the carefully tended white mustache, the exaggerated accent.

"I don't know, the old families, they don't come so often anymore, it's always these new people. Trendy, trendy. They follow the restaurant critics, and that's not so bad, but now we get all these people, they move to the city, have a good time, but they don't eat. They want a doggie bag, to bring the food home. It's everybody's got to be so skinny, like a fashion model. They don't order dessert. To come here and not eat the cannoli, what is that? You'll live a little longer? Who cares? Who'd want to live so long?"

It was a set piece, an aria he'd sung to many others; maître d' was a position earned by style. You go to the North End to eat, you don't want a young guy in shirtsleeves. You want an old-school maître d' in a suit, with the accent. This guy had put on his show so often, I wasn't sure he knew where showmanship ended and reality began. I tried to urge him back on course.

"These people ate an early dinner Friday night."

He peered at them blankly, placed a pair of reading glasses on his nose, and tried again. "They live in the neighborhood?"

"I don't know."

His tongue licked his lower lip. "Excuse me, please, but why do you ask?" What he meant was, Why should I tell you? Every once in a while I miss that old police credential, but this time I had a good response: The Gianelli pull, the mob grease.

"I'm sure Sam would appreciate it if you could help me out."

The mob was more respected than the police.

"The eighteenth?" He retrieved a logbook from under the stand, thumbed through it. "Maybe they had a reservation?"

I shrugged.

He showed me the list. "For two?"

"Yes," I said, although I didn't know for sure.

"Only the Imperiolis for two. Them, I know." He seemed happy. He hadn't had to rat out any customers.

"I'd like to show the photo and the drawing to the staff."

He sighed, weighing the inconvenience with the possible gain. The Gianellis were not to be crossed easily. "Come."

I followed him through wide steel push-doors into a kitchen that smelled of sage and garlic. A man in a white close-fitting jacket chopped carrots into dice at a counter. Another stirred pots of simmering stock. A severe young woman at a desk clicked icons on a computer screen.

"Della," the maître d' said, "the dinner servers are here yet?"

"Marcie's here. Gregory, no. I'm working the shift, and Mikey, too."

He turned to me. "I must go up front, but Della will help you. Please, don't take too long. And tell Mr. Gianelli when you see him, that we miss him. He should come back. Anything on the menu, even from years ago, we'll make special for him. He should call."

I nodded my thanks, and tried not to think about Sam coming back. I wasn't supposed to think about it. Whole half hours passed when I didn't think about it. Maybe soon, whole hours would pass without the reality of his absence chiming like a clock.

"What?" Della said, still moving her mouse, a frown line etched deep in her forehead.

"I want to talk to anyone who might have served a couple at dinner last Friday."

"Why?"

"Because your boss told you to help me out."

"And that's enough reason?" She glared at me, then shrugged her narrow shoulders. "Yeah, you're right. It is."

The cooks were listening in. I passed through clouds of fragrant steam, showed them the drawing and the photo, got no reaction.

"Let's go out front. Maybe Greg will show the fuck up soon. I'm tired of doing his work, too." The woman's anger seemed to transfer itself easily from me to the hapless no-show Greg.

The front-of-the-house staff were busily draping linens over tabletops, shuffling silverware, goblets, and plates. One, standing around, glanced up guiltily and started moving at double time as soon as he saw Della.

"Listen up," she said, with a mock bow in my direction. "You worked Friday dinner, form a line over here. The rest of you, keep plugging."

There was a murmur but they obeyed. You're a waiter, that's what you do: move now, complain later.

"This lady has some pictures to show you. Let's get her out of here quick so we can be ready to open."

There were four waiters in line. Two quickly disavowed all knowledge. I thought they might be illegals.

The third said, "Yeah. I had them." He was small and skinny, with earnest brown eyes.

"You're sure?"

"Not all my tables have fights."

"Lovers' quarrel?"

"That I didn't get. Maybe brother and sister, or business. No cuddle stuff, no handholding."

"What were they arguing about?"

"I stand around and listen, Della kills me, okay?" He shot her a glance, kept his voice low.

"The photo looks like him?"

"Not him, so much, but her. Her, I remember. She came in late. She was upset, hardly ate."

"Wait a minute. They didn't come in together?"

"No. I thought he was a single. Then she was there, before I even got around to clearing the other setting, so that was cool."

"Was the fight because she was late?"

"Like I said, I don't know. Jeez, really, I don't know, but maybe he was surprised to see her. Maybe he thought she'd canceled out and then she comes late, like a surprise?"

"What did she call him?"

"His name?"

I nodded.

He shook his head.

"Hers?"

"I'm getting a Jeannie, Janet, Julie, but I don't know. It's different names every night, you know?"

"Close your eyes."

"Huh?"

"Think back. What did they order?"

"Pasta. The tortellini for her, the penne for the man. No wine. Tap water. Cheap date, if it was a date."

"Who paid?"

"Cash. Ten percent tip, that's it. And I'm thinking they split the bill, but I'm not sure on that."

"You're sure about the cash?"

He nodded.

Damn. I'd been planning to ask for the credit card receipt.

"Either of them a regular?"

"Never saw either one before. She hardly ate, I remember that. The plate was full when I took it away. But she didn't complain."

"And nothing about the conversation? The argument?"

"I think, maybe, once, when I brought more bread, they were talking about the weather, the night sky. Dark, shadows, something like that?"

"If the man comes in again, call me." I handed him my card and a ten-dollar bill.

"And the woman?"

She won't be in.

I thought it, but I didn't say it. What good would it do?

CHAPTER 18

"Like I ever said I wanted to be a PI? My toes are nothing but blisters. I totally chose the wrong shoes."

"I didn't call about your feet, Roz." Mamma Vincenza's parking lot attendants had been a washout: They didn't recall the Volvo; they didn't know the whereabouts of the Gianelli Jag, and I was currently navigating a narrow North End street packed with pedestrians, delivery trucks, and through traffic.

"People, you ask 'em stuff, they're so fuckin' rude. Like guys, they rate this woman right off, you know, is she a hottie? One to ten on the babe scale?"

"Tell me about the car," I said.

"The car. Right. You know what the Registry's like; they don't do quick miracles, no wine into water."

"Water into wine."

"Whatever. Here's the deal. I mean, you'd think it was a stolen car, like the cops said, but there's a twist. I've got a contact says the plate was registered to a stolen car, all right, but a stolen Mercury, not a Volvo. So you got a switcheroo."

A Mercury had been stolen; its plate had turned up on a Volvo.

"The Mercury get recovered?" I asked.

"No."

I bit my lip. Could have been broken down for parts, sold out of state, burned, or driven off a pier. Possibly gotten rid of at the request of an owner who wanted to collect on the insurance.

The Volvo might have a brand-new plate by now.

"You want me to keep on it?" Roz said.

"If a standard check on the Merc's owner doesn't raise a red flag, give it up. Stay with the building. Any luck yet?"

"Zip, but it's a monster place. I'm talking to anybody moves their lips. I'm waving the photo and the drawing, and I'm getting zip. Wanna help out?"

"I've got my own to-do list. Oh, one other thing, Roz. The guy was carrying a bag. That could jog somebody's memory."

"A grocery bag, a briefcase?"

"More like a big tote bag, maybe canvas, maybe leather." I hadn't seen it clearly.

"Like a salesman, with samples?"

"Could be. Bye." I balanced a Styrofoam coffee cup in the rental's rickety cup holder, checked my watch, and made my regular call to find out whether Paolina had expressed a desire for my company. If she had, I'd have needed to make a U-turn and a mad dash in the wrong direction—which I'd have done, no questions asked. But she hadn't, so I was free to travel south to the Cape, a long trek and a gamble, but one that might pay off. On the small and insular Cape, people know their neighbors and notice strangers. The man who looked like the man in the photo might have friends or family there.

I took bumpy surface streets to the Dig tunnel, drove

135

underneath downtown to the Southeast Expressway. Traffic was surprisingly light.

Most of the Cape had seen stunning changes in the past twenty years, new houses rising from the marshes, summer shacks torn down and replaced with mansions. Demand for services had increased, taxes had skyrocketed, housing prices had shot through the roof, and suddenly sons and daughters couldn't afford to buy even the smallest house near the folks. It had taken years before the town councils caught on and called for a halt to development before it became wholesale destruction.

Large-scale development never took root in Nausett, the small town just beyond Marstons Mills, the place I'd singled out as "Ken's" most likely destination. If the man visited Nausett often, someone would know him. I could get his real name, find him, show him "Jessica's" picture.

Until she had a real name, she'd stay where she was. She'd be Jane Doe with a number that depended on how many other unidentified women had turned up on the Boston streets this year. It didn't affect the dead, being nameless; I knew that. But somewhere she had family. Somewhere somebody was worrying about her, searching for her. She was somebody's daughter, somebody's child. As pretty as Paolina, and now she was dead.

It was an easier drive in daylight, but the junker guzzled more gas than the cab had. Just past Marstons Mills, I pulled off the road at a small grocery and self-serve gas station combo. The store was bordered by a closed-for-the-season ice cream parlor and a vacant building with a FOR RENT sign. The wind whipped the scrubby pines across the street. Only stubborn plants took root here and survived.

A sign in the grimy window advised me to vote no on 6. A bell tinkled when I pushed open the door. The wind grabbed the door and slammed it into the wall.

The man didn't look up at the sound of the bell, but the slam got his attention. He was as gray as the weathered shingles, as bent as the trees, but he pasted a game smile on his face and nodded to let me know he was there to help.

A cooler hummed at the back of the store. I rummaged through the bottles till I found a Pepsi. More caffeine. The candy bars near the front desk looked fresher than the prepackaged dusty snacks on the wire rack near the drinks. I grabbed a Milky Way.

"Healthy eating," the grizzled man observed. "Good for you. I got nothing against junk. I like to see people enjoy what they eat. Plenty of time for rabbit nibbles when you're old and can't chew so good." He had an unexpected voice, thin and reedy, but pleasantly soft.

"Quiet out this way," I said.

"Mostly it is. Used to be, anyway. Back in the day, you were looking for quiet, you'd a picked the right spot. Up till the end of May, when all hell breaks loose."

"Tourists," I said.

"They pay the bills, God love 'em. Summers, we stock those rubber-soled beach shoes and all kind of suntan lotion. What they pay for tubes of goo, you wouldn't believe. I used to race around the whole summer, brown as an Indian. No cancer scares then. Scare you into buying anything now."

"You grew up here?" I stretched, trying to get the drive out of my spine. It was warm in the store and I liked the old-fashioned smell, wooden boards and dust and peppermint.

"Good a place as any."

"Prettier than most," I said. "What's with Proposition Six?"

"That's just what I'm talking about, why it's not so quiet. Demonstrations and stink bombs and egg tossing, that's not quiet like it used to be." He shrugged his narrow shoulders and started ringing up my purchases, plus the gas. "You don't live around here, do you? You lived here, I'd a seen you at the meetings. You'd be on our side, too. You don't look like an Indian, not with that pretty red hair."

"How much for the candy?"

"Hey, don't be thinking I'm prejudiced or nothing. They want to live here and pay taxes, fine. They want to set up their own damn country, let 'em do it somewhere else."

I smiled. "Weren't they here first?"

He pursed his thin lips. "You one of those? Think we should all go jump in the ocean after living here—what?—four hundred years or more? You always got your losers and your winners, right? What I say is you don't change the rules in the middle of the game."

"Which rules?"

"Weren't for the gambling nobody'd give a damn. Live cheek by jowl, and now they want a separate country, and nobody can tell me it's 'cause they want to exercise tribal customs. Who's keeping them from their tribal customs, huh? Not me."

"Is this about the Wampanoag tribe?" The Cape Cod Wampanoag was recently recognized by the federal government as an officially sanctioned tribe. It made a brief splash in the Boston newspapers.

"No, no, that's in Mashpee." He said it like Mashpee was hundreds of miles away instead of the next town over. "They got it all sorted out there. Nobody's gonna build no casino in Mashpee. I'm talking about the Nausetts."

I shrugged. I'd never heard of them.

He made a face, and started winding up like he was going to give a Sunday sermon.

"I'm looking for somebody," I said quickly.

"Sure you are. Nobody wants to hear an old goat rant. Anyhow it's all in Proposition Six. Vote's coming up in a special election, but if you don't live here, I'm not gonna bother you with it. What address you want?"

"That's the problem." I put the photo on the counter along with money for the Pepsi, candy bar, and gasoline. As he took the bills, I angled the photo so he could see it better.

"He live near here?"

"You know him?"

"Don't look familiar. What's his name?"

"He look like anybody you know? He ever come in here?"

He shook his head. "Some folks go to the big stores in Falmouth. Never come by here."

"He drives a silver Volvo. Maybe he stopped for gas."

"Maybe he did, but I couldn't say."

Gas station attendants used to be a reliable source of gossip. I regretted the self-serve pump, unwrapped the candy bar on the way out, took too big a bite, and got caramel stuck in my teeth. The candy bar was stale.

Most of the stores I passed had placards stuck in the windows saying yea or nay on Proposition 6. Several of the pro–Prop 6 signs were ripped or partially defaced by red paint or anti-6 signs. I slowed to read the billboard in front of a white-steepled Congregational church.

LIE DOWN WITH THE DEVIL, it said. GAMBLING AND OUR COMMUNITY. I missed the date of the sermon, but this time my balky subconscious automatically supplied the rest of the saying: "Lie down with the devil and wake up in darkness." I wouldn't have to attend the service to know the Congregationalist minister's take on gambling.

I tried a bank, a bar, and a real estate agency with no luck. I drove down residential streets, staring at cars parked at the curb or in driveways, not finding the Volvo. Finally, frustrated, with an overdose of caffeine thrumming through my veins, I decided to take the direct approach.

CHAPTER 19

Located on a stretch of road labeled Main Street, in between the Chamber of Commerce and a coffee shop, the Nausett Police Department looked more like a country store than a lockup. A sign pointed to a small parking lot in the rear. I pulled into the narrow driveway. The candy bar was a memory and I was hungry.

Nausett sits on a scraggy peninsula bordered by Mashpee and Cotuit. It used to be a fishing town in the days when the nearby banks yielded a plentiful harvest of cod. They'd just about jump in the boat, the old-time fishermen used to boast, but no more. The few who persist as commercial fishermen have to sail out to Georges Bank and beyond. The summer people and the sport fishermen gravitate to the fancier towns farther up the Cape, Chatham and Yarmouth, or ferry out to Martha's Vineyard and Nantucket. Cape Cod, summer playground for New York City and Boston, never had much in the way of industry. The Massachusetts Military Reservation covers some thirty square miles. There's a potato chip factory, some cranberry bogs. The salt air makes for hard farming and the year-rounders wind up renting their homes to the summer people to get enough cash to pay their ever-increasing taxes.

I sat in the car, the feeble heater eking out a stream of warm air, and did a quick review of cops who'd retired down the Cape. I knew the Martha's Vineyard chief from my Boston days, but couldn't recall anybody who'd left and headed to Nausett. No easy intro, no casual "driving down here and thought I'd look you up."

"I'd like to speak to an officer."

Maybe it was the earplugs in her ears and the MP3 player strapped to her upper arm, maybe the tattoo on the side of her neck, but the young woman who glanced up from the desk didn't have the air of a sworn peace officer. She had an original face, long and narrow with a defiant set to her jaw. She didn't wear the uniform, unless the Nausett department had a very casual dress code. Maybe a community volunteer.

"Detective Thurlow is right down the hall." She put an odd emphasis on the word *detective,* but I wasn't sure what that was about. Her manner was cheerful.

Thurlow, the first black man I'd seen on the Cape that day, had his boots on his desk and his focus on a window that overlooked the parking lot. His weary eyes said middle age, but his body, clad in navy slacks and a plaid shirt, said younger.

"Nice-looking car." There was amusement in his voice and challenge in his eyes. He was a good-looking man who knew it.

I slid my card onto the desktop. He reached over and took it.

I said, "I'm looking for a man."

"Private Investigations, huh? Cambridge? This legit?"

"Why would I lie to you?"

"Oh, I don't know. How about you're from a collection agency?"

"You sound like a cop," I said lightly. "Always suspicious."

"This man you're looking for? He lives in Nausett?"

"The idea was that you'd tell me."

"Long drive from Cambridge." He ran a hand over his face like he was checking whether he'd shaved. "Make good time?"

"Yeah."

"Sit down, why don't you? And tell me this, you play basketball?"

It seemed to come out of nowhere. "Why?"

"Cambridge. Cambridge Rindge and Latin, that's where Patrick Ewing played—and now his boy's playing college ball. You ever see Pat play at the high school? Nah, that would be before your time."

"I never saw him play."

"You play?"

I shook my head. "Too short." That's not true—and it's not the reason I don't play basketball—but I don't talk about the real reason. "You gonna help me out here?"

Cops are always curious. This one might not tell me whether or not he knew the man, but he'd want to see the photo. He had a calm face, quiet eyes. He looked like a man who governed his emotions. I hoped I'd be able to tell whether or not he recognized the Volvo man.

"So this some marital thing? Divorce stuff?"

I opened my mouth to deny any involvement in "divorce stuff," thought better of it, and nodded. If I started explaining why I was looking for the man, I'd be there a long time.

"You're not the wife?" he asked.

"No."

"Not itching for revenge?"

"No."

"Not planning to gun him down?"

"No."

"That's good. We hicks don't like that much."

He seemed to have the Cape chip balanced finely on his shoulder. Bostonians may envy the laid-back lifestyle they see on the Cape come summer, but they don't want to know about the hardscrabble winters. The Cape people envy the Bostonians their extravagant summer lifestyle. They can't help but notice the enormous wads of cash flashed in the trendy restaurants. They also can't help but notice that those same trendy places shut down when the tourists flee. And so it goes: the locals dependent on the tourists, but resentful as well. My home base, Cambridge, is like that all year round: townies versus the college kids who come in fresh each fall just to make the rest of the population feel poor, old, and uneducated.

I wasn't falling for it. The man's voice, not to mention his color, gave him away. "Hick, huh?" I said. "You sound like New York."

"Can't take the Bronx out of the boy, huh? I figured the accent was just about gone."

I shook my head. "How about it? Seems pretty quiet around here. What would it hurt to take a look, tell me if you know the guy?"

"Looks are deceiving. Things aren't that quiet."

"What, people throw tacks in the road at the rotary?"

"What do you mean?"

"I got a flat there a couple nights ago. Friday night."

"You were looking for this guy then?"

"Following him."

His eyes slid out the window, then came back to my face. "Let's see him."

I took the photo of my Volvo man out of the file folder and handed it to him.

"Huh," he said, after thirty seconds of silence. "Never saw him before."

Either he was a world-class liar or else he was telling the truth. My heart sank. Maybe Roz had already found someone in the tall office building. But she hadn't rung my cell, and she would have, if she'd gotten anything good.

The lanky tattoo girl wandered back and stood just outside the door.

"Hey, we got another one, Detective."

"Another what?"

"Disturbance call. Broken window over at the meetinghouse."

"Again? Well, damn, I'd better get over there and take a look."

"They're gonna want you to fingerprint the whole town next. I told them it's just kids."

"Rosemary, you're just supposed to take the reports."

"Right."

"I would have taken the call."

"You were busy with this lady. I said I'd tell you right away. And that's what I'm doing."

"Thank you, Rosemary."

"Detective."

No love lost between the two of them. I wondered whether she might have more connections in town than Detective Thurlow, maybe know my mystery man.

"I'm out of here," he said. "Call Mitch or somebody else on the council and tell them I'll be right there, okay? Politely?"

"Certainly, Detective."

"And show this lady out. Please."

Thurlow passed us in the corridor, putting on a jacket, hurrying. Rosemary deliberately slowed her pace and blew out a breath to display her annoyance.

"Lotta work, huh?" I said sympathetically.

"Plenty, without making his calls," she said.

"Sure is different," I said.

"What is?"

"I used to be a Boston cop. The idea of an officer rushing out of the station for a broken window—"

"Yeah, and as soon as they put in new windows, they'll break 'em again. Waste of time, you ask me. Leave 'em boarded up till after the election."

"This is about Proposition Six?"

"Damn straight it is. Kowtowing to the Indians, that's what the cops do best around here. They all want security jobs when the casinos come in. They know where their bread gets buttered. Now I gotta make that call. He gets there before I make it, he'll have my ass."

"I'll wait," I said. "I wanted to ask you something."

"About Six? You from the TV?"

I waited while she made two calls. She couldn't find Mitch, had to go with Ned.

"You know this man?" I put the photo on her desk as soon as she'd finished.

She took her time. "Cute guy. No, sorry. So you're not here about Six?" She sounded disappointed.

I took out the drawing of Jessica and placed that on her desk, too. Mainly I did it because I wasn't ready to leave yet, to make the long journey home without so much as a summer-shack clam roll to make it worthwhile.

"Hey," the girl said, craning her long neck. "Lookee there, if it isn't Julie Feathers. Hot damn, you know where she is?"

"Julie," I repeated. The *J* name fit with what the waiter remembered. Julie. Jessica. She'd kept her initial.

"Yep, she's pretty fresh on the missing list this time

out. Moves around, that girl does. Her daddy reports her pretty regular."

"Her last name is Feathers?"

"Detective Thurlow woulda been on it more except we're still all worked up around here. Not with Prop Six, or this window-breaking shit; that's just annoyance stuff. With that Danielle Wilder thing," the lanky girl said.

I gave her a blank stare. *Danielle Wilder.* I'd heard or read the name, I knew I had.

"First real murder we've had in this town in twenty-five years. She was just about Julie's best friend, Danielle Wilder was. A killing right here in dinky little Nausett. Thought I'd never hear the end of it, but all the fuss is finally starting to die down because word is they nailed the guy. That's the word on the street anyway. Some mob thing, guy with a vowel stuck on the end of his name. Boston mob, this guy who's real high up in the genuine mob. You wouldn't think it, down here."

"Boston mob," I repeated, thinking dead bodies, Las Vegas, thinking why is the name Danielle Wilder so familiar? "You happen to know the guy's name?"

"I'm not supposed to," she said meaningfully.

"I'll bet there's not a lot around here you don't know," I said.

She looked left and right before whispering his name, like she knew she was out of line. And before she said it, I knew it. I didn't need to hear it spoken aloud.

"What I want to know is why nobody's arrested him yet," she added resolutely. "People around here are starting to think the fix is in."

CHAPTER 20

I sat back in Gloria's guest chair and watched as her eyes grew rounder.

"Damn," she said. "I want to hear more."

"So did I. But Rosemary started getting phone calls. So I got out of there, drove around the block, and lurked till she finished her shift. We are best pals, Rosemary and me."

I now knew why the Boston police always used sworn officers on the desk. Rosemary not only had attitude, she had big ears and a mouth to match. We'd imbibed pre-dinner drinks at a local tavern; she drank like whiskey sours were a hobby.

"What did she say? Julie Feathers? What kind of name is that?"

"Local humor. Her real name is Julie Farmer, but she's an Indian, was an Indian, a member of the Nausett tribe, so the kids in the high school decided she wasn't a farmer, she was an Indian, and—"

"Injuns wear heap-big feathers."

"Right."

"Kids," Gloria said disapprovingly. When fellow students at her high school started calling her gimp, her three huge brothers sorted them out. Leroy still sorts out anybody who gives his baby sister grief.

I said, "I gave Rosemary Detective McHenry's name. Eventually she'll get around to telling Thurlow to contact the BPD."

"You didn't tell her Julie was dead?"

I shook my head slowly. "I wanted to get back first, flaunt the news flash to the Macs. Then I thought I'd run it by a friend first."

"Because of what this Rosemary girl said?"

Rosemary, alas, hadn't said half enough. She knew for a fact that Danielle Wilder, a legal aide, had been murdered three months ago, going on four. While she hadn't known the vic personally, she had seen her on occasion, and had given me great detail about Wilder's clothing, especially her shoes. Rosemary had assumed the crime involved lurid sex because of Wilder's clothes, not to mention all the hush-hush and whispers, but she had been vague on details. She seemed to think that Wilder's spike heels had incited the crime, and after a few drinks she'd wanted to discuss all the TV crime shows she had watched since she was seven. The main thing she had been crystal clear on was that Thurlow and the other locals were major-league irritated when the investigation was snatched out of their hands by the FBI.

"Feds, huh?" Gloria said darkly.

"Yep."

"And she said this Danielle Wilder is the woman Sam's supposed to have offed? I thought you said the murder bid was about something that happened in Las Vegas?"

"Sam said Las Vegas. I'm sure he said Las Vegas. But there was something about a woman on the Cape. I know that."

"How?"

"How do I know? I remember he said something."

"You weren't listening? What? How could you not listen to something like that?"

"It wasn't like that. It was like food or a movie, like last summer he went out to dinner with this woman or to see some show."

"I would have listened," Gloria said.

I was almost sure I remembered the woman's name. Danielle was a fairly uncommon name.

"What now?" Gloria asked. "How much are you gonna share with the Macs?"

"Yeah, here's the problem: They were pretty nasty when I didn't get Jessica—my client—Julie's ID right. So how are they going to react when they find out she's related, even in a very oblique way, to me?"

"It was a car accident."

"Hit and run. But only after the guy ran over her two or three times to make sure she was dead. They're treating it as a homicide and I don't like it. I mean, this woman comes to me out of the blue and hires me under an alias, and then it turns out she just happens to be the best friend of a woman Sam's supposed to have killed? If I were a cop, I'd say that stinks."

"Put it like that, I can see why you don't want to run it by the cops."

"Hostile cops."

151

"Why not go to Mooney?"

"What I want—what I need is to find out everything I can about Danielle Wilder. How she died and exactly when she died and why Sam's on the hook for her death, if he actually is. What the feds think they've got on him. Why they haven't made it public."

"Politics," Gloria said. "Feds, they got their own agenda."

Someone tapped lightly on the glass door and Leroy came in smiling. Even smiling, he looks threatening. It's his size.

"Hey," he said with a nod at me. "You're in the money."

"Me?"

"You gonna drive it around here? In this stinking weather?"

"I rented it, Leroy. I know it's a piece of junk, but I'm gonna make up my mind soon and buy something serious."

I wanted a fire engine red Miata. I wanted to live someplace where the weather was always sixty-five degrees with sunny skies and a gentle offshore breeze.

"No, no, I'm talking about the Jag," Leroy said cheerfully. "I'm talking about that deep blue chunk of heaven. Gianelli's XK smooth-ass ride."

"I don't know where it is."

He gave me a look. "Well, I do. You didn't park it in the garage, the old garage? I figured you put it there for safekeeping. I wasn't gonna tell anybody else."

"Wait a frickin' minute. Sam's Jaguar is in the back garage?" Gloria said.

"Come see. Either that or I'm having some kind of weird delusions, hallucinating and shit. Ask me have I been drinking, why don't you?"

Gloria couldn't leave the phones. I followed Leroy out the door and down the gravel path.

When Gloria had the garage rebuilt, only one part of the old building was salvageable, a brick three-door garage that she kept mainly to remember how ugly the place used to be. It was currently used for storage, mostly tools and old records. I hadn't been inside it in months.

While Leroy yanked up the old-fashioned garage door, my cell rang.

"Cops are here," Roz said. "Outside in an unmarked, waiting."

"You know them?"

"Same guys here before, to ask about Jessica Franklin. One black, one white."

"They didn't ring the bell?"

"No, just waiting."

Sam's car was dusty. I circled around to the front of the Jag. The bumper was bent.

Roz's voice seemed to reach me from a distance. "Carlotta?"

"Don't tell them you talked to me," I said. "You don't know where I am or when I'll come back."

I hung up without waiting for a reply.

The bumper was crumpled where it might have hit something or someone. The car was where I might have parked it. I had the car keys.

There was a connection between my phony Jessica Franklin and the woman Sam was supposed to have killed.

There were cops parked outside my house.

I couldn't go home.

PART FOUR

CHAPTER 21

No lock on the office door. Mooney considered wedging a chair under the offending doorknob. He decided against it, eased the folder out of the second drawer on the right, and emptied it on his desktop. Afternoon sunshine, slanting through the grimy window blinds, felt like prying eyes.

He patted the breast pocket of his shirt, stuck the despised reading glasses on his nose, and began, never skipping a word, working slowly, the way he always worked, but conscious that his heart was pounding too quickly in his chest. He wanted to move, not sit. He had a gift for street work, but paperwork was different, a slow, plodding task, sifting and resifting other officers' reports for tiny golden nuggets. Still, he kept going, because occasionally, mercifully, there came a click, a moment of grace, when a fact shifted in time or space and he saw the case in a new light.

Danielle Wilder's death wasn't his case. It hadn't occurred in his jurisdiction. He'd had to call in favors just to obtain the paper. The resulting file was incomplete; he didn't even know what was missing, and that made him edgy.

Not so edgy as he had felt doing nothing, not so edgy as he had felt when the Macs barged in with the news: the hit-and-run vic identified, and get this, she was a

*witness—no, maybe not a wit—but the best friend of
that broad got herself killed over in Nausett. TV called
it the "Red Ribbon Killing"? Remember? FBI
snatched the case; something major, something to do
with organized crime.*

There were news clips from Cape Cod and Boston
papers. The initial stories made Danielle Wilder's
death seem the sort of lurid sex crime that kept
mothers up nights waiting till they heard the familiar
tread on the steps or got the reluctant, dutiful phone
call: *I'm home, Ma, safe and sound. What did you
think would happen to me, huh?*

Mooney had no children, but in some way he didn't
understand or particularly want to examine, he
thought of them all as his kids. He was glad he hadn't
been called out to look at the body.

At twenty-seven, Wilder would have been insulted
by the word *kid.* The photo in the *Cape Cod Times,*
probably a high school graduation shot, made her look
demure and utterly defenseless, blond and lovely.
Young and never to grow old; Mooney hoped there
was some kind of grace in that, but the longer he
stayed on the force, the more he doubted the Catholic
certainties of his childhood. And he was sure as sure
could be that when he finally lost his faith, he'd lose
his calling, too.

It was a calling, the blue brotherhood, a variation on
the priesthood his mother would have chosen for him.
If he lost his calling now, after so many years on the
force—well, it was late in the day for alternatives.

156

The Macs were not his favorite team, but they were decent cops. It wouldn't take them long to make the connection. The FBI had labeled the Nausett killing mob-related. Nausett was mob; mob was Gianelli; the hit and run was Carlyle; Carlyle and Gianelli were an item. Once they followed the dots, Mooney expected an explosion: *Red Ribbon Killing linked to Boston hit and run.*

He pushed the clippings aside, turned to the slim section labeled NAUSETT. The first officer at the scene, Jerold Heaney, dispatched in response to a 911, Wednesday morning, 6:17 a.m. December 20. Five days before Christmas, it would have been barely light. Cold. Heaney had called for backup, strung yellow crime-scene tape. Heaney's superior, R. Thurlow, had arrived at 6:29 and set the machine in motion, making the call to the state police. A small-town force like Nausett's knew its limitations. When it came to murder, they called in the troopers. The state police had the CSU, the personnel.

Thurlow. Mooney pondered the name, wondered if he'd caught a break.

The scene had been sketched, diagrammed, photographed, videotaped, and searched by a four-man state team. Mooney studied the diagram, committing it to memory. The three-by-five color glossies were divided into three packets. The photographer had set the scene with wide shots showing sparse grass and gravel, dotted with old tombstones. In the distance, a small wooden building was sheathed in scaffolding, undergoing repairs. As Mooney flipped through the first packet, the focus narrowed to a small circle of rocks. The second packet detailed the placement of the body.

Mooney inspected the last packet, the close-ups, seeing them as from a distance, turning the ravaged body into a test dummy instead of a father's child. Later, after he had cleared the case, he could bring back her personhood, her outraged self. Whether he could bring himself back, he no longer knew.

Both knees raised and bent to her left side. Naked, except for black thong panties dangling from her right ankle. Part of him, the part that could never have taken the vows, noted the curves of breast and thigh, the faded tan lines from last summer's bikini. The cop in him said: no sexual positioning. So easy to spread those lifeless knees, but the killer had moved them, almost modestly, to the side. Mooney noted the dark bruising along the left side of the body, the swollen and distorted face, the thin red ribbon looped around the neck.

Mooney fingered the video; he didn't want to requisition a viewing room only to have some eager rookie, or worse, one of the Macs, ask which case he was reviewing.

He wasn't much of a believer, but he believed this: If a homicide wasn't cleared in the first twenty-four hours, the chances were good it would never get cleared. The first twenty-four were crucial. In the first twenty-four, if cops moved quickly, identifying the vic, collecting the evidence, interviewing the witnesses, they had their best shot.

A few of the cases that stayed stubbornly unsolved were whodunnits, but most of Boston's open uncleared cases were nothing of the kind. Mooney was in political trouble and he knew it. Last year's stats were bad and this year's likely to be worse. He couldn't guarantee even a forty percent clear rate, and anything under forty was unacceptable. Seventy-eight percent of his cases came from the same neighborhoods, from Roxbury, Dorchester, and Mattapan, and figured in brief newspaper paragraphs where the victims went unnamed, referred to as young black males. The stories didn't make the nightly news. Witnesses openly refused to speak to cops. Last week, the family of a fourteen-year-old victim had refused to allow the police in the house.

Mooney realized his lips were pressed into a thin line, his hands clenched. He sucked in a deep breath and made an effort to relax his neck muscles. This Cape thing wasn't one of those cases. The paper on his desk showed initial progress: the vic ID'd right off the bat, identification made at the scene by the responding officers. That was the thing about small towns: The cops knew the locals.

But evidence at the scene had been sparse; the winter ground rocky and hard. No useful footprints. The man who had called in the body, a cemetery worker named Gordon, hadn't seen the crime. There were no nearby doors to bang, seeking witnesses.

Mooney paged through the state police documents. Troopers had interviewed the decedent's acquaintances, but Mooney found no mention of any argument, any violent conflict that might predictably end in murder. Small-town residents, unafraid of gang retribution, they had seemed eager enough to talk about Danielle Wilder. Still, the clock had ticked past deadline on this one; the case had taken on a refrigerator chill. The FBI had abruptly taken over. Then silence.

Mooney had learned about the secret indictment by luck: A woman he used to date, Magda, was a court reporter. Daily, he had anticipated the arrest warrant, the headlines: MOB BOSS GIANELLI NAMED IN CAPE KILLING.

The headlines never came. The feds might have been hoping that if they kept silent, Gianelli would reenter the country, get caught before he knew they were on to him.

That wouldn't happen. Mooney had seen to it personally. Not because he owed Gianelli; he didn't owe Gianelli an ounce of spit. He'd done it for Carlotta, so she wouldn't prove her stubborn loyalty by giving her lover a phony alibi. Failing that—Mooney had to admit, even given her remarkable blind spot about Sam, she probably wouldn't go so far as perjury—failing that, so she wouldn't spend her days at Cedar Junction, never quitting the man who lived for her visits.

At the time, he'd thought he could live with it. Now he wasn't sure.

When he'd made the split-second decision, he hadn't known the facts. Mobster and murder; that was all Magda had told him, that Gianelli was connected to a murder, and Mooney had made the easy link and assumed the murder was a mob affair. Murder was murder, sure, but the crooked men who worked the game knew the risks. His informant hadn't mentioned that this victim was young, female, and lived outside the world of organized crime. She had never hinted that the case was Nausett's "red ribbon" murder.

Did he know the facts now?

He squinted at the close-ups of the corpse. Was it plausible that the cops had made the ID? He reread the statements, both uncertain, both grounding the identification on a small rose-shaped tattoo on the woman's ankle. He could buy it; men noticed women's legs. The woman worked as a paralegal; she'd visited the station on business.

He fingered the piles of paper. No notification of grieving parents, no interviews with stunned siblings. He separated the reports, dividing the interviewees into groups, grouping them by category: family, friends, neighbors, colleagues.

Colleague, colleague, neighbor, colleague. If the mix spoke to the vic's life, it said she'd worked too many hours.

She had been a legal assistant. Most of those interviewed were personnel from the law office of Hastings and Muir, one of the oldest Cape Cod firms, headed by a Hastings still. Bradley J. Hastings, forty-eight years old, former town selectman, had made the formal ID. Again, Mooney wondered about the girl's lack of family.

Wilder had worked at Hastings, Muir, three years, almost four, excellent worker, energetic, a go-getter. Hastings was shocked, aggrieved, angry, as if the murder were an insult to the community, to the small-town expectation of law and order. The interviewer, a trooper named Thorpe, had led the man down expected pathways: When did you last see the victim? Were you aware of any enemies, any arguments, any disputes?

Mooney read a second interview, a third, with increasing frustration. He didn't know Thorpe or the other troopers who'd conducted the sessions. He didn't like the pattern of the questions, the follow-ups, the gaps. No one had mentioned Gianelli, much less accused him.

Julie Farmer. The name of the hit-and-run vic stood out like it was printed in neon. Age: twenty-one. So she was even younger than the Nausett vic, Danielle Wilder, who had been her best friend. Danielle had been Julie's mentor, her idol. He read the brief transcript twice. Julie Farmer had voluntarily come to the Nausett station, consented to the taping. Even with her own words on the page, Mooney found he wasn't getting what he needed. Had she hesitated before answering, spoken freely, kept things back? She didn't mention Gianelli by name, but she did talk about a man, an older man, Danielle's ex-lover, a guy with a reputation as a tough guy. . . . Maybe the feds had interviewed her again. Maybe she'd remembered the name.

Mooney raised his fingers to the bridge of his nose, adjusted his glasses, massaging the tender area underneath the nose pads. He needed a copy of the federal file, but he didn't have a single friend left at the bureau who'd be likely to pass it over. He couldn't risk a formal request. If the feds found out he'd requested the file, their suspicion that he was involved in the leak to Gianelli would harden into certainty.

Dammit, why were the feds even involved? Because Gianelli was organized crime? Mooney tapped his desktop with his pencil point until the lead snapped. The Boston feds were in the doghouse, had been ever since mobster Whitey Bulger had skipped town leaving a legacy of outrage and lawsuits. The revelations kept coming: Senior agents had used Whitey as an informer. In return, they had kept him apprised of government moves against him, including the names of potential witnesses, several of whom had been subsequently murdered. Transfers, trials, and dismissals had followed swiftly.

He could see why the bureau would want to take down Gianelli. Taking down Gianelli would lift their grimy reputation out of the gutter. But how had they made the connection? Where was the evidence linking him to the "red ribbon" crime?

Mooney went back to the photos. Given the lividity, the obvious bruising on the left side, the victim hadn't

163

been killed in the graveyard. She'd been killed some-place else, then moved, her body repositioned, the red ribbon and black panties left behind to fuel tabloid headlines.

Where had she died? Where was her car? Why had she been dumped in a cemetery? Was it close, convenient, meaningful? Nausett, on the ocean, had plenty of boats, and a mile or so of shoreline. Why not take the body out to sea?

All Mooney had, besides the piles of paper on his desk, were questions. He didn't even have a copy of the ME's report. His trooper buddy hadn't included it in the file and no way could he request it and not get somebody from the bureau demanding to know why.

He eyed the thin red ribbon, looped around the vic's neck like an untied bow on a Christmas gift. Had the doer loosened it? When and why? Again why?

He pulled the phone closer, tugging the long cord. He would have to go for the ME's report, take his chances. The ME might have nothing; the feds might have gone with their own lab, but he doubted it. They were quick enough to take advantage of local resources, the state police lab in Sudbury if not the ME's office in Boston. He might have to make several calls—

The knock on the door was followed so closely by the two officers, he barely had a chance to cover the file, let alone sweep it into a drawer.

"I must have said, 'Come in.'" Mooney had never

liked McHenry, the big man. Too much arrogance there, an old-fashioned bull.

McHenry opened his mouth, but McDonough spoke first. "We got something here, thought we ought to tell you." The smaller man, ill at ease, rocked slowly on the balls of his feet.

"I knew there had to be more to it, a private eye making a dud ID!" McHenry, pleased with himself, jumped into a rundown of the Nausett case: Sam Gianelli was the mobster the dead girl had dated. Not only was the hit-and-run vic a bosom buddy of the Nausett vic, but Gianelli was cozy with Carlyle. The hit-and-run vic must have been blackmailing Carlyle, threatening to take what she knew about the murder to the cops—

"Motive's for lawyers." Mooney kept his voice even, like they were talking about the weather, the remote possibility of snow. "Motive doesn't put Carlyle behind the wheel."

McHenry's smile widened and Mooney thought he'd never seen a less attractive grin.

"Got the vehicle," the big man said proudly. "Impounding it now, some garage in Allston. So we'll contact the feds. They'll want in on this baby."

"She doesn't have a car." Mooney wanted to recall the words the minute they left his tongue, but he didn't bother to amend them, to turn the self-incriminating statement into, "I heard she didn't have a car." Let the Macs think what they wanted to think.

The big man said, "Vehicle's registered to Gianelli.

How do you like them apples? Judy's gonna work it, and I'm betting she'll not only make the match with the vic, she'll put the lady in the driver's seat."

Judy Bisset, a criminalist in the CLU, specialized in trace evidence. She was good, but she wasn't a miracle worker. She couldn't leave all her other work to concentrate on a single hit and run. It would take time to make the match.

"No reason Carlyle wouldn't be in the vehicle, if it belongs to Gianelli." Mooney spoke calmly but his mind was racing. "What does she say about it?"

"Can't find her. Nobody seems to know where she is." McHenry made the words into a challenge.

"Well, when you pick her up—"

"We've got enough to talk to the feds," the big man said stubbornly. "If there's a link between the cases—"

"That's okay, McHenry, good work. Get your report on my desk and I'll take it from here."

"But we were—"

"I'm already on my way across the street, so I'll handle things with the bureau. McDonough, why don't you hang on a minute?"

McHenry lingered a beat too long, then pivoted on his heel. As soon as his footsteps died, Mooney said, "I was looking through the personnel files. You're up for a department citation on the trash-fire thing. Congratulations."

"Thank you, sir." The smaller officer ducked his head and turned to go.

"So how did you get onto the car?" Mooney hoped he had made the question sound like an afterthought.

"We did the hotline thing in the papers. Got it on the news."

"Guy leave a number?" Mooney wasn't talking about a phone number. Often, tipsters didn't want to be identified, but if there was reward money involved, there was a department protocol. The caller would leave a five-digit number instead of a name. If the tip panned out, the tipster could use the number to collect the cash.

"No name, no number," McDonough said.

"A do-gooder," Mooney said.

"I guess."

CHAPTER 22

Outdoors in the bracing chill, Mooney didn't bother to pretend he was on his way to some mythical confab with the bureau at the JFK Building across the street. He moved like a man on autopilot, backing the Buick out of the lot, racing down busy streets to the Central Artery, the underground maze of the Dig, and headed south.

He drove skillfully, weaving the lanes with a sense of purpose as well as speed. He hadn't gone to the feds. Instead he had made his choice. This was it. Now was the time to take time. He had it coming, hadn't taken a vacation in years. He was going to go back to what he was good at: street work.

In Boston, too many local bad guys knew him by sight. More and more, he was the wrong color, the wrong nationality. He spoke the wrong language. He didn't blend in; he stood out. All that would be different on the Cape.

The crush of traffic temporarily defeated the urge for speed. He accepted bumper-to-bumper traffic on summer Friday afternoons when Bostonians rushed to the Cape, but now, midweek in winter, he wondered what the deal was. Were people slipping off to open summer homes with no hint of spring in the air? Were they fleeing the city for some unknown reason, following the evacuation routes that had sprung up post–9/11?

As he drove, Mooney tallied his mistakes. He had believed Magda when she'd relayed the news about Gianelli, but he hadn't pressed for details. Mistake number one. Once he knew more about the case, he had continued to keep quiet, to protect Magda, to protect himself. That was number two. Then he had avoided Carlotta, knowing the feds suspected him of leaking to Gianelli, aware that Agent Dailey was on his tail. Mistake number three.

But the biggest mistake was this: Because he had wanted Gianelli arrested and out of the way, he had never questioned the case. Not his jurisdiction; not his problem, he had told himself. Now, with Carlotta involved, it was.

He considered McHenry's take on the hit and run. Julie Farmer, the girl who'd been killed by a car in the

North End, was Wilder's friend, and in the Macs' scenario, she had come to Carlyle not as a client, but as a blackmailer: *I am a witness; I saw what your fiancé did.* To the Macs, the story made sense. To Mooney, it had all the hallmarks of a frame. He doubted the Macs or the feds would see it his way.

Carlotta wasn't where she ought to be, wasn't answering her cell phone, wasn't picking up her home phone. Roz was answering, but she wasn't talking, and Gloria, who always talked, wasn't talking either. Mooney couldn't sit calmly at his desk and watch the chips fall. He needed to move, take action, make waves. The Wilder case was the beginning, the place to start, and this much he knew: The investigation had been bigfooted. The Nausett cops and the state troopers had barely had a chance to sink their hooks into the case before they had been ordered to give way to the FBI.

A blue Pontiac cut him off. The driver gave him the finger and Mooney smiled. He thought they ought to display the finger on the Massachusetts state seal.

With his own criminalists and evidence techs working full-speed, Mooney thought a week might do the trick. It would take at least a week to study paint chips and glass fragments, make the necessary microscopic lab comparisons, decide whether or not they had the right vehicle. If the Macs went to the bureau, the feds might steamroller the job through their own facilities. Could they do it faster? Would they try? Putting Gianelli away would be a feather in somebody's cap. Mooney wondered if the cap would belong to the red-faced agent Dailey.

Hingham. Marshfield. Duxbury. Traffic thinned the farther south he drove. The Sagamore Bridge, a notorious summer bottleneck, was easy sailing and once past it, he didn't need to consult any maps. Mooney's family, dozens of aunts, uncles, and cousins, used to gather on the Cape when he was a kid, back when it was affordable. They'd pile into the backs of pickup trucks, drive to Dennis or Falmouth or Yarmouthport, watch Cape Cod league baseball games. The price was right: free for all; bring your own beach chairs. If you caught a foul ball, you had to give it back.

Route 6 had been a narrow two-lane road then. Suicide Alley, they had dubbed it. Now he took the third exit off the divided highway, heading south to Nausett. He told himself he'd need to watch it, not come on as the city cop visiting the country cousins, avoid any wiseass remarks about sweeping up dead animals off the roads or babysitting drunken tourists, as though these cops weren't real cops, just traffic enforcers, guys with easy, placid jobs.

He had a big-city chip on his shoulder, but at least he knew it. Most of these guys were okay, guys who'd grown up in the places they served, the best kind of cops, with the pulse of the town in their blood, who knew names and families and history going back three, four generations. Sometimes the intimacy backfired: Kids from bad families had it held against them, became the usual suspects rounded up for every petty offense, but mostly it worked out fine.

Jesus, he was nervous. Nervous about a case, playing with his head, going around the investigation instead of plunging into it. He had told himself for years that all his cases were personal, but now this one was, and it felt different.

He thought he knew her, knew Carlotta, but how far would she go? If she had crossed the line with a lover, how far would she go? Women in jail, most of them were there because they'd joined forces with the wrong man.

Gianelli was the wrong man. Moon felt his jaw tighten. He knew Gianelli was the wrong man because he, Mooney, was the right man. But if he was the right man, if he'd always been the right man, why didn't she see it, too? Why hadn't he done something to make her see it?

He remembered her in uniform, the first day. Defiant because it was no use pretending to be demure, not with the hair and the height. There early; there late. Reliable, reasonable, always passed over, always given the crap assignments, never complaining. When he'd given her a break, she'd given him suspicion in return.

The timing had never been right.

Signs caught his eye, multisyllabic Indian place names: Attaquin, Ashumet, Santuit. Placards urged him to vote for Proposition 6, to vote against it. A vote against Proposition 6 would KEEP NAUSETT SAFE. A vote in favor would MOVE NAUSETT INTO THE 21ST CENTURY!

Long after she had left the department, when he was alone on stakeout, he'd hear her voice in his head, low and clear, with a husky undertone, a faint hint of smoke. They would engage in imaginary dialogues, alone in the dark, but whenever he picked up the phone, determined to reconnect with the real woman, the ring went unanswered. She was dating some other man. She didn't want to get involved with a cop. She was so damn stubborn.

When she had been part of his team, he had felt younger, more alive. Maybe it was the feeling rather than the woman he yearned for, the moment relived, youth and promise before they yielded to age and compromise.

As a child he'd mispronounced that word, *compromise,* in school. Reading aloud, he'd said *com-promise* and the teacher had corrected him. His cheeks had burned with crimson fire; a girl had giggled. Now he thought he'd been right about the word: an undelivered promise.

He scanned the roadside, the low trees, the cranberry bogs, the stunted, wind-scoured foliage. A square brownish sign read, HISTORICAL SITE: NAUSETT BURIAL GROUND. There was an arrow pointing at a diagonal to the right. He turned before he thought.

It might not be the scene of the crime, but it was the scene of the discovery of the crime. A place to begin, a sidetrip that would satisfy an itch and delay the visit to the Nausett cop house, the questions he should have asked weeks ago and hadn't.

The small building with the scaffolding, the one in the photos, turned out to be a church, which puzzled him. He had assumed the Indians of the Cape weren't churchgoing Christians, but he had been wrong. They were "praying Indians," early converts to Puritan and Pilgrim ways, he learned from a sign affixed to the boarded-up house. Beyond the scaffolding, the grave-yard seemed haphazard and disorganized. No neat rows of crosses, just meandering circles of stones, clumps of trees, occasional tombstones. Few of the stones had carving; few bore names. The crime-scene tape was long gone. The rains had come and gone; the snow, too.

There was more than one circle of stones. He was scanning the trees, the small church, trying to make the scene in front of him match the photos, when a dour-looking man, wearing a heavy wool jacket, chinos, and workboots, emerged from a distant guard shack.

"He'p you any?" The man's jaws worked a wad of gum.

"This place private?"

"Nah, open to the public, dawn to dusk. Get a lot of picture-takers, grave-rubbers, tourists. In season."

It wasn't exactly a question, but the man seemed curious.

"This where that woman was killed?"

The guard smiled through the gum wad. "Yep. I'm the one found her."

Calvin Gordon. The man matched the stats in the file: sixty-three-year-old army vet; partially disabled; shoulder injury. The bad shoulder wasn't noticeable under the heavy jacket.

"Musta been something," Mooney said.

"Believe it." Small and wiry, the man looked every one of his years. His seamed outdoor skin had seen too much sun.

"You mind talking about it?" Mooney said.

"You a reporter?"

"Hey, if you've got other stuff to do . . ." Mooney let the sentence die. Gordon would have to be bored, bored and cold, he thought. Talking would be better than standing around thinking about how cold it was.

"Where ya want me to start?" the man said. "The beginning? Well, ya know, this here's a quiet place, mostly someplace tourists stop in the summer and it sure wasn't no summer, back December. I spent my time in the guardhouse up yonder."

"Bad night?"

"Cold, misty. Didn't hear nothing; no kids giggling. Weren't no beer cans in the morning. When there's beer cans, I go right out, pick 'em up. Only respectful. Folks buried here."

"Not much you can do about kids."

"You got that right. They drink beer and they're lookin' for someplace to do it. Some of 'em like to sit on the gravestones and drink, but mostly the only trouble I have is on Halloween."

"But the day you found the girl?"

"Can't rightly say why I left the guardhouse when I did, but I always walk around near dawn. There ain't no schedule to it. I don't have none of those key-in-the-lock deals like they got over to the army barracks. Nobody comes and checks up on me if I don't turn a key right to the minute. I wouldn't work a place like that, where they don't trust a man."

While Gordon spoke, Mooney reviewed the man's background. Honorable discharge, he recalled. Employment history: paint factory, fishing boat, trash collection. Dismissed once for fighting, once for drunkenness.

"First off, I thought somebody drunk a few too many. Then, when I got closer—Man, it was that ribbon. That horrible face and then that loopy, curly ribbon." The guard stopped abruptly and Mooney remembered that the guard's footprints and vomit had contaminated the crime scene.

"Where did you find her?"

Gordon gazed at Mooney speculatively, then beckoned him to a small rectangle of out-of-the-way grass, leading him respectfully around stones and markers.

Mooney sighted on the scaffolded church, moved left till the angles lined up. Why here? he wondered. Why not behind that scrub oak? What made this the best spot to dump a body?

The guard shack stood at the mouth of a narrow road. The small meetinghouse church, the scaffolding, blocked the sightlines. The guard wouldn't be able to see this area.

"There another road over there?" Mooney nodded his head to the left. A car seemed essential.

"Yep. Through the trees. That's how they must a come."

"They?"

"He. Whoever. Whatever."

The grass near the stone circle was mashed flat—by the body, by the feet of the investigators, by raccoons, for all he knew. Mooney wondered what he had thought he'd see that nobody else could see.

"You didn't hear them? No engine, no car doors slamming?"

"Hey, I used to hear pretty good, you know? Now? Too much loud music, I guess, and I'm not really supposed to talk about this stuff. Cops already figure I'm the one blabbed about the ribbon. That ribbon shit got in all the papers."

"Did you recognize her?"

"Hey, people don't hardly even look like people when they're dead like that. This wasn't no casket viewing where they're all prettied up. The light wasn't good either, kind of cloudy and broken." Gordon paused. "She wasn't wearing clothes, none at all. But that don't mean it was a sex thing."

Mooney raised an eyebrow.

"Well, I figured sex, right at first, but then I said to myself if it's some kinda sex thing, why aren't they in some hotel or her place or his? I mean, he didn't jump her and rape her here. No way, not with no noise, not with weather like that. And why's he gonna dump her here? This here is an Indian burial ground, right?"

"Right," Mooney said, because the man seemed to want an answer.

"And she sure ain't one of them, blond girl like that. Blond all the way down, you know? I figure she was put here for a reason."

"You do?" Mooney tried not to sound pushy, just encouraging.

"Good as saying, You live with 'em, you die with 'em. Dead girl hung with the Indians, she did, friends with the tribe. I figure that's why the FBI took over. They do all that hate crime stuff."

"Somebody killed her because she hung around with Indians?"

"You don't believe me, but that's 'cause you're not from around here. Proposition Six, you probably don't even know what it means."

"You're right there."

"It's no big deal, the tribe says, just is the town gonna sell them a chunk of land."

"But you think it is a big deal."

"Well, hell yeah. First off, where's a bunch of poor Indians—they're always crying poor-mouth, too— gonna get all this money to buy the land? And then, look at it, you sell the Nausett a chunk of land, you might as well say they gotta right to be a tribe. That's one of the things they look at, the government. Does the town recognize the tribe? Selling land to 'em, that's flat-out recognition."

"It makes a difference, this recognition business?"

The guard gave Mooney a look like he'd just landed

on the planet. "You're not from around here, all right. Casino gambling, man! Slot machines and dice, and all the trouble that brings on this earth and in the kingdom to come. Oh, they got a church here, but take my word, most of the Indians don't belong to any church but the holy church of money, high church of the dollar bill. They get themselves recognized as a tribe, next thing you know, this place is all gonna be a parking lot. Pave paradise, put up a parking lot. Folks round here don't like that."

Mooney didn't think Calvin Gordon had just come up with the words, "holy church of money, high church of the dollar bill." The man sounded like he was reciting lines from a speech, maybe a sermon.

"Once they get the land," the guard said solemnly, "they'll build a casino and it will be part of the Indian nation. It won't even be Nausett anymore."

CHAPTER 23

Bobby Thurlow strode down the corridor into the light and Mooney knew he'd caught his break. It was the same man he had known half a lifetime ago, still slim and fit, hair shorter, flecked with gray in sharp contrast with his ebony skin. A good cop who'd seen things he didn't want to see, started drinking a little too much, wised up, and gotten out when the getting was good. Bobby Thurlow had known who he was and how much he could take, a rare combination in a cop.

"Jesus, izzat you?" Thurlow's bass rumble was lower than low.

"In the flesh." They shook, Mooney's big hand all but disappearing in Thurlow's massive grip.

"How the hell are you?"

"Good. Fine."

"On vacation? I heard you never took a day off."

"I'm working, Bobby. I could use some help." The walls were more than partitions, but less than sound-proof, so Mooney kept his voice low. The young receptionist at the front desk was too close and all ears.

"Robert," the man corrected. "Here, I'm Robert."

"Robert," Mooney said easily.

"Boston needs my help?"

"Me. I need your help."

"How about we go for coffee? Tastes like crap from the machine I got here, swear to God, worse than that crap we chugged in the city."

Mooney waited while Bobby—Robert, now—arranged to have an officer cover a DARE meeting on Sharp Street and reminded the receptionist to phone the school principal to reassure him that the grounds would be patrolled. The station, light and airy, painted white, seemed more like a real estate office than a police station. The lanky receptionist wasn't even in uniform.

Mooney assumed that "coffee" meant anything from a long walk to drinks to dinner. He hoped it meant food, an early dinner, maybe a clam roll at one of those shacks near the ocean that he remembered so vividly from childhood. They probably wouldn't be open yet, not before tourist season began.

Mooney offered his car, but Thurlow said he ought to take a cruiser, just in case something came up. The best place was within easy walking distance, always supposing an old cop like Mooney could manage to move his bones a few blocks in the cold, but Thurlow felt naked without the car. Conti's had great atmosphere, good draft beer. You could get Sam Adams seasonals, a few smaller local brews on tap. Big fat burgers, too, although those oughta be avoided. Maybe once a week Thurlow slipped and gobbled one, but he worked it off at the gym.

Downtown Nausett was a single traffic light, church on one corner, police station on another, town hall across the way. Unmetered parking lined the quiet street. Conti's had both a counter and booths. Bobby—Robert—Thurlow hailed the man behind the grill like a friend, ordered two tall Sam winter lagers.

They chose a booth at the back, sank onto cracked red leather.

Thurlow said, "So you want a job? I'm surprised sometimes the whole damn force doesn't invade. It's quiet here."

"Pretty, too."

"The ocean, man; I love living near the ocean."

"You're in charge, hiring and firing?"

"Hey, I'm the chief, but mostly I go by 'Detective.'

Rosemary, that's the reception girl, she hates that, likes to tell people she works for the chief, but it sounds wrong to me. I mean, it's me and one other guy, most of the year. I hire help in the summer, deputies. And they keep telling me I'll get to hire another full-timer some day. We could use it. I had to hire myself a part-timer to patrol the schoolyard tonight."

A skinny brunette waitress brought their beers in frosted glasses. She offered menus, big eyes, asked whether they'd like to hear the daily specials.

"Don't you go tempting me now, Liza."

The waitress smiled at Thurlow's rumbled response and subsided with a raised eyebrow.

"Besides," Thurlow went on, "down here, 'chief'—well, to me—sounds like I'm trying to set myself up as a kind of counterweight or something to the Indians. So you looking to work on the Cape? Security?"

"I'm looking for help on a case."

"I thought you said personal."

"It is." Mooney found himself reluctant to explain.

The Nausett detective chewed his lip. "This the Wilder thing?"

Mooney nodded, sipped his beer. Thurlow wasn't the smartest detective Mooney had ever worked with, but he was up there.

"First killing we've had since I came, and that makes it one more than I thought I'd see."

"What would you say if I told you I'd heard rumors

it was a hate crime?" The tall glass felt slippery in Mooney's hand.

Thurlow smiled. "I'd say you been gabbing with Mr. Mouth down the graveyard. I'd say you shoulda talked to me first."

"Look, I don't want to step on your toes."

Thurlow's grin broadened. "Hell, this case my toes are squished so damned flat already, it don't make much never mind."

"What's your gut tell you?"

"Hate crime?" Thurlow shook his head. "We got ourselves a situation here with the special election coming up. Had some busted windows, shit like that. That's why we're patrolling the school. But broken windows are one thing and killing is another. Hate crime? You go into any bar or café or church meeting around here, you'll get yourself seventeen other theories."

"Such as?"

"Oh, well, lemme see now. Wilder was pregnant by the police chief. I swear, that little gem was on this pissant local crime Web site—you know about crime Web sites, right? Print any piece of crap you want, sign it 'anonymous.' And what else? The vic was stealing from some old guy—I think his name was Bloomquist or Bloomberg—stealing from his trust, in it with her employer, old Hastings, except that's a crock, too. There is no Bloomquist or Bloomberg, and Brad Hastings doesn't need to steal any money, because he's rolling in it already. And the vic was just a paralegal assistant, did library research, looked up deeds and crap."

"What about casinos?"

"Mr. Mouth again? Casino gambling is still illegal in Massachusetts, whether the tribe owns the land or not. And from what I hear, it doesn't matter what the crackpots or the gossips say, because the case is cleared, tied with a ribbon, just like the vic."

"So how come they haven't made an arrest?"

"I'd like to know that myself."

"They keeping you in the loop?"

"I call the DA every now and again, ask him why the hell he doesn't arrest the son of a bitch so I can stop having to listen to every single asshole on the Cape thinks he solved the crime. We got this woman calls the station all hours, trying to get us to pick up her ex-husband. Says she's scared he's the killer. I figure she calls whenever she bangs the guy and he walks out on her again."

"Halprin was working it, right?" Mo Halprin was the state trooper who had copied Mooney the partial file.

"Yeah, Hal's okay. The staties, you know, they let you in on the ground floor. They know what it's like, small-town politics. They know you got to be able to tell people what's going on with a case. The feds don't give a warm dish of spit." Thurlow snorted and drank the foam off his beer. "Look, what's your interest here? I mean it, rumor is the feds got their man, a Boston dude, a player, all mobbed up."

"I heard the same rumor," Mooney said. "I'm not sure I buy it."

"There's also a rumor that you hate the federales. You playing cowboy here?"

"The feds come in, they don't know what the locals know. Am I right?"

"Yep. And they don't bother to ask because us locals are too plumb dumb to polish their brass."

"So I'm asking you," Mooney said. "I want to know why they settled on this guy."

"Gianelli."

"You know him?"

"Never had the pleasure. I know about him, from when I worked Boston, but I never had much to do with OC. I wouldn't recognize him, and I didn't know Danielle Wilder was hooked up with him. We get all kinds of summer people. Nobody gives me a heads-up when a killer rides into town."

The waitress came by to see if they wanted to freshen their drinks. Mooney nodded. Thurlow switched to tomato juice and Mooney, who wanted something to eat, wondered whether the cop had a one-drink limit.

"Buffalo wings any good?" Mooney didn't want to take time to study the menu. The wings were advertised on a blackboard behind the bar.

"The mozzarella sticks kill," Thurlow said.

"Some of those, then."

The waitress made a note on her pad and left.

Mooney said, "You know what they got on Gianelli?

Forensics? CW?" *CW* was bureau shorthand for a confidential witness.

"You trying to give the feds a black eye? Gunning for any agent in particular?"

"It's just this thing you got here doesn't sound like a mob hit." It wasn't an answer to the question, but Mooney hoped Thurlow would let it slide.

"I know what you're saying. Mob hit is two in the head, body in the trunk. You working for somebody on this?"

"Is that a polite way of asking if I'm trying to help out the mob? You know I don't work for them."

"And you want me to trust you on that, right? I guess you figure I owe you?"

When Thurlow was a Boston cop who drank too much, he'd been accused of roughing up a suspect, administering street justice. Mooney had intervened and steered the officer into counseling. Back then, Mooney had worried that Thurlow was one beat-walk away from swallowing his gun.

The waitress came by with fresh drinks and a plate of mozzarella sticks, fried and greasy, smothered in marinara sauce.

"I just want you to talk to me," Mooney said as she walked away.

"About?"

"The vic, what was she like?"

Thurlow looked at him for long seconds over the rim of his tilted glass, then set it down, grunted, and stared into space. Mooney thought he had hit a dead end, come up empty. He had already reached into his pocket for his wallet, so he could put down cash for the drinks and food, when Thurlow sighed and started talking.

"Prettiest girl in town, probably. High school sweetheart. Sort of girl guys make assumptions about. I mean, right, you're not supposed to, but all those years watching TV, you see this blond dreamgirl and what are you gonna think about, IQ or cup size? Personality or swaying hips?"

"So you knew her?"

"Strictly business, Moon. You know the type: popular girl, trophy girl, the one you have to be man enough to win. Big-city looks, but never left town. Got as far as Cape Cod Community College. Had some kind of deal with the place she worked where they'd send her off to law school. An up-and-comer. Not your most likely candidate to wind up strangled in a graveyard."

"A lot of men in her life?"

"More than a few, but some dude drinks a little too much on Saturday nights sorta pales in comparison with a mob capo. So, yeah, there are guys I would have questioned, but it was taken off my plate. Taken off the state plate, too."

"If it's not a hate crime, why the feds?"

"I wondered about that, too. How's this? The Indian Country Crimes Act and the Major Crimes Act, both part of your very own Federal Criminal Code, give the FBI the responsibility and jurisdiction to investigate murders in Indian country."

"You looked that up."

"Damn straight, I did."

"The graveyard counts as Indian country?"

"Yep. Body was found there, and it's technically reservation land under the jurisdiction of the feds. But don't ask me why they wanted it, because I don't know why."

"I want to know how they latched on to Gianelli," Mooney said quietly. "Nothing will come back on you."

"Like I never heard that before."

"You never heard it from me. You want one of those burgers?"

"Yep, but I'm not gonna eat one."

Thurlow helped himself to a mozzarella stick instead. Mooney took a second. They were awkward to handle, sauce and grease dripping onto the plate, but Mooney thought they were about the best bar food he'd ever tasted.

"Did they find where she was killed?" he asked.

"Not that I know of. Could be they're just being tight-lipped about it."

Tight-lipped about the scene of the crime and loose-lipped about the identity of the killer. Mooney thought the combination unlikely.

"I know they went through the vic's apartment," Thurlow said. "It's still sealed off. Woman rents it out had another tenant lined up. I hear from her all the time."

"Hard to rent a place after the tenant gets murdered?"

"It's not that. Wilder was planning to move out, go off to law school somewhere in D.C. The new tenant was all lined up before the killing. And the place was neat as a pin, so Wilder wasn't killed there. We did the usual, ran a check on all the hot-sheet motels, but nobody had themselves a murder site. Or else the help just cleared up the mess and called it a day." As Thurlow spoke, his cell phone buzzed, and he yanked it out of his pants pocket.

"Yeah?" He reached for a paper napkin and wiped his mouth. "Jeez Louise, yeah, two minutes. Hang on, boy, I'm on the way."

Mooney, anticipating a quick departure, slapped a twenty on the table.

"Wrap up those cheese sticks," Thurlow said. "We'll chomp 'em later."

CHAPTER 24

"Town used to be so quiet," Thurlow said. "You're carrying, right?"

"Yeah." Mooney quickly fastened his seat belt and stowed the mozzarella sticks, sauce already starting to soak through the napkins, in the dash compartment. The patrol car shot down the street like it had been launched from a cannon.

"Well, I don't want you shooting any of these little pissants. This is penny-ante shit. Hazeltine, that's my part-timer, thinks he's got a couple of them cornered down at the schoolyard."

"Broken windows?"

"Taggers."

The cruiser's blue lights flashed, but the chief kept the siren silent on the dark and deserted roads. In a couple of minutes they were pulling into a driveway, screeching to a halt.

"Flashlights in the trunk," Thurlow said. "Grab the bullhorn, okay?"

The cruiser's headlights blazed a pathway.

"Hazeltine's got 'em in the courtyard." As he moved down the driveway, Thurlow snapped on his Maglite. He moved the beam left, then right, until it illuminated a man in uniform crouching beside a hedge.

The man hurried over. "One got away. Shinned over the wall. But somebody's still there." He pointed vaguely north.

"Mooney, Hazeltine."

"Hey, with three of us, we can nail 'em." Hazeltine's narrow face was young and eager, his nose red with cold.

"Don't point your light at me," Thurlow said.

"Sorry."

"Where you figure they are?"

"That big platform thing with the ropes and ladders? Jungle gym? There's a slide down the left side. I think they're on top, drunk, or one of 'em is. Somebody puked out front."

"Drinkers and taggers the same group?"

"Let's go get 'em!" Hazeltine was almost dancing in his excitement.

The sound of shattering glass broke the night.

"Dammit! School committee's gonna chew my ass!" Thurlow grabbed the bullhorn out of Mooney's hand and yelled, "Come on outa there with your hands up!" His amplified voice distorted, but the words were clear enough.

"Shee-it," said a low voice. A second person laughed and Mooney thought the laughter sounded feminine.

"I'm giving you till three. You come out, we talk things over, and see what we've got. You make us come in there, you're headin' to jail in cuffs, understand what I'm saying? Okay? I'm gonna start counting. One. Two—"

"Gimme a minute." A girl wearing tight jeans and a hooded top walked blinking into the pool of light. Mooney thought of the word *sashayed*.

"Get around the other side," Thurlow yelled. "Somebody's on the roof."

Mooney easily outpaced Hazeltine, racing counterclockwise around the long low building, flashbeam bouncing over grass and dirt. Ahead he heard a scrambling and a curse. Mooney knew he was running after a schoolkid, a dumb tagger, but he was still wary, because he was on unfamiliar turf, because he might take a tumble, because in the pitch dark, the unknown kid might turn out to have a knife or a gun. Mostly he felt exhilarated, the fresh air and the action conspiring to make him feel young. Or maybe it was just the beer.

Hazeltine, who'd taken some sort of shortcut, popped up ten yards ahead. "Stop it right there!"

"Don't shoot me. Sweet Jesus, don't shoot." The tagger was down on the ground retching.

"Put the gun down." Mooney was more worried that Hazeltine might shoot himself accidentally in the foot than fire deliberately at the scrawny, defeated figure in the grass.

"Don't you barf on my shoes," Hazeltine yelled.

"You got him? Good." Thurlow came around the corner, leading the bold young lady by the arm. "Let's see who we got. Miss Eberlee didn't want to snitch."

"Oh, Luke," the girl said mournfully, "you coulda got clean away."

"Izzat Luke Fellman? Tell me that's not Luke Fellman. What the hell you think you're doing, Luke? Your momma is gonna tan your ass."

"Shit," Luke said.

"Okay, let's see what you're in for, you two."

"Oh, come on, I don't feel so good."

"You're gonna feel worse, Luke. Plenty worse. Who was the third genius?"

"Huh?"

"One of 'em got away," Hazeltine said.

"Bullshit," said the girl.

"Donna, you oughta wash that mouth out with soap."

"Fuck that," Donna Eberlee said with grim satisfaction. She looked about thirteen years old.

"Okay, why don't you two show me what you been up to?"

Hazeltine said, "They were working on the front windows."

"You putting bad words where the little kids gonna read 'em? Shame on you."

In the eerie glow of the flashlights, the school was revealed as an old clapboard house, with a long low wing added on each side. While Thurlow scolded, the group moved around one wing to the front.

GIVE THE INDIANS BACK THEIR LAND!
NO MORE BROKEN PROMISSES!
OPEN LAND. NO CONDOES FOR RICH FOLKS!

Hazeltine read each statement out loud. It wasn't the kind of stuff Mooney had expected, not from the appearance of the two kids. The boy was short and slight, maybe fifteen at most. His hair was wispy and fair.

"What's the story, here?" Thurlow said. "Donna?"

"Go fuck yourself."

"Donna's a hard case," Thurlow said. "What am I gonna do with you, Donna?"

"Just take me in and book me."

"Bill," Thurlow said to Hazeltine. "You call Mrs. Schneider over to the—"

"Come on!" Donna said.

"Donna wants to do time," Thurlow said to Mooney. "She doesn't like it at home, wants to go to reform school."

"Fuck you," said Donna.

Thurlow said, "You really want to go to that reform school so bad, Donna, you tell me what happened here tonight and maybe I can help you out."

"Shut up!" It was the boy's first offering since he'd begged them not to shoot.

"C'mon, you two," Thurlow said. "I'm interested in how come you're suddenly politically involved here. Your momma tell you to write this stuff, Luke?"

"They gave him fifty bucks," said Donna. "He promised to split."

"Hell I did! You get ten, that's what I said."

"Who's 'they'?" Thurlow asked.

"The boogeyman," Luke said.

Donna just about fell over herself laughing. "Yeah," she said. "The boogeyman, like Luke said."

"Injuns," Luke said. "Heap-big ones. War bonnets and face paint."

"You little creep," Thurlow said.

"Don't you call him names," Donna said.

"Here's a name for you: Liar. Turn out your pockets, the both of you."

"I got no pockets," Donna said defiantly. "You try search me, I'll scream my head off."

"Luke?"

The boy's right pocket made a crinkling sound and a slip of paper fluttered to the ground along with a fifty-dollar bill. Mooney held the paper to the light. Whoever had written the phrases to be copied had spelled *promises* and *condos* correctly.

"Hazeltine?" Thurlow said.

"Yeah."

"Take Miss Eberlee home. If you give him any crap, girl, he'll handcuff you to the door and you'll answer to me, understand?"

"I want my money," she said.

"You come down to the station tomorrow then. And bring your ma with you."

"You old fart."

"One more word outa you, girl—"

"And what?"

"Take her home, Hazeltine. We'll take care of Luke."

Mooney didn't envy the young cop, but the girl followed him wordlessly. She seemed to have lost most of her swagger.

"Okay, Luke, who gave you the money and the list? And don't 'boogeyman' me this time. I don't impress as easy as your girlfriend."

"Some guy. Um, he was kinda tall, wore those wire-rim glasses, little goatee. Tall skinny guy, long dark hair, probably one of those Indian nuts."

"How old?"

"Old. Maybe thirty."

"And he gave you this list? He write it out for you?"

"Yeah."

"Well, I appreciate you telling me that."

"What are you gonna do with my money?"

"I thought maybe you'd help me with that."

"How?"

"Let's go give it back," Thurlow said.

"Huh?" the kid said.

"Mooney, you watch this little pissant while I make a phone call, okay?"

CHAPTER 25

Thurlow angled the rearview mirror so he could keep an eye on the kid in the backseat. Mooney, who hadn't had a chance to ask the police chief what he was up to, wondered whether the mozzarella sticks would be worth eating cold.

The cruiser pulled up in front of a weathered gray bungalow on a winding road. Stunted trees fronted the lot. In the yellow glow of the porch light, in spite of the cold, two old men rocked on a saggy front porch. One wore a banded hat and smoked a slim cigarette; the other, his skin as dark as Thurlow's, puffed on a stumpy cigar.

Thurlow parked the unit on the brown, beaten grass by the roadside, among a cluster of cars. Mooney noted three elderly Detroit rust heaps, two pickup trucks, a maroon Lexus, and a sky blue Mercedes.

"Where the hell are we?"

Mooney was glad the kid had asked.

"Listen up, Luke. You know what a lineup is?"

"Yeah."

"There's lots of people here tonight. I was gonna come on over anyway, pay my respects, but what you said gave me an idea."

"Yeah?"

"First off, you're gonna behave like a human being, okay? No yelling, no loud talking. You stay with me and we walk around and when you see the man gave you the note and the money, you just lean over and tell me about it, real quiet. Okay?"

"I don't have to do it."

"Right." That was all Thurlow said, but there was menace behind the word.

The kid heard it. "Will I get to keep the fifty if I do it right?"

"I don't want you acting up, hear me? This is a solemn thing, like church. Old man lives here lost his granddaughter. Did you know that girl, Luke? Girl named Julie Farmer?"

Mooney lifted his eyes to the mirror, found Thurlow watching him, not the kid. Mooney thought the Nausett cop had thrown out the name the way a fly fisherman might cast a line, trying to see whether Mooney would bite, whether he knew about Julie Farmer, whether something about the Farmer case had brought him to town.

"At least I won't be breaking the news," Thurlow said. "That sure used to suck."

"Want me to wait?" Mooney wasn't sure why he didn't want Thurlow to know he was interested in this crime, too, but he had learned to trust his instincts. He no longer knew Thurlow well, wasn't sure where the man's allegiance might lie.

"Suit yourself, but you won't be intruding. Everybody in town knows Mitch Farmer, and most of them will be here. His granddaughter, Julie, she lived with the old man, off and on. Girl had some history; nothing awful, drunk a few times, runaway. Good girl, mostly, big pretty smile. She ran off again, only this time she got hit by a car. Hit and run. Mitch had already come by, filled out a missing persons. I'd have made the ID eventually, but we got a tip from a Boston PI. A woman?"

Thurlow hadn't worked with Carlyle, Mooney was certain of that. They had both been Boston cops, but it was a big department and the years of service hadn't overlapped, Thurlow calling it quits before Carlyle had shown up.

"Mitch Farmer, the old man, he's a high councillor of the Nausett nation."

"That a big tribe?" Mooney asked.

Thurlow's brow wrinkled. "Some say the Nausett nation is really a subset of the Mashpee Wampanoag. Since the Mashpee Wampanoag just got themselves recognized by BIA, that might stick a fork in the Nausett tribal claim."

"What do you think?"

"Well, according to the feds, there's a set of seven things you gotta prove to be a legit tribe. The Nausett have been going through the process for as many years as I've been here."

"What seven things?"

"Got me, but somebody here will know. Mitch Farmer says there's—what?—sixteen hundred tribes in the Americas—and he figures the Nausett oughta know who they are."

"BIA's Indian Affairs?"

"You probably don't hear from them much."

"We get the whole rest of the alphabet: ATF, DEA."

"PIA. That's for Pain in the Ass." Thurlow's deep voice rolled with easy laughter. When the kid in the backseat snorted, Thurlow said, "You gonna cooperate, Luke?"

"I want my money."

Thurlow shrugged and opened the car door. The blast of cold air tingled against Mooney's ears.

"Guess I might as well tag along," he said.

After the Nausett nation buildup, the house was disappointingly ordinary. Mooney would have preferred some kind of traditional Indian dwelling, a cookstove instead of an electric range in the cheerful yellow kitchen he glimpsed through an archway. The crowd didn't fit his image of Indians, either. If he'd been forced to guess, he'd have labeled most light-skinned blacks. A few looked more Hispanic than African-American. One or two younger men had let their hair grow long enough to braid into a single pigtail at the back.

"You want feather headdresses, you gotta come back during pow-wow time," Thurlow, at his elbow, said solemnly.

Mooney stared at the ground, embarrassed that he'd been caught gawking, even more embarrassed by the realization that his stereotypes, like Luke's, had been culled from late-night movies.

Most of those present in the sparsely furnished front room that ran the length of the house were men, all ages and more than a few economic levels, matching the variety of cars on the street. Jeans and workboots outnumbered suits. Mooney looked for a man to match Luke's description. Quite a few wore small soul patches that could be called goatees.

Thurlow marched directly through the crush until they were facing a man who met every particular of Luke's description: tall, thin, dark long hair, wire rims. Luke looked dumbstruck.

"Anything you want to say, boy?" Thurlow murmured.

"I want to go home."

Thurlow kept a hand clamped on the boy's bicep, but otherwise ignored him. "That you, Andrew?"

"Robert." The tall man's eyes lit. "Glad you could come by. Uncle Mitch will appreciate it."

"I'm sorry for your loss," Thurlow said. "You don't happen to know this fella, do you?"

Luke squirmed uncomfortably.

"Isn't that Jody Fellman's boy?"

"Don't suppose you hired him to write a few words over on the school house? Paid him fifty bucks?"

"You kidding me?"

"Luke?"

"I musta made a mistake." The boy stared at his sneakers.

"Thanks for your time, Andrew. Mooney, I'm gonna take this young man back to his momma now, then I'm gonna come back and stay awhile. You want me to drop you at your car?"

"Will you be long?"

"Ten minutes. Fifteen, max."

"If nobody minds, I could stick around till you come back."

Andrew with the wire rims said, "No problem. Have something to eat. Make sure you talk to my uncle when you get back, Robert. Okay? He's got something he wants to ask you."

The Nausett cop propelled the boy across the room and out the door, and Mooney knew that Thurlow, intentionally or not, had given him a gift, a chance to find out more about Julie Farmer, Danielle Wilder's best friend.

The crowd was packed more densely at one end of the big room. That was where the girl's family would likely be, seated around a low coffee table, accepting condolences. Mooney retreated to a sideboard covered with partially demolished rings of coffee cake and discarded paper cups. He scanned the length of the room. The few women looked ordinary. No fantasy Indian princesses with dark curtains of hair and beaded moccasins. Clusters of men, quietly chatting, drinking from Styrofoam coffee cups. Mooney found himself trying to pick out possible BIA agents.

A man in a cheap gray suit looked familiar, but he was such a standard type—medium height, brown and brown—that Mooney couldn't decide whether he'd previously seen Gray Suit in a lineup, a cell, or a uniform. Mooney made his eyes continue the sweep without seeming to pause. Had he once sat across from the man in gray at a conference table at the JFK Building? The blue-suited man standing next to Gray Suit was murmuring into a cell phone. A wide-bellied coffee urn sat on a card table. An ice chest held beer, and whiskey bottles dotted the tabletop.

Mooney decided to avoid the men who might be feds. He ducked into the yellow kitchen, overhearing shreds of conversation on the way.

"October, I'd have said you were crazy you said seventy-eight percent turnout. I'da thought half that, half that, for a special election."

"Twenty-one years old. Damn shame. Mitch relied on that girl."

The people seated at the long oak table were stuffing envelopes with printed flyers. SUPPORT 6! was the header. VOTE YES ON 6! SPECIAL TOWN ELECTION! MAY 18!

This was where most of the women hung out; here, in the kitchen, stuffing envelopes. Only one male was seated at the table, a scruffy, long-haired teen.

"If you wanna sit down and fold some flyers, that would be fine."

The young woman had come up behind him. She wore a flower-print dress that rode easily over a plump body. A halo of frizzy dark hair framed a pale doll-like face.

"No, that's okay," Mooney said. "I can't stay long."

"You against us?" she asked, an edge in her breathy voice.

"Proposition Six? Don't know much about it. Came to pay my respects."

"Well, take one. Read it. We'd get so much more done in the big room. We had a meeting scheduled for tonight, but—well, you can't hold it against her, poor kid."

"Julie?"

"She was alive, she'd be with us, so we keep going. Her family believes in the tribe's future just the way she did. Come on. Take a look."

The handbill she thrust in his face was bright canary yellow.

SUPPORT 6!

Your friends and neighbors of the Nausett Nation wish to make an investment in beautiful Nausett, traditional homeland of our people.

These acres adjoin land we already own. For 400 years, Nausett Nation land has been an asset to the community, green and open to all. Why trust an outside developer who could subdivide and resell the land?

Do you want apartment complexes and condos— or acres of beautiful trees? Shopping malls or open space?

Don't be misled by our opponents; there are NO PLANS TO BUILD A CASINO in the town of Nausett.
Support the Nausett Nation! Support open space! Vote Yes! Special town election. May 18.

"I don't live in Nausett," Mooney said.

"Oh, okay." The girl sounded disgusted. "None of your business. I get it."

"Sorry. Is there, um, a bathroom?"

"Down the hall, first door on the right."

Mooney didn't turn in at the first door on the right. He passed a bedroom that made his nose wrinkle with the musty smell of age, kept moving until he found a narrow staircase with a spindly railing. The girl's bedroom was probably upstairs.

"Can I help you?" The man blocking the upstairs hallway had a head of fine white hair an aging movie star would envy.

"I'm just going to dump my coat."

"The family is putting coats downstairs. The small room off the front hall?"

"Must have missed it." Mooney could recognize an expensive suit when he saw one, mostly because the cops he knew wore stiff cheap suits all the time. He wondered who this white-haired hall monitor might be. "You know the house, Mr.—?"

"Not well. The councillor asked me to bring him down some cough drops." The man stood smack in the middle of the narrow corridor. "I hope I got the right

203

ones. So many cold remedies these days. Side table looked like a regular drugstore counter."

Mooney felt he had no choice but retreat. He clattered down the staircase, wondering whether the white-haired man had heard his footsteps. He didn't normally make much noise when he walked.

"I'm pretty much a stranger here," he said politely when he reached the bottom of the flight. "Mooney's the name." He stuck out his hand so the man couldn't ignore it.

"Hastings."

The lawyer, Mooney thought. In his sixties, but well preserved, the man had fair skin, a healthy pink complexion, gray eyes. The elegant suit, tailored to take a few pounds off a slight paunch, would go nicely with the Lexus parked on the grass.

"Hastings and Muir." Mooney made himself sound enthusiastic. "I remember your sign from when I was just a kid. You've been practicing here a long time. Your father before you, right?"

"My grandfather, too." There was deep satisfaction in the lawyer's voice. "I thought you said you were a stranger."

"You a friend of the family?"

"Hastings and Muir has represented the Nausett nation for fifty-eight years. My father represented the tribe and my grandfather before him."

"Then you've seen this." Mooney displayed the yellow handbill.

"Are you considering which way to vote?"

"I don't know as much about it as I should," Mooney said truthfully, "but somebody was warning me to vote no, otherwise we'd have a casino in town faster than you can whistle 'Dixie.' Because a Yes vote would make the Nausett a legal tribe. Is that true?"

Hastings's smile seemed to cover a layer of impatience, as though Mooney had asked a question he'd answered far too often. "A Yes would help the tribe get recognized a little faster than they otherwise might, but they will be recognized eventually. It's only a bureaucratic slowdown that's holding up the process now, a backlog of tribes. As for a casino, that would be up to the legislature."

"This same person told me it didn't matter about the vote because the Indians wouldn't have the money to buy the land anyway. Said it would be way too expensive."

The lawyer shook his head sadly. "I'll bet you that person is not a homeowner. Every homeowner knows you don't put down full price when you buy a piece of property."

"A mortgage?"

"The tribe has a strong relationship with community banks. There's a wide consortium of interests, both public and private, that feel the land purchase can only help the town."

"So you're in favor of it?"

"Mr. . . . . Mooney, is it? Think about it. These are the people who greeted our ancestors when they came to the New World. You know Corn Hill up in Truro? That's where the first Pilgrims off the *Mayflower* stole the Nausett's seed corn so they could survive that first winter. Some people wonder what right we imagine we have to 'recognize' the tribe at all, but it's a legal process, one that has been too long delayed. My father always thought he'd see the day the Nausett were honored with recognition. I'm certain I will see the day, and this vote can help make the difference."

"Well, bravo," said Robert Thurlow. "That's one heck of a stump speech, Brad. I see you two have met."

"Mr. Mooney's a friend of yours? Well, I apologize if I was making a speech. Everything all right, Chief?"

"A little trouble at the schoolyard."

"Not the windows again?"

"Pro-Nausett slogans, but I think they might have been financed by the opposition."

"What do you mean?"

"Well, I figure pro-Indian propaganda spray-painted on a school is gonna rile voters up against the tribe. Kind of a double game, you know what I mean?"

"Clever," the lawyer said. "If that's what's going on. Have you spoken with Mitch yet? I know he wants to talk to you."

"I'll head right over."

Hastings said, "And Robert? You haven't heard anything about an arrest yet?"

"No. I'm sorry, Brad."

"It would make people feel better if they'd just get it over with." The lawyer sounded wistful.

"I know it would," Thurlow said. "I'll let you know if I hear anything."

"Thank you."

"Danielle Wilder's boss," Thurlow murmured as the white-haired man moved away. "You make the agents in the front room?"

Mooney nodded.

"Indian Affairs. Bureau, too. Maybe they think the hit and run's a hate crime. I gotta see the old man." Thurlow set out toward the family gathering, Mooney traveling in his wake, thinking about other possibilities: that McHenry had gotten impatient, that Big Mac had a buddy in the bureau.

Mitch Farmer, enshrined in a heavy dining room chair, had a weather-beaten face and ramrod-stiff posture. His bearing gave him dignity in spite of the brown short-sleeved bathrobe he wore over a cranberry sweater with holes in the elbows. One by one, people approached, patted him gently on the back, touched his shoulder.

He nodded solemnly to each one, clasped an occasional hand. Thurlow worked his way through the throng. Mooney followed.

"I'm sorry about this," Thurlow said when his turn came. "Real sorry, Councillor."

Brown eyes looked out from a nest of gray wrinkles. "Robert, thank you for coming."

"Anything I can do?"

"Help her come home," the old man said. "She should be home."

207

A middle-aged lady wearing too much makeup stood at the old man's shoulder. She nodded vigorously. Mooney thought she might be drunk, then he decided she was probably the old man's daughter, mother of the hit-and-run vic. Her eyes looked as red and exhausted as the old man's.

"Julie is still in the city," Farmer said. "Her body. Ask them to let her come home."

Thurlow explained the routine in an unexpectedly gentle voice. Then he introduced Mooney as a Boston officer who might be of assistance.

"I want to know whether she was drunk," the old man said. "Can they tell that? If she was drunk?"

"Yes," Mooney said.

"She was stubborn. She had to do everything her own way, and she always knew what was best. Once that girl got the bit between her teeth, she ran with it. But I don't believe she was drunk. I won't believe it unless they tell us."

"I'll see what I can do," Thurlow promised.

"Do something. We're supposed to be so patient and long-suffering. People die waiting. You understand? We die waiting."

Mooney followed the old man's eyes as he raised them to glance into a mirror over the sofa. The men who looked like federal agents watched with unblinking eyes.

As if he'd sensed the outside interest, the old man lowered his voice. "Come talk to me later, Robert. I'm very tired, too tired now. Come talk tomorrow."

CHAPTER 26

Outside, fewer cars on the grass verge. Overhead, a thousand stars. Mooney, used to the murky night skies over Boston, stared straight up, awed, and felt like a rube when Thurlow said, "Let's get in the car so I can get the heat on."

"So what was the deal with Luke and Andrew?"

"Not all the Nausett are in favor of this Proposition Six thing. I mean, it's like everything else. No organization represents all the members on all the issues, and some of the Indians are scared of what this could mean, worried about the gambling and sin and whatever."

"Andrew in the opposition?"

"I don't know. But the boy had a run-in with Andy a while back, dumped trash on his lawn, got caught, and had to do community service. So I figured Luke was lying about who hired him, trying for a little payback. Plus I thought maybe somebody at the gathering would come over, show more interest than they should, but that didn't happen."

"But you think it's like you said to the lawyer, a double game?"

"Could be. There's an undercurrent for sure."

"Think the land's the thing? Somebody else wants to buy the same land the Indians want to buy?"

Thurlow eased the patrol car onto the roadway. "Big chunks of land don't come on the market often down here. Every town with money is trying to buy land, set up conservation reserves, conservation trusts. Nausett's poor. We have to sell, and good Cape land this close to the sea, well, it's pure gold."

"Developers interested?"

"Hell, I'm almost as beat as the old man. I take you back to your car?"

"Yeah. And recommend someplace to stay the night. A B-and-B?"

"All closed for the season, but if you're not fussy, you can have my comfy living room couch."

"Your wife'll be okay with that?"

"That's how I know the couch is comfortable. I spent a lot of time there before she left."

"Sorry."

"I'm not."

Forty-five minutes later, Mooney sat on the lumpy sofa in the dark, listening. The toilet flushed, the sink gurgled, the floorboards sighed. The faint squeak of bedsprings subsided and Mooney peered at the battery indicator on his cell phone. It was charged, but the service signal was weak. He dialed Carlotta, waited, pressed end as soon as the message started.

He didn't keep any numbers on speed dial. He knew what cops could do with a recovered cell phone, and the knowledge made him cautious. He memorized numbers, considered it mind training, like crossword puzzles. He punched the numbers for Gloria's cab company.

"Let the other lines ring," he said.

"I'll lose money."

"Consider it an official call."

For a moment he thought she had hung up on him; then, after several clicks, her voice came back on the line, still deep and melodic, but flustered.

"Moon, I was going to call you. Look, she didn't know the car was here—"

"Did you know? He garage it with you?"

"I don't run a parking lot. Hey, what can I say? Carlotta was looking for that car, looking for Sam's Jag. She didn't have a car and no way he'd mind if she used his."

"She had the key?"

"I don't know."

Gloria had paused a beat too long before her reply. Carlotta would have had to have the key, Mooney thought. Otherwise what good would the car do her? Why would she be looking for it?

"Where is she, Gloria?"

"I don't know."

"You're the worst liar I know."

"Leroy drove her to Logan."

Jesus, that was like taking out an ad in the paper: guilty, guilty, guilty.

"She'll be back soon," Gloria said. "Maybe tonight."

"Where did she go?"

"I don't know."

"Which terminal?"

"I'm not saying."

"International?" He couldn't bring himself to mention Gianelli's name, to ask whether Carlotta had gone to him, joined him in whatever elegant place of exile the mobster had picked.

"Mooney, she didn't run. She'll be back. She said she'd be back, so she'll be back."

Mooney couldn't think of anything else to ask.

"Can't you call off the dogs, Moon? You know Carlotta's not the kind to run some girl down in the street."

"Can't do it," he said.

"I got calls, Mooney. Good-bye." Gloria's voice had turned to ice.

CHAPTER 27

"Hey, hey, rise and whine, pardner."

Mooney's eyelids felt like they'd been glued shut. He tried to remember where he was. Yawning and stretching, he rediscovered that the police chief's couch was too short.

"Couch sucks, huh?" Thurlow's voice was thick with sleep, but the man was dressed and ready to go. "Lied to you about that. But I made it up to you big-time. You eat cornflakes?"

"You made it up to me with cornflakes?"

"I made phone calls."

"To?"

"I had to call Rosemary, find out if the station burned down since last night, but that's neither here nor there. You eat cornflakes?"

"Yeah."

"I been dating."

"Good for you."

"I date this girl, Amy Gerson, works over at Hastings and Muir. I called her."

Mooney ran the name Amy Gerson through a mental file, didn't recall it from the state police interviews. "You ask her about Danielle Wilder?"

"No," Thurlow said. "Use the blue towel in the bathroom."

Mooney didn't ask why Thurlow hadn't questioned his girlfriend until the two men were at the kitchen table eating cornflakes drowned in semi-sour milk.

"I haven't questioned her because I don't want what happened with my wife to happen to us."

Mooney spooned cereal. He wouldn't have taken Robert Thurlow for a family inquisitor, but it was an occupational hazard. Long ago, when his own marriage was breaking up, his wife had once inquired, mid-argument, whether he wouldn't be more comfortable shining a light in her eyes. The memory was unpleasant.

"Cops must have talked to her."

Thurlow shook his head. "I doubt it. She went out sick couple days after the killing. Then, by the time she was back, FBI had gone on to other things. Amy was pretty disappointed."

"I didn't get much from Hastings last night."

"Cornflakes gonna be enough? You got yourself some exercise last night. At least."

"Hey, it was fun. I haven't run after schoolkids in a while."

"Just like Boston. Big-time broken-window bust."

"Really, I had fun. You want me to dump my sheet in the wash or what?"

"Let it be."

Mooney doubted his spinal column could endure a second night on the couch. "So what's your take on this special election?"

"The property thing? Sale seemed like a foregone conclusion, then some group, Citizens for Good Cape Government, yeah, CGCG, got hysterical, said it wasn't about the tribe buying the land, said it was about casino gambling."

"Is it?"

Thurlow rested his spoon on the edge of his bowl. "You know what? The Bay State's one of fourteen left in the union got no casinos and no slots. And what's our nickname? Taxachusetts."

Mooney nodded.

"I hear the tourists. That's what they say: 'Massachusetts liberal' and 'Taxachusetts.' You know how much Connecticut makes off of Foxwoods? Guaranteed? A hundred million a year is what and that's not counting Mohegan Sun. You know, I live here, year-round, and the taxes on this shitty little house go up every year, and they scoot up by a lot. I want good services. I want plenty of policemen and firemen and trash collectors and new roads and open space. So where's that money gonna come from?"

"State lottery?"

"See what I mean? The state's already in the gambling business. What's the big deal with slots and casinos if it gives everybody a break on the property tax?"

"Organized crime—"

"Bullshit. They got a study—a Harvard study, no less—says there's no increase in crime goes with Indian-run casinos. What—you think people in this state don't gamble? They drive to Connecticut is what they do. Buses roll out of Boston every hour for Mohegan Sun and Foxwoods. Three-quarters of a billion bucks moves out of state every year heading to Connecticut with love from Taxachusetts. What—you think they stop gamblers at the state line?"

Mooney remembered buying a state lottery ticket once, back when they were brand-new, a novelty. Won fifty bucks and he'd never bought another one. Sometimes he'd bet ten bucks on a football game.

"Local Indians interested in casino gambling?"

"Couple tribe members spent some time at Foxwoods last year, checking it out. Who in their right mind wouldn't be interested in running a casino?"

"Is Citizens for Good Cape Government a religious group?" Mooney remembered the fervent cemetery guard, the way he'd tossed off the phrase, "high church of the dollar bill."

"Don't know. They haven't thrown any rowdy parties or broken any laws I know of. You ready?"

"Coffee?"

"We're gonna pick up Amy, go for coffee. That good with you?"

"And you'll just lead the conversation around casually to the Wilder thing?"

"I got a plan for that."

"What?" The way Thurlow smirked, Mooney figured he was screwed.

"Remember that business in Truro? The Worthington killing? They had writers coming out of the woodwork, reporters, novel writers, everything in between. I'm gonna tell her you're a writer."

"She'll buy that?"

"How about a retired cop who's a writer?"

"Retired? I look that old?"

"After a night on the killer couch? You kidding?"

"I don't know."

"Hey, c'mon, you must know a couple big words."

"Asshole."

"That's one. Oh, and keep this in mind: Technically," Thurlow said judiciously, "far as Amy knows, I'm still married."

CHAPTER 28

"You been seeing this lady long?" Mooney asked.

A driver yielded right-of-way to the patrol car at a four-way stop, waving a friendly greeting. That sort of thing didn't happen in Boston. Mooney decided he felt more at home cruising the Combat Zone, eyes darting sideways to catch movement in the dark alleys.

"Couple months," Thurlow replied. "We'll pick her up at Hastings, Muir."

Mooney was uneasy about the writer cover story, too; he would have felt more convincing and comfortable posing as a low-life drug dealer. He had already checked his cell phone twice, called his home phone, screened messages there and at the office. Carlotta hadn't returned his call. If she'd left the country, he was wasting his time, spinning his wheels.

"Hey," he said, "did she own a car? Danielle Wilder?"

Thurlow nodded and Mooney wished he had a key that would unlock Thurlow's mouth, make the man talkative, free with information.

"You'll like this one," the Nausett officer said. "Her car's gone."

"Gone?"

"Nice car, too. Volvo or Saab, one of those. Can't remember which. Kind of showy. She parked it on the street, so somebody might have stolen it, I guess."

"Is that what the feds guess?"

The police chief shrugged his shoulders and made a left turn down another quiet street.

The law office didn't look any more like Mooney's idea of a law office than the Nausett police station resembled his idea of a cop house. It could have been a big old family house except for the signboard over the wide front porch. The maroon Lexus was parked out front.

"Here she comes," Thurlow said. "Is she a looker or what?"

Dark hair framed a thin eager face. Not strictly pretty, but fresh and bright-eyed. She floated to the passenger door, stopped, hand on handle, surprised to find the front seat occupied. Mooney, looking up at her, thought she was way too young for Thurlow.

"Amy, meet Moon, my old buddy. He just might make you famous."

"Oh, famous, huh? I could do famous."

Not with that screechy voice, Mooney thought, as she declined his offer to move and climbed into the backseat.

"Who do you figure should play her in the movie, Moon?" Thurlow was laying it on thick; the chief had evidently decided to have some fun. "Me, I'd go straight for Angelina Jolie. Can't do better than Angelina Jolie."

"You talk such shit, Rob," the girl said. "Where are we going? I got a meeting in an hour. And papers to get ready before then."

"Moon here is writing a book about your girlfriend, Danielle."

"Shit. You can just let me out at the light."

"Come on, Amy. He doesn't have to use your real name. He can call you Deep Throat, huh?"

"Well, I sure wouldn't want to be seen with him. I don't know about this."

"I was going to take the both of you out for coffee, but how about I go in and grab takeout? Then you two can stay in the car and talk?"

"Are you going to use a tape recorder or a videocam? Will I have to sign a release?"

Thurlow was grinning.

Mooney felt woefully unprepared. "Um, this is preliminary work. I'm not sure there's a book in it."

"Are you kidding? Of course there's a book."

"You gonna write it, Amy?"

"Maybe I should, Rob."

"Go get us some coffee," Mooney said.

When Thurlow left the car, Amy hopped out, too, and they embraced in the parking lot. Mooney cracked the window and eavesdropped shamelessly.

"Looking good," Thurlow said. "What are you wearing under that coat?"

"Old clothes, moron. They're repainting the place. Again. I don't want to spoil my good stuff. You take me someplace nice, I'll wear something nice."

The girl strolled partway to the coffee shop, then hurried back and slid into the driver's seat. Hard to tell about her figure under all the coats and scarves, but her legs were fine in tights and heels. Her scent held a hint of lemon.

"Let's start with the office." Mooney, who had grabbed a pad of paper and a stubby pencil off Thurlow's kitchen desk, made a meaningless squiggle. "How long have you worked there?"

"Wow, since forever, since high school. I was an

intern there. My mom was a law office secretary. She liked it a lot, so I thought I'd give it a try. I'm a demon keyboarder. I like being in the front room, meeting people."

"Is it a big firm?"

"For this town, I guess. It's the biggest."

"And what do you handle?"

"Realty, wills, all that stuff. We represent the local tribe, too, the Nausett nation."

"How many lawyers, besides Hastings?"

"No Muirs anymore, but there's two other guys, Joe Kepple and Blake Ganley. Blake only comes in part-time. He's about ninety."

"Support staff?"

Amy shifted her legs. "Look, I don't have much time. You want to know about Danielle, ask."

"Okay. How long did she work there?"

"She got hired after me. But she got to travel. Washington and New York, and tons of other places."

"You handle real estate in other cities?"

"I think it was all to do with the tribe."

"So Danielle was involved with the tribe?"

"Not so much. She just liked to seem more important than she was. The whole thing with her getting killed, I keep thinking how much she'd enjoy all the fuss. She'd be the one angling for a big movie star to play her onscreen. She always had to be the center of attention. You don't take many notes."

"I have a good memory."

"You have stuff published?"

"In the pipeline." Damn Thurlow. Mooney had no idea how familiar she was with authors or publishing houses. He thought he ought to have written something, for credibility's sake. "Where were you when you heard about Ms. Wilder's death?"

"At the office. Nobody got any work done."

"People were shocked?"

"Hey, we all warned her. A woman dates a mobster, what does that say about her?"

"That depends," Mooney found himself saying. He forced himself back into character. "You knew about that? Knew his name?"

"Oh, yeah. Her Sam, her sweetie. She liked the money he spent on her, that's one thing. Danielle was an expensive girl. She really got off on glamour. She always wanted you to think she knew stuff you didn't know. I mean I'm a secretary; I'm not a paralegal, and she made all this big deal about how she understood shit I didn't understand and she was gonna be a lawyer and I was gonna be nothing."

"I heard the thing with the mobster was over."

"Who says a guy like that is gonna take no for an answer? But yeah, it was over, as far as she was concerned."

"Was she dating somebody else?"

"She wasn't the knitting-a-scarf-on-Saturday-night type." The claws were out. Amy was the first person Mooney had met who was obviously glad Danielle Wilder was out of the way.

"Did Danielle hang out anyplace? A bar, a club?"

"That December, she was totally devoted to work. I mean putting in extra hours was nothing to her. Shining up to the lawyers, and boy, did it work, them paying to put her through law school."

"They have a program for that?"

"They're not sending me to any law school if I bust my ass for a thousand years."

"But she wasn't dating anybody in particular?"

"Oh, there was a guy. At least one. She was extremely available, you know what I mean?

"And this guy?"

"I don't know that I'd call him 'anybody.'"

"Another lowlife?"

"I don't really know who he was." The admission cost her. "I saw Danielle at some store, at Radio Shack, yeah, and she didn't see me, or if she did, she didn't bother saying hello. She was with this guy, very cute. She called him Kyle, I think. Yeah, Kyle, and she was like ordering him around, hold this, hold that, and he's following her around like he's in heat, you know? She had him holding cords and gizmos, like maybe she was going to have him set up a new stereo."

"Could he have worked there, at Radio Shack?"

"This was definitely not a clerk. Nice overcoat, good haircut. A girl can tell."

"You ever see this Kyle around town?"

"Nah."

"But you figure him for a boyfriend?"

"A fallback guy, maybe, the way she bossed him. So she didn't get cold at night, like a blanket or something. Probably wasn't worth the effort, finding a man who could stand on his feet when she knew she was leaving town."

"Kyle have a last name?"

She shrugged.

"You have any idea what she was working on? Before she died?"

"She was just showing off, putting in extra time like that."

"Did she seem worried about anything, different in any way?"

"She was always stuck up as hell. Oh, you're going to hear nothing but flowers and lace now she's dead, and how good she was to her old granny, but I think somebody oughta tell it like it is. What do you suppose happened to Rob? I better honk the horn or something. I get in big trouble I take too long a break. Danielle never did. No, she was a 'professional.' Me, I'm dirt."

"You've been very helpful, Amy."

"Just don't use my name in the book."

CHAPTER 29

"She's something, huh?" Thurlow watched his girlfriend trot back up the walkway to Hastings, Muir, balancing her takeout coffee in one hand and waggling the fingers of the other over her shoulder in farewell.

"She gave me a name: Kyle."

"A player?"

"Possible boyfriend, post-Gianelli."

"Must be young," Thurlow said. "My momma's generation didn't name their babies Kyle."

"No last name."

"First name doesn't chime, but I don't have a lockbox memory. Let's see if he comes up in any of the friends-and-family chats."

"I didn't see any family interviews."

"Wilder girl didn't have much: only child, Dad dead, Mom traipsing around Europe, some stoned left-over hippie, didn't even come to the funeral. Grandma's in a nursing home in Falmouth. Told her Danielle was dead, but she's got that Alzheimer's so she's probably still waiting for her little girl to visit. Kyle, huh? Least it's not John or Pete."

"Jason or Alexander."

"Yeah, I'm sure behind the times."

When they pulled into the police station lot, Mooney said, "You go ahead in. I want to see if I left something in my car."

The thing he'd left was his portable phone charger. He thought about phoning the commissioner or calling in sick with some phony complaint that would explain his absence, excuse his reckless behavior, but he didn't feel like lying. Pretending to be a writer had taken it out of him. He'd had enough lies for the day.

He tried Carlotta's number, waited out the message and the beep, left a terse "Call me." He figured Gloria would have phoned him if Carlotta had been picked up by the Macs and tossed in jail, so he tried another number instead.

Even though he was on the list of approved callers, it was a struggle to get through to Paolina. Miss Fuentes could call *him,* a cool-voiced receptionist informed him, when *she* felt like it and had time to do so. He could not expect to get through whenever he felt like it. Mooney bit his lip and listened to the long hours and frustration behind the receptionist's tone. He didn't want to use his rank, doubted it would work. Instead he sympathized with her difficult job, emphasized how deeply he'd appreciate her taking personal responsibility to put the call through, promised he'd never break protocol again, and breathed a sigh of relief when he was finally switched to her room.

"Paolina?"

She sounded groggy. He hoped they weren't keeping her on some medication that made her voice so flat and dull it was barely recognizable.

"Who is that?"

He identified himself.

"How are you, honey?"

"Okay, I guess. Are you coming to see me?"

"I need your help, babe."

"My help? I can't even go outside without permission. They watch me all the time."

"Carlotta calls you, right? Calls the desk, anyway."

"Why?"

"Paolina, do you trust me?"

Her voice got so quiet, he had to strain to hear her. "You came and got us in Miami."

"You know I'll always come and get you, the same way Carlotta will always come?"

"I didn't ask her to. I didn't—"

"You didn't want what happened to happen. I know that and Carlotta knows that. Nobody has that power, Paolina, to make things happen the way they want them to happen. But you do have one power right now that I need."

"What?

"When Carlotta phones, take the call. Put her on the list of acceptable visitors. Tell her you need to see her now. As soon as she can get there."

"I . . . Mooney, I can't . . . I don't . . ."

"You won't have to see her if you don't want to, but I need to talk to her. I have to see her, and you're the only one who can bring her to me. You know I'd never hurt her, right? I'd never hurt you?"

"I don't know."

"Please."

"I'll think about it."

"Set it up. And when she calls, tell her to come."

"Can I tell her about you?"

"Paolina, I can't make you do what you don't want to do. But if you mention me, she might not come. And that would be bad."

"I'll think about it, Mooney."

"I'll come see you anyway. Soon."

"Where are you?"

He glanced at the low buildings and windswept trees. "I'm near the ocean, honey. On the Cape."

"It's too cold for the beach."

"How about I bring you some seashells?"

"Bring them soon."

Mooney hung up. If Roz wasn't so maddening, he might have tried her again, but she wouldn't tell him where Carlotta was even if she knew.

The civilian receptionist was talking on the telephone so Mooney pointed to his chest, then pointed down the hall to let her know he was expected in the chief's office. At the bulletin board, he paused reflexively to take note of the wanted posters. The yellow sheet he'd picked up last night at Mitch Farmer's house was affixed nearby, its VOTE YES! headline partially obscured by a salmon-colored VOTE NO! The Citizens for Good Cape Government handout had a more professional look than the Indian flyer. Mooney untacked the negative broadside, folded it, and stuck it in a pocket to study later.

"Your car still there?" Thurlow asked. "Good. I hate it when crooks boost cars from the cop lot."

Mooney settled into a chair. "That old Indian guy, Farmer, the one who said he had something to tell you, he call?"

"I'll go by and visit later, once I check with the Boston ME about his granddaughter." Thurlow opened a file drawer and started rummaging. "Kyle, right?"

"Your Amy sure didn't have much use for Danielle Wilder."

"Yeah, but don't go looking at her for the killing; she has a great alibi."

Sleeping with the chief, Mooney assumed from the wink. "People at Farmer's house last night, most of them Indians?"

"Hard to tell, huh?" Thurlow seemed amused.

"Lay off about the feathers, okay?"

"Remember those seven federal criteria I was talking about? For being a tribe? One of them goes something like this: All those on the current tribal roll must have documented their descent from people identified as Nausett Indians by the Commonwealth of Massachusetts back in the 1800s when the Nausett nation was administered as a tribe. Okay? Well, you can imagine, there are problems."

"With the documentation part?"

"Hell, yeah. See, lots of folks intermarried with the Indians back then, but they weren't proud of it. Changed their names, so people wouldn't guess, so the kids wouldn't be called half-breeds. Wasn't real fashionable to be an Indian then. Not like now when they got claimants coming out of the woodwork because everybody knows how much money the Connecticut Pequod are raking in. But the government's got it figured. You have to be one-sixteenth Nausett to qualify."

Mooney shook his head. "Sounds like octoroons down in New Orleans."

"Worse. I don't even know a name for one-sixteenths. And I don't see anybody named Kyle in these files."

"Me neither," Mooney said. "But I never got to read anything from the feds."

"That makes two of us," said Thurlow.

"I wonder if the DA feels like sharing."

"Doubt it."

"Still . . ." Mooney let the word hang there.

"Haven't I paid off that favor yet? Let's go through these one more time before you get me in more hot water. And then we'll ask Rosemary."

"The receptionist?"

"Hell of a gossip. Usually, I try not to encourage her."

They were almost three-quarters of the way through Nausett's accumulated paper on the Wilder case when the phone rang. Thurlow picked up and his head snapped back. He said yes and no, hung up, blurted, "Hang on to your hat."

Heavy footsteps pounded down the hallway, followed by a knock on a door that opened before Thurlow had finished saying, "Come in."

Today's suit was gray, not blue, but Mooney recognized the first man anyway; he'd been at Mitchell Farmer's house, supposedly paying his respects to the bereaved Indian. He was closely followed by Dailey, the red-faced special agent from Boston, and Thurlow's big office seemed suddenly too small.

"Can I help you?" Thurlow said. "My receptionist—"

"We asked her not to bother you."

"That's her job, bothering me. You Boston or Washington?" Thurlow, bristling, wanted them to know he knew who they were, men dressed like that, shoulder holsters bulging their left armpits.

The man in gray said, "Washington. Agent Farrell. Indian Affairs." Farrell not only displayed credentials, he doled out business cards as well.

Dailey didn't have the chance to introduce himself, because Thurlow stood and said, "Let's go to the conference room. That way you can sit down."

"We don't mind standing." The beefy Dailey shifted his feet to a wider stance. He looked like an offensive lineman gone to seed.

"I mind," Thurlow said. "Hurts my neck looking up."

To help the police chief seize control, Mooney stood, too. He eased out the door and hung a right, figuring the others would follow, figuring the conference room would have to be farther down the corridor. It was two doors down and looked like it did double duty as a lunchroom. A small refrigerator hummed in the back left corner.

The four men stood, one to each side of the rectangular table, and finished the introductions. Thurlow asked whether anyone wanted coffee. No one did, but the dynamics of the situation had changed. The visitors subsided into squeaky metal folding chairs. Thurlow and Mooney did likewise and the tension eased slightly.

"Now, what can I do for you gentlemen?" Thurlow asked.

"We're a little curious about BPD's involvement."

The Indian Affairs man had a voice as bland as his accent. A cookie-cutter of a man, he seemed to have no oddities. If he turned to crime, Mooney thought, he'd be a shoo-in; no one would be able to identify him.

Dailey said, "What he means is what the hell do you think you're playing at?"

Thurlow said, "I thought Washington was running this, not Boston."

Dailey said, "I asked him a question." Meaning Mooney.

Mooney ignored the Boston fed, focused instead on Gray Suit. "How's this? I'll tell, if you'll tell. What's BIA's interest in Wilder?"

"You don't owe him any fucking explanation."

If Dailey hadn't protested, the BIA man might not have told. Dislike of Dailey registered in Gray Suit's eyes, and his voice grew even blander. "Hearings are currently under way in the District concerning the legitimacy of the Nausett tribe. A Miss Julie Farmer requested a meeting. And since she said she was a close friend of Danielle Wilder's, we intended to listen to what she had to say."

"Why is that?" Thurlow said.

"You don't know?"

"Too many secrets around here."

"Danielle Wilder was scheduled to testify before a Senate committee."

"State senate?" Thurlow sounded surprised.

"U.S. Senate. Washington. Concerning the influence

of organized crime in Indian affairs. Originally, Miss Wilder was scheduled to appear as a witness for the tribe, to assure the senators that there was no mob influence in the Nausett nation."

"Originally." Mooney caught the man's emphasis and tossed it back.

"Miss Wilder had changed her position. Mid-December she said she could produce evidence that certain mobsters were working to gain control of the tribe. Real evidence. Possibly tape recordings."

"Shit," Mooney said under his breath.

"What?"

"Nothing."

"What happened to Wilder makes it difficult for us to accept that the Farmer girl was in the wrong place at the wrong time." The Indian Affairs man looked straight at Mooney. "I assume Boston Homicide must have a hot lead, sending in somebody of your stature."

"A hit and run is a wrongful death," Mooney said.

"Yeah, well, your boss seems to think you went AWOL," Dailey said. "He wants you back in harness. Now, as in today. And we don't want you mucking around in our case."

"That doesn't include me, does it?" Thurlow said. "Mucking around? Our case? Seems to me both these girls were Nausett girls, my girls, and now you're telling me they were both killed by organized crime? Both by this Gianelli bastard?"

"Second one can't be Gianelli," Dailey said.

"Why not?"

"Ask your pal." He turned his eyes on Mooney and lowered his voice. "Some of the guys don't believe you tipped Gianelli off, say it isn't your style, but I think you're just the sort to pull a play like that."

Mooney clamped his jaw.

"And once I prove it, you can kiss the job good-bye. Pension, too. The BPD will take the hit on this, and it's time. The bureau's taken a lot of crap about keeping mobsters out of jail. This time we're going to put one in."

Mooney decided not to ask whether any mobster would do.

Thurlow said, "Look, we just got a possible lead on one of Wilder's former boyfriends, name of Kyle?"

Farrell, the Indian Affairs man, turned on Dailey. "For chrissakes, you mean nobody at the Boston office has told them? If you guys didn't try to play it so close to the vest, this kind of thing wouldn't happen."

Thurlow said, "Yeah, why not tell me? You got the goods on Gianelli? CW? Or what?"

Farrell folded his arms across his chest, and a look that might have been faint satisfaction flitted across his inexpressive face. "I don't think we'll have to rely on any confidential witnesses. Not when we've got DNA."

"Well, okay, that's pretty final." Thurlow nodded. "Wish I'd known so I could spread the word around, calm folks down when they start ranting about how the killer's still out on the streets. That's pretty final, all right. All they had in the Worthington case was DNA and that guy sure got nailed. Jury convicted first-degree."

DNA. Dammit all to hell. Mooney, who'd been listening with increasing dismay, swore inwardly and thoroughly.

He'd been right, but he'd been wrong, too. Danielle Wilder's death hadn't struck the right note as a sex crime. So much for his vaunted street smarts and investigative skills: Turns out it wasn't a sex crime. He had tried to eliminate Gianelli as a suspect and he had discovered the man's true motive instead. Gianelli must have been trying to move in on the tribe, trying to find a way to use them as a gateway to get the mob "legitimately" involved in Massachusetts's casino gambling future. Wilder, clever girl, had found out. Wilder had threatened to expose him.

There was solid DNA evidence. He might as well go home.

What would he tell Carlotta?

PART FIVE

CHAPTER 30

I had already lifted my hand to knock when I noticed the small button to the right of the door. The high-roller suite sported a doorbell and why not at the going price? I sucked in a deep breath and pressed my index finger to the glowing disk.

The woman who answered the bell looked every bit as expensive as the high-ceilinged room and the sweep of deep pile carpeting. She wore a clingy silk sheath in an icy blue that matched her eyes, and for a moment I thought of Katharine, Big Tony Gianelli's latest wife, Jonno's mother. This woman, just as formidably well-groomed, was younger.

"Solange," I said.

Her wide eyes did a careful survey of the hallway. The penthouse suite was on a key-only floor. She had every right to demand how I'd gotten access, but instead she regarded me with calculating eyes in which I thought I saw a glimmer of recognition.

"But don't I know you?"

When I gave my name, she nodded gravely, and opened the door wide. The vast living room, by far the most sumptuous rental accommodation I'd ever set eyes on, was ivory and gold, with furniture in the style of some former king of France, all swirly and gilded. Plump pink cushions dotted overstuffed gold sofas that contrasted nicely with heavy rose velour drapes. A fur throw rug decorated the marble floor in front of the gas fireplace. Classical music played, a light air, piano and orchestra.

I won't lie; I'd thought about faking it, offering a phony business card with a new name, wearing a wig. But I'd seen Solange once before. Her face was burned into my memory and I'd thought it possible that she would remember me as well.

Sam travels to Las Vegas fairly often. I'd accompanied him twice, once more than I should have. I'm a slow learner when it comes to men.

The first time I was nineteen and it was easy to forget exactly what kind of business meeting his business trip fronted. There were plenty of other conventioneers, guys from United Fruit and amalgamated arms, and I sold myself on the story that there were worse things in the world than some quaint old-country protection racket. The first time, I gawked my way along the Strip, amazed that so many grown-up kids wanted to see gaudy replicas of real places. The Venetian only gave me the itch to see the real Venice, minus costumed actors steering phony gondolas.

I got bored as hell during the day. The nights were fine; we had tickets to any and every show around, but, tell the truth, the town's attraction eluded me. Too many lights and mirrors. It seemed garish and cheap, a smooth gigolo with no soul.

The next time I went back, I was a grown-up. I stuck too close to Sam and saw things I wished I hadn't.

There was this woman, a pseudo-Frenchwoman named Solange, probably Susan at home, who looked at Sam with ice-blue eyes that altered when I entered the room. When she wasn't aware of me, Solange regarded Sam with a proprietary gaze that told me volumes about what he did when my cop work kept me home. When I brought it up, he said he wouldn't be questioned, wouldn't be treated like one of my suspects. I got angry, left off being a suspicious cop, became judge and jury instead. We broke up, not for the last time.

If "something happened in Las Vegas," I had decided Solange might know about it. I was grateful for her unusual name.

I was able to describe her; I doubt there was a woman I could have described better. She was drop-dead gorgeous. Tall, the way Las Vegas showgirls are tall, with long tawny hair. I thought she was a pro, a demi at least, a showgirl who rented out for the occasional evening or two with a top-of-the-line clientele.

I thought I could find her quickly. I did.

She worked the Bellagio and she was very little the worse for wear. I thought her eyes were harder now, but my own aren't baby soft anymore, so who am I to talk?

"You are not here to make trouble?" she said coolly.

"Not for you."

Her mouth smiled but her eyes stayed wary. "I have not a lot of time."

"Mr. Strathmore never leaves the gaming tables till one."

She pivoted on a pair of the highest heels imaginable, glided over to a wall of fancy stereo equipment, pondered a variety of dials before choosing one and lowering the volume of the music so that it faded into the background. When she turned to face me, her features were expressionless. "What is it you want?"

"Sam was here in December?"

"You should ask him. You are going to marry him. So you can ask him." Her face was curiously immobile, but her eyes seemed to mock me.

"Can I buy you a drink?" I asked.

"I cannot leave the room."

"That shouldn't be a problem. They have room service, right?"

She considered the gold wristwatch on her slim left arm before deciding. "White wine and do not put it on Strathmore's tab. He will check."

"I wouldn't dream of it."

She floated across the carpet, and sank onto the largest of the sofas in front of a cluttered glass coffee table. The clutter consisted mainly of bottles, nail varnish in several different shades, polish remover, clear plastic containers of orange sticks, files, and cotton balls. Until Strathmore returned to the roost, it looked like the agenda had been doing the nails while listening to music.

I located an ornate phone on a gilded table. A leather folder nearby looked like a menu.

"And you wish to talk about Sam?" She had slipped her shoes off and was scrutinizing her toenails. The polish looked good to me, but she soaked a cotton ball in acetone and started removing it.

I nodded, then said yes, out loud. She wasn't looking at me.

"Make it champagne then, please."

"Will I get my money's worth?" Her intonation was still vaguely French, but not so much as I recalled. I wondered if her accent had faded or if she only made the full effort with men.

"Oh, you'll get what you want."

I ordered a bottle of overpriced bubbly, hung up, and shoved a chair close enough that I could study her eyes. When she glanced at me, I said, "I don't want you to tell me what I want to hear."

"Bullshit. Everybody wants to hear that."

"I'd prefer the truth."

She gave a silvery practiced laugh. "And which truth is that, *cherie*? I have stories for all occasions."

"I don't have time to play games."

"Oh? And what kind of game do you play, coming here? Is Sam with you? Maybe you're getting married in the Elvis chapel? Maybe you want me to be a bridesmaid?"

A wineglass with a lipsticked rim sat on a low table by the stereo. She'd already had a drink or two, which was a good thing, I decided.

"Which color are you going to use?" I said, holding up a vibrant crimson, then a soft pink.

"I don't know. Why don't you choose for me?"

"What does Strathmore like?"

"I haven't known him long enough to say."

We went back and forth like that, whiling away the time until the champagne arrived. I didn't want any waiter interrupting. His arrival didn't take long. When the penthouse suite wants champagne, the penthouse suite gets it right away.

I can't say that the waiter was surprised to find two women in the room. He was a fiftyish Latino with eyes that made me think he hadn't been surprised since he was five years old. He did the whole routine, displaying the label, popping the cork, catching the fizzy liquid expertly in crystal.

I paid cash, added a healthy tip, and saw the man out the door. By the time I got back to my seat, Solange was pouring herself a second glass.

"Please, turn the music up a little," she said.

It took me a moment to find the volume adjustment. The piano was firmly in charge, playing a progression of quick, trilling notes that ran lightly up and down the scale. Solange had closed her eyes to listen more closely.

"You like this piece?" I asked.

"I love it. I adore it. I used to play Chopin quite well. Does that surprise you?"

"No."

"Bullshit. Of course it does. You think you know me because you have an idea of who women are who sleep with men for money. I was once a student at a conservatory. Very promising, they all said. You don't know me."

"I never said I did."

"Look, why don't you pack up and go home? I won't tell him you came here. Trust me, you don't want to ask questions; you don't want to know. Men come here, they do what they do, and they leave it here. It's time out, playtime, free play, whatever. It's got nothing to do with you, nothing to do with what your life will be. There's this place and then there's the wife at home and the children and the parent-teacher groups and painting the house, yes? It's like Tina Turner says, you know? 'What's love got to do with it?' Love's got nothing to do with what goes on here. It's like a business."

"Yeah," I said, "it's like a business." I fanned ten fifties out on the coffee table.

The money made her eyes grow warier.

"Solange," I said, "I don't know you. You could be a concert pianist with a worldwide reputation. But you don't know me either. Okay? We don't need to know each other." I tapped my index finger on the spread of bills.

"Why—?"

"You don't want to know why."

"What is it you want?"

"Christmastime," I said. "From December nineteenth to the twenty-fifth. Was Sam here? With you?"

She hunted around the room until she found her bag, a small clutch made of deep blue leather. Her calendar was leather-covered, too, and slim. She guarded it so I couldn't see the pages and I wondered whether she kept it in some sort of code.

She looked at me with speculation in her eyes. "*Cherie*, if you were about to divorce the man, I could understand. But you are not married to him yet. You will not collect one dime on this, no matter what I say."

"But you will. If you answer."

"He was here. With me. Yes, he was here, and then he came back, right at the beginning of March, just— what, not a month ago—yes. He asked me about December, too."

"Your glass is empty." I poured her more wine and asked about other dates. Then we talked about classical music. She told me how she hadn't been quite good enough, how she felt sick to her stomach before she performed. It took time, but I didn't want to be direct; I thought she might lie if she sensed I valued her information too much. Slowly, I led her back to the night of December 20. The night Danielle Wilder was killed. She seemed very sure of the date, of the fact that Sam had definitely been in Vegas.

"Which hotel? Here? The Bellagio?"

"He moves around. Most guys like one place, but he likes to move. Always a nice room, but never the top of the line. Keeps it toned down, not showy. I don't mind. Some men are just dazzle and no guts. You ought to marry him. Someone should."

"Would you?"

"I don't know. Maybe."

"In December? Where did he stay?"

"At Caesar's, I think. When I close my eyes, I see a lot of marble." She'd seen three-quarters of a bottle of champagne. "Yes, Caesar's Palace."

"And then, in March, you said he asked you about the December trip?"

"Just to see whether anybody had questioned me about it."

"Had they?"

"No. But he said, if they did, I should say I remembered nothing. I shouldn't talk about it. That's what he said: Don't get involved. As though he would have to tell me that. I go on a limb for no one. He was very sweet. He didn't want me to get in any trouble. He said I might want to disappear if anyone started asking. He gave me money."

"If who started asking?"

"I assumed a man. Should I be frightened of you?"

"No."

"*Cherie*, you don't think he's fooling around with another man? Sam? So what are you after here? I may be a little drunk, but I'm not dumb."

If she was drunk, I've never seen a woman handle it better. There was nothing sloppy about her; she just downed the golden liquid like it was ginger ale and never missed a brushstroke on the nail varnish.

"Did Sam tell you who might be asking?"

"I'm certainly not dumb enough to name any names."

"Did he give you a hint?"

"You don't name names around here."

I circled around and went at it again and again. I don't think she knew who Sam was worried about. If she had, she'd have spilled it, just to get rid of me. She didn't want me in the room when Strathmore came back, that's for sure.

I gave up on her at a quarter to one.

Hours later, after visiting Caesar's, New York New York, the Mirage, the Venetian—practically every hotel and every hotel detective on the Strip—exhausted and stinking of cigarettes, I got ready for bed.

I could still hear the echo of Solange's voice: *"You ought to marry him."*

Marry a man who'd proposed marriage to me at the beginning of March, then flown to Las Vegas to spend a few days and nights with a tawny-haired showgirl.

I was hearing her accented voice for maybe the twentieth time when my cell rang. The impulse to ignore it died as soon as I doublechecked the unfamiliar number.

CHAPTER 31

Gravel crunched as I turned onto the winding road, and I welcomed the noise, willing it to keep me awake. Stay with the crunch, I ordered myself, flicking a strand of hair off my nose. Stay away from the silent grass, the lurking ditch.

Paolina's summons had grabbed me and shoved me on board eight hours before the flight I'd considered my earliest possible return; after her call, I'd have rented a private jet if I'd had the money. I've never been good at relaxing in metal cylinders, so I hadn't slept on the plane.

The collegiate buildings rolled by, red brick, yellow brick, old and older still. I negotiated the abrupt turn into the parking lot and rolled the rental to a stop. I used the rearview mirror to determine that the shadows under my tired eyes were seriously dark, decided it couldn't be helped.

As I fumbled with the unfamiliar door handle, I heard the snick of another door opening. Mooney emerged from the nearby Buick and I blinked, wondering how I could have missed the vehicle's presence.

"Bring the handcuffs?" I made it light, but I scanned the area for undercover units as I spoke.

He folded his arms and gave me a look. "Where in hell have you been?"

"I can't talk now. Later. Paolina called and—"

"Paolina will wait. She's still not sure she'll see you."

My turn to stare at him.

He said, "Yeah, I got her to call you. Actually I told her to leave word at the desk that she wanted you to come, but she couldn't sleep and—Anyhow, she found an unattended phone."

"Excuse me? You used a sick kid to—"

"I'm trying to keep you out of a cell. Fat lot of good you'll do her in jail."

"You didn't tell her—"

"I didn't. And I didn't bring backup either." He raised his hands in a gesture of surrender.

"I tried to talk to you, Moon. Weeks ago."

"And I should have listened, but I didn't. Let's get out of the cold, okay? I had my reasons."

He was right about the cold. The wind tore at my thin jacket.

I said, "Paolina first."

"Talk first."

"No way."

"You're stubborn as a goat."

"Mule."

I got to see my little sister only by Mooney's good graces, with Mooney present, for less than half an hour, and while she barely spoke, Paolina looked better. Her hair was shinier, her eyes more expressive, her gestures less restricted, looser, as though something deep inside her had relaxed for the first time since her kidnapping ordeal began.

The best thing, the terrific thing, was that she played me a tune on the pipes I'd sent her, a tune she remembered from Colombia. Her fingering faltered on the seven slender reeds, but her pitch was true, and I found the accomplishment miraculous for a girl whose instrument is percussion. When I asked whether I could bring my guitar sometime, try to play along, she didn't say no. She didn't say anything, but she didn't say no.

Moon stayed with her while I spoke with her doctor, and I'll admit I was jealous. She seemed to prefer him to me, after all we'd been through. Part of me realized that was the problem: all we'd been through. I knew another component of the problem as well: Paolina was looking for a man to replace her lost father. Knowing didn't make the ugly green monster pack up and fly away.

Aaron Eisner met with me in his perfect room. I wondered whether the glossy plants were the same ones I'd admired last time or whether they'd been replaced by some service that whisked in lush substitutes in the middle of the night while the cleaning staff polished the spotless windows.

"How is she?"

"We're trying to help her identify and manage her anger."

"Without cutting herself."

"She is not cutting herself here."

She wouldn't have access to a blade, so I wasn't sure he should take much credit for that.

"How do you do it? Identify and manage anger?"

"Mainly through talking therapy."

I had been yanking my hair and unaware of it. My hand froze in midair.

"We try to encourage her not to swallow the anger. So it won't fester and come back to her years from now. Or never go away. Things were done to her—"

"Physical things. In Colombia?"

"I can't break her confidence. I'm sorry."

He didn't sound sorry.

"Paolina told me you've taken the initial steps to become her legal guardian. Is that true?"

"Yes."

"It might be better if it were done sooner rather than later."

"Is her mother—?" I was glad when Eisner interrupted, because I didn't know how to finish the sentence. Disruptive? Crazy?

"Her mother wants her released immediately."

"Can you stall her?"

"I would have to state unequivocally that Paolina is a danger to herself or others."

"And that would do what?"

"She's a juvenile, but she's old enough to be in the shady region. The records might alter her chance of returning to a public school environment. Safety issues are—"

"For Christ's sake, she's not going to shoot up some high school cafeteria."

He said nothing and I realized that there wasn't much he could say.

"What does Paolina want?" I said. "Is she happy here? Is she okay?"

"She feels safe here," he said.

"She played me a song on the pipes." I don't know why I said it. It forced its way out of my mouth. If I hadn't said it, I think I'd have started to cry.

"Did she?" Eisner said. "That's a very positive sign."

Mooney was waiting when I got out and he started right in on me, flinging the same questions he'd opened with before, as though I owed him answers.

"Where in hell have you been?"

"Las Vegas."

"Sudden urge to play the slots? Hey, are you okay?"

I must have nodded, but I don't think I did it very convincingly.

"Come on, let's get outa here."

The next thing I knew I was seated in a cafeteria-like place, a lunchroom in another building on the McLean grounds, and there was a steaming mug of coffee near my right hand. I picked it up, took a tentative sip, and said, "December twentieth, the night that woman died—"

Mooney, across the table, cradling a mug of his own, said, "Let's give her a name. Danielle Wilder."

"Major OC figures from all across the country met in Las Vegas. Sam was there."

"Sure he was. You're not the only one who's been traveling, Carlotta. I went down to Nausett. Gianelli had a damn good reason to kill Danielle Wilder."

"What? He wanted to marry me, but he was afraid I'd refuse him because Danielle could prove he wasn't a virgin?"

"Keep your voice down. That's not what—"

"He's a psycho sex killer? You think I wouldn't have noticed? Okay, what?" I could tell he had news, and not good news, either. I drank coffee while he outlined his stay in Nausett. I heard about Thurlow, the police chief, and Julie Farmer's bereaved grandfather. He mentioned the warring forces for and against Proposition Six and possible casino gambling. A woman named Amy had identified a man named Kyle as a possible suspect, a post-Gianelli boyfriend. It all sounded promising until he got to the Bureau of Indian Affairs, to Danielle Wilder's intent to testify about organized crime involvement in the Nausett tribe.

"So there's your reason," he said. "She gets pissed at Gianelli, decides to change her tune. Maybe because of you, because Sam's going to marry you and not her."

I shook my head impatiently. "Didn't you hear me? He was in Vegas."

"I suppose you have proof?"

"An eyewitness." My opinion of Solange's impact on a jury must have shown on my face.

Mooney raised an eyebrow. "Really?"

I let out my breath in a sigh. "But I doubt she'd testify. And it gets worse: Every record with his name on it is gone. The guest register's been altered; Caesar's Palace says he canceled at the last minute, and none of the other hotels have him booked." I hadn't been able to check airline passenger lists, but Sam rarely used his real name when he flew anyway.

Mooney was shaking his head. "Carlotta, let me get this over with. There's DNA."

At first I thought I'd heard him wrong. "Who says?"

"The feds say."

"What do they have? Semen? Hair? Where did they run the tests?"

"Is it just me or does it sound like you're snatching at straws? It's DNA, Carlyle."

"Which, you would agree, is as good as the lab tech who runs it."

"Jesus. What will it take?"

"Sam didn't kill that woman."

Mooney said, "Listen to yourself. You're saying the DNA is wrong?"

"I'm saying it could be. Or the feds could have stage-managed it."

"The feds fixed the DNA? Was that before or after they killed Kennedy?"

"It was while they were letting Whitey Bulger run free." I reached across the narrow table, tilted Mooney's chin so I could see his eyes. "Look at me. Do you think I ran over that girl, Julie Farmer, with Gianelli's car?"

"No."

"Why?"

"Jesus, Carlotta. I know you."

"And I know Sam." I was uncomfortably aware of the thin ice I was skating across. I felt like one of those moms they interview in newspapers, the kind who says what a good boy her Joey was, before he shot up the school.

"Maybe you have a blind spot there," Moon said.

"Sex? You think I'm blinded by sexual attraction?"

"It happens."

"You going to turn me in?"

"I ought to, for your own good, for your own safety."

A doctor with a short white jacket and a stethoscope hanging around his neck sat at the edge of our table and smiled apologetically. For the first time I realized that the other tables were crowded with medical staff, visitors, patients. My eyelids felt like they'd stick together if I blinked.

"Don't you have work?" I asked Mooney wearily.

"Don't worry about it. I went AWOL."

"You what?" I goggled at him. Mooney and the force are inseparable, two sides of a coin.

He shrugged. "Work's not life, Carlotta. Someday, you know, someday down the line, I'm gonna pull the pin, retire or burn out, and the BPD's gonna march on without me."

I took a long look at him, reliable as air, round Irish face, straight brown hair slanting almost to his eyes, blue button-down Oxford cloth shirt, gray gabardine suit pants. And I thought: He's changed. Lifting my coffee cup, avoiding his eyes, I remembered the first day I'd met him, the no-nonsense leader of the team, how I'd been attracted by the warmth of those brown eyes, determined not to look into them too deeply, not to react to any glint of admiration or shared amusement. I wasn't going to mess up at work. Mooney had been my boss—an attractive man, but my boss—and I'd drawn a line.

"The job's not the same," he said. "The technology,

the forensics. Department's doing this thing with gun-shot echoes, setting up these noise detectors: A gun goes off, we're on it. Computers. Everything's computers. And the killings are different, too. When you go to the scene and there's two twelve-year-olds down and a thirteen-year-old kneeling in the blood, and he says he didn't see a thing." Mooney's voice ran down and I thought he could have been me, years ago, explaining why I had to leave the job.

"So you're AWOL," I said. "And I'm on the lam."

"In the wind," he said. "On the lam—that's old mob talk."

"In the wind," I echoed.

"So what's our next move?"

Our move, I thought. I liked it: *Our* move.

Sleep, my eyes said, but really I wasn't so tired as I'd been on the drive. Seeing Paolina had worked on me like a tonic. The caffeine was starting to kick in, too.

"We need to go back to the beginning," I said.

"Where is the beginning? I thought I'd find it in Nausett, but—"

"The beginning is Jessie Franklin."

"Julie Farmer," Mooney corrected. "Who came to you with a cock-and-bull story about getting married to Barbie's Ken."

"Ken," I repeated. "Julie, Jessie. Ken, Kyle."

"Huh?"

"What did this guy in Nausett look like? This Kyle?"

"Never saw him. The witness described him. Handsome. Six feet, blond, in his twenties."

"Julie. Jessie. Same initial, right? So maybe's it not Barbie's Ken, maybe Julie wanted me to follow Danielle's Kyle."

"I see where you're going. Maybe."

"So why don't we go nab my file, see what Roz has got—"

"Carlotta, I wouldn't go to your place if I were you."

"What?"

Moon smiled. "The Macs aren't bright, but they're not stupid either."

CHAPTER 32

While Moon tried to goose the Buick's heater, I returned my rental near a busy suburban Holiday Inn. Together, driving toward Cambridge, we fell easily into the banter of the patrol car days, when no matter how wretched the assignment, the camaraderie kept us going, kept me sane. Some days we'd driven this very Buick. I knew its quirks: why the passenger door didn't open, why Mooney had never gotten it fixed.

Maybe it was exhaustion, maybe the situation, but the sudden appearance of the Boston skyline seemed almost surreal from Arlington Heights on Route 2. The bright sky hurt my eyes. Traffic lights seemed to send mysterious blinking signals. Cops were hunting me, lurking outside my house, and here I was, sitting next to a cop, the sun glinting off his dark glasses. I envisioned bold-faced *Herald* headlines: PI WANTED IN HIT AND RUN.

In spite of stop-and-go traffic, we were sharing a back booth at Mary Chung's before Roz, the spy I'd phoned en route, came in from the cold, wearing an outfit Mata Hari might have envied, carrying my guitar case.

"You loose?" Mooney said severely as she approached.

"None of your fucking business."

"He's not talking about your morals," I said.

"Is anyone following you?" This time he spoke the way a father might talk to a slow two-year-old.

"I know what you mean, copper. If they were, you'd be in deep shit, huh?"

Roz and Moon don't mix well. They can't get by appearances. She assumes he's as conventional as white toast. He buys her outward bizarreness as interior confusion.

She said, "First of all, they're not interested in me; they're waiting for Carlyle. Second, I didn't bring a suitcase, which might have looked suspicious; I brought a guitar case."

I'd told her to do that on the phone, so she shouldn't have taken credit.

"Third, I walked into Harvard Square, freezing my ass, so I could see they weren't behind me. Nobody even got out of the car. It's too cold to walk, in case you haven't noticed. I'm dying, by the way. My fucking toes will have to be amputated."

"Tea?" I said.

"Then I took the train to Kendall instead of Central, and cabbed back. Believe me, there is nobody on my tail."

She plunked the guitar case on the floor and shoved into the booth next to me. I poured tea from the metal pot, dribbling it on the tabletop.

"Don't worry," she told me, "I packed it just the way you said."

I'd asked her to pad the guitar, layer it with the T-shirts and underwear I'd need to prolong my exile. I hated taking my Gibson out in this weather, but I wanted it nearby, in case Paolina let me visit again. Maybe, I thought wearily, I could bunk at McLean.

"I didn't want to fuck up again," Roz said earnestly. "I know it's my fault you're in this mess."

"What?" Mooney said.

Roz glared at me. "You didn't tell him?"

I poured tea into a second thin round cup.

Roz addressed Mooney across the table. "Look, the client snowed me. Old Jessie/Julie whatever, she says, 'Oh, I really want to see her, I really need to see her, how can you slip me in to see her?' And I fell for it, like a sucker from the sticks. I told Carlotta she was a friend of mine."

"So that's why—," Mooney began.

"Friend of a friend," I said firmly.

Roz said, "Don't try to make it better. Then I didn't check her out because she seemed so harmless, so totally genuine. I screwed up once, but I'm not going to screw up again."

"Roz," I said, "quit beating yourself over the head. I didn't check her out, either. She was that good, Mooney. If she walked in here right now, and I wish to hell she could, I'd probably believe her all over again."

A cheerful waitress took my order for suan la chow show. Mooney, a coward about super-spicy food, went with pan-fried Peking ravioli. Roz ordered ma paw tou fu and I could see Moon suppress a shudder at the thought of wriggling tofu.

Roz had brought the case file. I wiped up the spilled tea with a wad of napkins before spreading the paper on the tabletop.

"Okay. Before I knew Jessie Franklin was Julie Farmer, when I was trying to find out who she was, I decided the best bet would be to track down the guy she'd hired me to follow."

"But that was a made-up story," Mooney said. "The wedding and all that."

"She went out of her way to hire me. She paid me. Story or no, she wanted 'Ken' tailed. The question is why."

Mooney nodded. "What kind of car?"

"Volvo. Silver, with a stolen plate. Roz and I split up the workload."

Roz gave a delicate snort to indicate that she'd been given the bulk of the scut work. I ignored her and started reading her notes. As soon as I finished with a page, I passed it to Mooney, a distant but familiar ritual. I'm the faster reader.

While I'd interviewed the genuine Jessica Franklin and visited the Nausett police, Roz had tackled the tall building in Kendall Square where "Ken" and his oddly shaped tote bag had spent some twenty-two minutes. Twenty-eight different businesses, ranging from mail-order novelty sales to financial management companies occupied the building. The two top floors were real estate management; the next two, a giant scientific equipment firm. The smaller the outfit, the lower the floor.

I passed the list to Moon. He ran his finger down the column of names while I read Roz's accompanying report.

She'd decided to be an insurance investigator, dressing conservatively to suit the role, which meant serious cover-up of flamboyant tattoos. Her patter: A man had been injured falling over a mop and pail in a hallway.

"Sometimes, when I got bored, I said he fell over a ladder." She was reading over my shoulder, offering running commentary.

She had varied the floor number of the incident, depending on the suite she was currently investigating. First, she had asked whether anybody in the office had noticed the offending mop and pail or ladder.

"Some people swore they did. They must have been even more bored than I was."

Whether she got a positive or a negative, she had hauled out her pictures. She'd drawn three, each with the same basic bone structure displayed in the photo of the musician that Jessie/Julie had given me.

Had anyone seen this guy? Did anyone know his name?

Mooney and I swapped pages. The food came, the suan la chow show so strong it made my nose run.

I rummaged for tissues, said, "What did you say if anybody asked why you wanted the guy's name?"

"I told them he might have witnessed the accident with the bucket. I didn't want anybody to think he was in any kind of trouble."

"Good."

Nobody had identified the man, but two of the outfits had struck her as hinky. She had starred them on the list. One was a political consulting firm, the other a start-up software shop. She pegged the software guys as a porno ring in disguise.

"You write a decent report," Mooney said grudgingly.

Roz fluttered her eyelashes and giggled. Always appropriate.

Mooney's cell phone plays a jazz riff. He looked uncomfortable when it sounded, like he'd meant to tune it to buzz and forgotten.

"Yeah," he said into the mouthpiece. "Just a minute."

He got up and moved into the corner of the room by the coatrack.

"Bad reception," I said to Roz.

"Lack of trust. Where you gonna stay?"

It was way too cold to sleep on the streets. "Maybe the Y."

"The Y? Like they don't have cops checking there all night?"

"Gloria can find me someplace—"

"Gloria? As in Gloria who's being watched because they found Gianelli's Jag in her garage?"

When Moon came back, there was a light in his eye. He scooted into the booth and spoke to Roz.

"You checked the car the guy was driving. 'Ken'?"

"Couldn't get past the stolen plates. Off a Mercury. Mercury owner was an old goat who'd lost the car years ago, didn't know the plates were still on the road."

Moon turned to me. "Wilder's missing Volvo is silver."

It was another link between "Ken" and Kyle. I liked it, but I didn't think it accounted for the glint in Moon's eye.

"Look, Roz," he said hurriedly, "can you get on the Web or the phone or whatever, find out about a Senate hearing in D.C.? The subject is organized crime and Indian tribes. See if the names of witnesses are published in the minutes."

"My senator owes me," Roz said smoothly.

I raised an eyebrow. Far as I know, Roz supports total anarchy.

Again, Mooney told Roz what a great job she'd done on the files. I realized he was trying to get rid of her. I'm not sure she did.

"What's up?" I asked as soon as Roz had cleared out.

"Thurlow, the cop from Nausett I was telling you about, called. Remember I said he took me to see Julie Farmer's grandfather, the tribal high muckymuck? The old guy who was so upset."

"Yeah, well, I ran over his granddaughter. Why not be upset?"

"He wanted to speak to Thurlow privately."

"About?"

"We don't know; he had a heart attack this afternoon. Minor one, if anything happens to a guy that old can be minor. His daughter called Thurlow, wants him to come by the hospital. Thurlow thought I might want to be there, too."

"The feds all but rode you out of town on a rail."

"They aren't invited. We won't stay long."

"We?"

"You go home, you've got trouble."

"Moon, I'm running on empty. Not food. Sleep."

"You'll sleep on the way down." He stood expectantly and when I'd put on my jacket and hefted the guitar, he took my other hand and tucked it around the bicep of his right arm.

CHAPTER 33

I positioned the Gibson carefully on the floor of the Buick's backseat and said, "Moon, I don't know. I'm pretty exhausted."

"Just keep me company," he replied easily. "You sleep. I'll drive."

"Can we even get there before the end of visiting hours?"

"You think I can't badge my way into a hospital? With the local police on my team? And you can't go home. Or register in a hotel under your own name or—"

"Moon," I said, "let me put it this way: I don't want to corrupt you—"

"Be my guest. Corrupt away."

"What I mean is, I don't want you losing your job because of—"

"Go to sleep," he said.

I couldn't sleep, not at first. I closed my eyes, but the Buick's engine whined and I couldn't find a comfortable spot in the passenger seat no matter how I tilted it. I replayed Mooney's tale of the time he'd spent in Nausett like it was an old movie on late-night TV, kept coming back to the DNA evidence. If I could talk to Sam, he might be able to clear things up. Maybe Eddie Nardo knew where he was, how to find him.

I didn't want to think about Sam or Las Vegas. Sam

had asked me to marry him, then gone straight to Solange. It didn't bear thinking about.

I woke when Mooney touched my shoulder.

"Christ," I said, "I hope I didn't snore."

He smiled suggestively.

"What's that supposed to mean?"

"Just all the times the guys on the team assumed you were sleeping with me, I'd say sure, you fell asleep sometimes in the unit."

"You didn't righteously deny it?"

"I kept hoping it would happen."

"You didn't do anything to make it happen."

"Damn straight. Harassment charges staring me in the face."

"And after?"

"After you quit? I felt like all I did was bring up bad memories. You'd gotten too close, like a sister or something."

"Hey, bro."

"I don't feel that way now."

The car's whiny engine was still. Outside the passenger window, two gulls fought over an unsavory morsel in an empty parking slot. I could barely see a sliver of gray ocean to the southeast. There had been moments in this car, I remembered, when we'd looked at each other and the heat had risen till I'd been surprised the windows hadn't fogged. But nothing had come of it.

He'd been the boss. I wasn't about to offer myself up to the sneers of coworkers and I wasn't about to quit my job. That was part of it, but had I resented his steady march upward through the ranks?

"Hey, I know," Mooney said, "you're engaged. I shouldn't run my mouth. I shouldn't—"

"Are we in Falmouth or Hyannis?" I said, interrupting because I didn't want him to apologize. Christ, he didn't need to apologize.

"Hyannis gets the emergencies." He got out and turned away, facing the ocean, shoving his hands deep in the pockets of his pants. I clambered across the console and we walked toward the swinging glass doors, his shoes kicking gravel, mine silent.

Inside the hospital, we didn't need to show any badges. The two of us strolled unchallenged to a central bank of elevators, the cranberry-jacketed desk attendant recognizing and accepting us as people who knew where they were headed. Signs on the walls cautioned us not to talk about our patients in public spaces. Moon hit the button for the fifth floor. The elevator smelled like a hospital elevator, pungent with disinfectant.

The doors opened and I recognized the officer pacing the hallway as the man who'd failed to identify my photo of "Ken."

"Big trouble," he said as he hurried over. "Mitch just went into some kind of shock. They hauled him into the operating room. Catch the elevator door and let's beat it down to three."

"They won't let us in the OR," I said.

"She's a friend," Mooney said. "She used to be on the force."

"We've met." Thurlow's voice was cool. "I think I might have asked if you knew her?"

"I don't think you did."

Thurlow shifted his dark eyes between the two of us. "Whatever. Looks like I brought you down here on a goose chase, so that makes us even. Damn, but I wish I knew the old man's daughter better. Julie's mom."

Moon said, "You think she knows what the old man wanted to tell you?"

"Alma won't talk to me. She's pretty near hysterical, lost her daughter, maybe gonna lose her father, too."

"Is she on three?" I asked.

He nodded. "You want to take a run at her, be my guest."

Mooney said, "Has she talked to the feds? BPD?"

"My guess is no."

The elevator door opened on an overlit corridor. Thurlow nodded us to the right-hand branch of the hallway.

"Waiting room," he said.

I said, "What does she know about Julie's death?"

"Hit and run. Nothing more than that."

Shaded lamps in the waiting room made a circular pattern on blue gray carpeting and the lighting felt restful after the fluorescent glare of the hallway. The furniture looked like it had been donated by an elderly recluse with a passion for floral upholstery and overstuffed pillows. I didn't have to ask who Mitch Farmer's daughter was, because there was only one pretender to the throne. Even if there had been ten other women in the room, I wouldn't have had to ask. If Roz had taken her drawing of Julie and aged it twenty years, that would have been the mother.

Her dark head was bowed and her lips moved as though she were praying. An elegant white-haired man held both her hands in his. If his clothing had been less expensive, I'd have pegged him for a clergyman.

Mooney murmured, "Brad Hastings, tribe's lawyer."

When the woman heard our footsteps, she glanced up like a startled gazelle. "How is—?"

"We can't tell you anything about Mitch," Thurlow said. "I'm sure they're doing everything they can. Brad, you heard?"

The white-haired man said, "Terrible. I got here as soon as I could."

Thurlow introduced us. He gave Alma a last name, Montero, for which I was grateful. She looked like she needed every shred of dignity she might be offered. Her dark skirt had gray smudges on one side, as though she had leaned against a dirty wall. A trail of crumbs was caught in the wool of her off-white sweater. Her eyes looked wild and I wondered whether she'd been drinking before this latest crisis broke over her head, or since. When Thurlow said Mooney was with the Boston police, the lawyer's gray eyes narrowed.

"Julie," Alma Montero whispered.

Thurlow said, "We'd like to ask you some questions."

"Now?" The lawyer's single word was a sober protest.

Thurlow stared at his shoes, rebuked. "We know it's not the best time."

"Alma, honey," the lawyer said gently, "if you don't feel up to this right now, and I can't see how you would, you tell them. They know it's not a good time."

"Good time?" The dark woman got jerkily to her feet, like a puppet whose strings had been yanked. "What does it matter, Bradley, good time, bad time? The question is, what good will it do? What earthly good?"

"Now, Alma—"

"Did any of you see her? *Did you see my baby?*"

Outside the window, gulls shrilled and called.

I took a step forward. "Yes. I did."

She raked me with those wild eyes and my throat tightened.

"I helped the police identify her. I saw her before she died—and after."

"You're a doctor? Did she suffer, did she say anything, did she know—?"

"Mrs. Montero, what I mean is she came to me for help. Before she died."

Her penetrating gaze narrowed. "Then why didn't you help her? If she came for help? Why?"

It took an effort to meet those accusing eyes. "If Julie had been honest with me, I might have been able to help her, but she wasn't. She didn't trust me, but I don't know why. I thought you might be able to help me find out."

"It's my fault." Her voice wavered and broke. She repeated herself once, then again. Then she couldn't stop saying it. "It's my fault."

Thurlow made a noise. "Now, Alma, I'm sure——"

She turned on him, regret changing to fury in a flash. "What the hell do you know about anything? Have you ever borne a child? Nursed a child? Raised a child?"

"Calm down now, Alma. Just calm yourself. Maybe you shouldn't deal with this right now." The elderly lawyer tried to catch hold of her hands again, but she wasn't having any.

The more Thurlow and Hastings told her to calm down, the more distraught she got. I thought it was likely she'd smack Thurlow's face. When she turned on Mooney, demanding to know whether he had children, whether he'd "borne them, nursed them, raised them," he, at least, recognized the futility of rational response, raising both hands in surrender and shaking his head.

And I heard myself say, as if from a long distance away, "I had a child, Mrs. Montero. I gave birth to a child and I lost her." I barely recognized the distant voice as my own. It sounded like I was speaking from the far end of a long tunnel, my voice as hoarse as the call of one of the screeching gulls. My neck and back ached from sleeping in the cramped car, from trying to sleep on the plane. "Mrs. Montero, please——"

"I'll talk to her," Alma Montero whispered through tears. "Just to her. You men, you go away. You get the hell away."

CHAPTER 34

"You okay?"

It seemed like days had passed instead of hours. Mooney and I were pulling out of the hospital parking lot in the inky darkness. The air felt damp and fog swirled under the streetlamps. Even the gulls were quiet.

I nodded.

"And that's it? That's all she knew?"

"You heard what I told Thurlow," I said.

"I thought you might have held something back. The lawyer being there, and—"

"No." I twisted in the passenger seat and stared out the blank window. Alma hadn't been observant enough to help us catch the killer of her child.

She'd heard them talking, her only child and her father, who were "thick as those thieves you hear about," united in their love of all things having to do with the Nausett nation. Alma, a woman who had grown up wanting only a "normal American life" like the lives she saw on TV, who had married a "regular American guy," who avoided anything remotely Native American, had felt completely excluded.

I'd edged her back to the comment she had made, that it was "all her fault."

"It's my fault because I'm the one made Julie live with him," she'd told me. "She didn't want to, but he was getting so feeble, so old. He couldn't stay in the house alone, so I told her it was her duty. I convinced her, and then she got so involved in all that tribal business, and I thought that's okay then, my father will forgive me, for Julie's sake. She already had his last name. I gave her that, did that for my father, slighted my own husband, when she was born, but it wasn't enough for him. He wanted her and I let him have her. It's my fault because I didn't want to take care of my father, not after the way he treated me. I should have, but I couldn't. I couldn't live there, like a child again, like a failure of a woman. And if Julie hadn't gotten so involved with the tribe and that—"

A woman in a white coat had peeked into the waiting room and interrupted. There was no news about Mr. Farmer, but if we'd like some coffee, there was a cafeteria on Level One. I'd shooed her away and tried my hardest to restart Mrs. Montero's monologue.

"Your daughter was upset about something having to do with the tribe?"

"I don't know, I don't know. It was about that girl who got killed, Danielle Wilder. Something Danielle had told Julie or given to Julie."

"You heard your daughter and your father talking about this?"

"Yes. Talking. Arguing."

"Was this before or after Danielle's death?"

"After. After, and my Julie said she needed to do something, and my father begged her to wait until after the election. He said if people knew, the proposition would never pass, and there would be no way to save the tribe."

"And what was it?" I'd said gently. "The something she had to do?"

"I don't know. I didn't hear. But Julie was so determined. To do it."

"Was it going to the police?"

"She never said police. I would have remembered police."

"The FBI? Did you ask her? Later on?"

"You don't understand."

I'd waited while she walked to the window, tilted the blinds, and stared out at the parking lot. "What don't I understand?"

She hadn't looked at me, just peered through the tilted blinds. I hadn't said anything. Either she would go on talking or she would stare out the window forever, or at least until a doctor came in and gave her news about her father, one way or the other, favorable or unfavorable, life or death. Minutes had passed. I'd listened for the gulls, but couldn't hear them. Maybe they'd been flying out over the dark ocean. Maybe, I'd thought, I'd still be here when they shrilled out a harsh greeting to the dawn.

"I was drunk." Alma Montero had spoken so softly, I'd held my breath to hear her better. "I'm a drunk. I drink and then I forget. I forget and then it comes back to me in a haze, so I don't even know now if I really heard it or if it's true. I drink." She'd turned to face me, taken a single step toward me, and sunk on her knees to the floor. "What kind of a mother drinks and lets her daughter die? And now, look what I've done."

"What? You can tell me. It's okay to tell." I kept my voice low and gentle, unthreatening, but still I got no answer. "Did you argue with your father? Did you try to find out what was going on between him and Julie?"

Tears leaked from her eyes and ran down her cheeks. "Yesterday. I went after my dad. I yelled at him and he's so old. I told him he had to tell me why Julie died—and look what's happened, look what's happening, look what's—"

"Calm down. Relax. You didn't mean anything bad to happen. You didn't know this would happen."

She'd nodded faintly.

"Was he at home when he passed out?"

"In Julie's room, in her bedroom. He kept going there, just sitting in her chair, on her bed. I drove him to it. I said such terrible things—"

I'd stayed with her. I'd patted her hands. I'd brought her coffee. But she didn't know. She had no idea why Julie would have come to me under a fake name, pretending to be somebody else, although Alma stressed that her Julie had always been a fine little actress, a girl who starred in all the high school plays, a talented girl who could laugh or cry on request.

Mom wasn't overstating the girl's talent, I'd thought. Even knowing, as I did, that Jessie/Julie's story about her fiancé had been a total lie, I still believed in her basic premise, that it was somehow crucial to the girl that I follow "Ken" on that Friday night, follow him and report back on where he'd gone and whom he'd seen.

A pink-cheeked doctor eventually came by and said Mr. Farmer had suffered a "minor ischemic episode." When Mrs. Montero looked at him blankly, he translated: a stroke. She hung on the word *minor.* He said they would know more in the morning. He seemed hopeful. Yes, she could stay with her father for a while. His vital signs were stable.

Alma had grabbed my hand like a lifeline. In the stifling room, the sound of the old man's breathing was raspy and hard. It took Mooney's help to transfer her grip from my arm to a nurse's arm.

All that, all that, and maybe I had been talking to the wrong person, coaxing the wrong person, and who knew if the right one, Mitch Franklin, would ever be able to recall what his granddaughter had told him before she died? The stroke certainly could have impaired his memory. Dammit, if I hadn't been going on no sleep and coffee fumes, I might have gotten more from Alma, steered the conversation down more productive paths.

"There's a B-and-B on Mass. Ave. between Porter and Alewife," I said to Moon after the speed of the car and the smoothness of the road told me we'd reached Route 6. "Or I could crash at the Marriott in Kendall Square."

"I don't want to drive all the way to Cambridge. What if the old guy can talk in the morning?"

"You can't stay in Nausett. The feds told you to clear out."

I think I fell asleep again, because the next thing I remember we were pulling onto a gravelly lane in the darkness, up a steep incline, and the car was coming to a stop.

"Where—?"

"Am I? Welcome to the country estate of the Mooneys. Believe me, nobody will find us here."

"Where—?"

"Are we? You know Marshfield? The Irish Riviera, tucked in between the Cape and Boston. Welcome to the Mooney family summer shack. And when I say shack, I mean shack. There are some fancy summer places around here, but this isn't one of them."

"Beds?"

"Beds, air mattresses, sleeping bags. I'm hoping for running water and heat, but I haven't been here in years. I think I remember an outdoor shower."

"You'd have to break the icicles off."

"I'm hoping for indoor plumbing, too."

"You have a key?"

"As I recall, on a hook to the left of the door."

"Trusting."

"Nope. Everybody owns a place down here is a cop."

The street was narrow and rutted. In dim yellow light from a distant porch, the shadowy houses looked small and worn. "Then we'll probably get shot as trespassers."

"No, but within half an hour, if the grapevine holds, all my distant relatives will know I brought a woman here in the middle of the night. Smile for the cameras."

"Mooney—"

"C'mon, let's get that guitar out of the cold."

There were two main rooms, one up, one down, connected by a contraption that was more ladder than staircase. The room on the bottom level had a tiny bathroom in a curtained alcove. The top room had a galley kitchen against a narrow wall, a child-sized refrigerator, a two-burner stove.

"I remember when they put in the ladder." Mooney stood under a forty-watt bulb that had sprung to life when he tugged a string. "Before that, you had to go outside, run around the back, and come in again on the second floor. It's on a slope. My uncle Tommy built the bottom level, and then another uncle—Cy, I think—came along and tacked on the second story."

"It's like a doll house," I said.

"Don't tell my uncles that."

We discovered sheets and towels in a cardboard box under a saggy bed. I sorted through the bedclothes while Mooney started the space heater rumbling; it was a gas-fueled metal box with small blue flames visible through the front grille. The room didn't get much warmer. The sheets didn't match.

There were three cans of warm Michelob in the barren fridge. Mooney plugged the unit in and fiddled with dials till it whirred and chugged. The sole item in the cupboard was a bag of stale pretzels.

"Up or down?" Moon asked. "Down will be warmer. Up gets the better bed."

"Down."

The bathroom was the draw.

Of course, once I crawled into bed, once I could sleep, I couldn't get to sleep. The hiss of the space heater and the whirr of the refrigerator combined in an oddly syncopated beat that seemed as loud as a jackhammer. I got out of the narrow cot, wrapped myself in the thin cotton blanket, and checked on the guitar, wondering whether it would ever sound the same after so much time in the cold. I had told Roz to loosen the strings, but old instruments are delicate, temperamental.

Softly, using harmonics and muting the strings, I tuned it. Most of what I play is loud, driving country blues, and I didn't want to wake Mooney, but I didn't want to let go of the guitar either. It felt good in my hands, solid and sure. I started out sitting on a fat sprung armchair covered with a chenille throw and wound up on the wooden floor, huddled near the space heater, just holding Miss Gibson, and moving my fingers over the strings.

I tried to remember the melody Paolina had played on the Andean pipes, but my fingers kept slipping into more familiar patterns. I didn't sing it, but Rory Block's "Lovin' Whiskey" kept running through my head, first the opening riff, then the strong bass line, then the words, one particular line: "If wisdom says to let him go, well it's hell, because you just don't know, what it's like to love a man who's . . ."

Block ends the line with "lovin' whiskey." I used to think of it as "lovin' cocaine," which was what Cal, my ex, did. Loved that stuff more than he loved me, for sure. I thought I'd have to write a whole new line for Sam; "Lovin' other women," didn't scan.

I was thinking about Sam, but it was Mooney who cleared his throat in the darkened room. I hadn't heard his feet on the ladder or seen the door at its head open or close.

"You can play louder if you want," he said. "You look good, sitting there."

"It's dark. You can't see me."

"Yes, I can."

I didn't know what to say to that. Maybe he could, by the glow of the small blue flames.

"You haven't lost Paolina," he said.

"What?"

"What you said to Alma Montero. That you had a child and you lost her."

I played a chord. Then another. The notes drifted away like smoke. "You weren't paying attention, Moon. I didn't give birth to Paolina. I wasn't talking about Paolina."

Alma Montero's confessed drunkenness lay heavy on my shoulders. Maybe it was because I was exhausted by the weight of her guilt in addition to my own. Or maybe it was because it was late at night after

277

a long day, and so dark and quiet. I don't know what made me do it or why, but I found myself telling Mooney what I had never told anyone, not my best friend, not my lover, and it helped somehow that I was holding the guitar. It seemed like I was alone in the dark, telling the story to an old guitar that already knew all the sad stories in the world. The small blue flames flickered.

Here's the secret: When I was fourteen years old I gave birth to a child. I gave up that child for adoption, but I keep her or him in my heart. I never saw that baby, never held that baby, but I grieve the separation both for the child and for myself, the self I once was. I divide my life that way, before and after. I hold it in my heart. I never tell anyone.

"Does Sam know?" Mooney's voice: gentle and far away.

"No."

"The father?"

"As far as my parents were concerned, it was an immaculate conception."

"You never told them?"

"I never told anyone." I shook my head no, but found my mouth moving again. "My high school basketball coach."

"Jesus," Mooney said.

"I never told."

"But you don't play basketball. Sorry. That was a stupid thing to say."

"But true. I don't play anymore. When I went

back—Well, the volleyball team had a woman coach."

"You went back to the same high school?"

"No other choice."

The door at the top of the ladder opened and then closed. I heard it this time, and the refrigerator whirring and the heater hissing.

"You want a beer? Still pretty warm?"

"No."

I heard the snap and sigh of a pull-top.

"I'm glad you told me." Mooney must have been barefoot, because I didn't hear steps, not even the creak of wood, but his voice was close.

"I didn't mean to."

"Did you ever try to find her?"

"I don't know that it's a her. They wouldn't tell me if it was a boy or a girl. They wouldn't let me see her. Him. It was a different time, you know? Then, you had a kid out of wedlock, you were branded. They made all your decisions for you."

"You never tried to find the baby?"

"No."

"You could do it."

"Break up a family? Why would I do that?"

"You don't know, Carlotta. Maybe the baby wants to find you. You could wind up making a family, not breaking it. Anybody would want to know who their mother is."

"I don't know, Moon."

"I'm glad you told me," he repeated.

"I'm sorry. Like I said, I didn't mean to. Don't think you understand me now, okay? Do me that favor." I didn't understand myself, I wanted to tell him. "I'm just tired."

"Cold?"

I nodded.

"If we had a fireplace instead of this damn space heater, we could toss another log on the fire. Scooch over." He took the chenille throw off the armchair, draped it around my shoulders, sat cross-legged next to me on the floor. "Sip of a Michelob? It's not bad for flat stale beer."

"No, thanks."

"Know what I think?" he said. "I think you meant to tell me. I think you wanted to."

"Why? Why would I do that?"

"You want me to know what a terrible, sinful person you are. So I'll pull away from you and feel good about not loving you anymore."

"Really?" The chenille wrap smelled like dust.

"Didn't work. If you want to prove how terrible you are, you'll have to do better than that." He leaned over and kissed me, the kind of long slow kiss that leads to other kisses. Nothing remotely like kissing a sister.

Nothing sisterly about my response.

Maybe I went to bed with Mooney so I could prove to him how unworthy I was. Maybe I did it to pay Sam back for his betrayal. I don't know or care to contemplate the reason, but in the end there was no reason. It seemed inescapable, inevitable, the fitting end to a day that had begun with a rocky airplane flight. Might as well crash and burn, I thought, as I squeezed him close and tasted his long-forbidden mouth. Crash and burn.

Then there was no sound but the harsh intake of breaths, the long slow exhalations. There was darkness and satisfaction and sleep.

CHAPTER 35

I could see my breath. The puff of steamy fog joined the dust motes hanging in a shaft of light from a high window. I could feel Mooney heavy on my left shoulder. When I turned my head, my cheek brushed against a tangle of dark hair. I should have felt terrible and guilty, and I didn't. I felt comfortable and inexplicably happy, as though I had come home after a reckless, way-too-long journey, and that made me wonder what the hell I thought I was doing.

"Don't move," Mooney murmured. "Good morning."

"Jesus, Moon, I'm sorry I—"

"No," he said. "Take it back."

"What?"

"I don't want to hear it. No sorry or guilty or sad songs this morning—not unless you really mean them."

I didn't say anything. I didn't know what to say. After my divorce, after Cal left me, I went through a stretch of bad times and one-night stands. I was careful then, to drive my own car, to carry cab fare, to leave myself an escape hatch. There was nothing careful or planned or safe about what I'd just done. What we'd just done.

"Carlotta Carlyle, listen to me. If we never ever do this again, it will make me very sad, but I will live with it. I'm all grown up. I'm here because I want to be here. I can't think of anyplace else I'd rather be. You are not the sole mover in this. You don't get to be sorry for my supposed ruin."

"Moon—"

"You want me to apologize, I will. I'll take full responsibility. I'll say I'm sorry. I took advantage of you. You were exhausted. I took you here to my frigid little love nest. I got you drunk on champagne and caviar—"

"I'm starving," I said.

"God, so am I."

"There's no food."

"Cans," he said. "There always used to be cans. In a cardboard box somewhere. I hope there's an opener."

"I'll use my teeth."

"Oh, no, don't waste them on the cans." He shifted and squeezed in close in the narrow bed. "Jesus, you know, I'm eight years older than you."

"How do you even know how old I am?"

"I read your file, child."

"Sam's ten years older than me."

"I don't want to talk about Sam."

Neither did I.

"God, you're beautiful."

"Don't say that."

"Why?"

"I'm not," I said. "I know what beautiful is and I don't like lies, so it makes me uncomfortable."

"What's beautiful?"

"If movie actresses and models are beautiful, then—"

"They're not. You're wrong. I'll never lie to you. It's my personal opinion that you are beautiful, and I have a right to it. I have a right to my own opinion. For example, in my personal opinion, it's too damn cold to get out of this bed unless we get some exercise first. That's just my opinion, what's yours?"

His opinion coincided exactly with my preferences. After we'd made love, we lay close together, breathing too quickly, his arm cradling my shoulders.

"Mooney—"

"What?"

"I'm not good at this."

"Oh, yes, you are."

"I don't mean sex; I mean love. I mean happily ever after—all that stuff. When you make a lot of mistakes, you lose faith."

"I don't make those kind of mistakes. I used to but I've changed."

"Hah. What kind of mistakes do you make now?"

"Mistakes of cowardice."

"That's a lie."

"The purest truth. I have wanted to do this since the day I met you, but I was afraid, and even if you're doing this to get even with Sam or to show me what a bad girl you are, or because you were too tired not to, I don't care."

For a moment I wondered whether I could possibly have told him those things, blurted them out loud in a fit of indiscretion. Certainly my tongue had run away with itself last night. But he kept on talking, so I didn't have to ask.

"I just want you to stay with me."

"You deserve someone better."

"It's not that easy to get rid of me, Carlotta, and I don't want to argue with you on an empty stomach, okay? Let's find something to eat instead."

Wrapped in a blanket, feet stuffed into overlarge sweat socks, I joined him in a quest for provisions. Under the same bed that had hidden the box of bed-clothes, we struck gold in the form of tin. Canned spaghetti and meatballs. Spaghetti-O's. Ravioli-O's. The entire Chef Boyardee bonanza.

"What do you like for breakfast?" Moon said. "I don't know what you like, except ice cream and Chinese food that burns your tonsils."

"No ice cream. I've got frostbite."

"I'm not sure anybody filled the oil tank. We could go out."

"I'm not fussy."

"Saying no to breakfast ravioli does not make you fussy, Carlotta. What do you like?"

"Honestly? Eggs."

"I'll get some."

He was dressed and gone almost before I could protest.

I went about getting ready for the day more slowly. If I hadn't, I might have banged my elbow harder in the cramped shower stall. By the time I got out of the shower, the hot water was a memory and it felt like my toes were encased in ice. I dressed by layering just about everything I owned.

Then I shamelessly snooped. Photos of long-ago summers crowded one paneled wall, making me feel like I'd stepped into a family album. I tried to find Mooney as a kid, spotted two possibles, so alike, I couldn't be sure which one was him. I knew so much about my ex-boss and so little. Some of what I knew I'd forgotten and some of it I'd ignored, and now I wanted to know everything.

After a while I climbed the ladder to see whether there was a likely frying pan near the stove. Mooney had left in such a hurry that he hadn't loaded his pockets with the things he'd removed last night. His nail clipper was on a bench near the bed. I unfolded two sheets of paper, one yellow, one salmon colored, and read about why I should and should not support Proposition 6.

Wait a minute.

The frying pan forgotten, I clambered down the ladder, the flyers clenched between my teeth. Where had I put Roz's file? In my bag? In the guitar case for extra padding? I opened the case and there it was, the report on the Cambridge office building. I shuffled papers, ran my hand down the list of firms till I found the political consulting firm she'd marked with an asterisk.

My cell phone had little charge, not much service. "Roz? Can you hear me?"

"Where are you?"

"Why were you suspicious of the Consortium Guidance Consulting Group?"

"What? You want me to call you back? On another line?"

"Just tell me about the consulting group."

"The cops are still hanging around. And Eddie Nardo—"

"It was one of the companies in the Cambridge building."

"Oh, okay. Consortium Guidance Consulting, right. They didn't want to talk politics. You ever meet any political wonks don't want to talk or flirt or show off how clever they are?"

"You sure they're political? 'Consortium Guidance' is pretty vague. They could guide investors or corporations or—"

"Desk man said they did political polling."

"Did they seem like a front?"

"There was work going on. It wasn't a maildrop or anything."

"Any reaction to the pictures?"

"That was the thing. One guy, like, he opened his mouth to say something, but another guy shut him up, overrode what he was going to say with how busy they were and how I'd have to go now. I mean, he could have just been a prick, but I didn't like the vibe."

The vibe. How much could I trust Roz's intuition?

She said, "And I think they knew about the bag."

"The bag?"

"Remember? The tote bag type thing your guy carried? When I described it—I mean, I leaned over the desk and drew it on a piece of scrap paper, and I got this weird silence. You still there?"

"Yeah, yeah. Look, don't go back there, Roz. Don't spook them, but find out about them. Who owns them, exactly what they do, who they work for."

"Okay. And I made some calls about the senate committee. The lobbying is fierce on all sides."

"How many sides are there?"

"More than you'd think. Really, this has nothing to do with whether or not the Nausett are a tribe. Everybody knows they're a tribe. It's about gambling and how many gambling empires there ought to be. So, like, other Indian tribes are not necessarily pro-Indian. It's 'I got mine, Jack, and screw you.'"

"Huh?"

"Think about it. Here I am, a member of the Connecticut Pequot and I am sitting pretty. New Englanders are pouring into my state begging me to take their money, and then all of a sudden, it's not bad enough the Mashpee Wamps are probably gonna open a place in Middleton or New Bedford, but here come the Nausett. How many tribes are gonna split the pot? So it's not anti-gambling types doing the lobbying, it's pro-gambling folks, too. You got your do-gooders, your religious—"

"Keep on it." I had my finger poised to disconnect.

"You don't want to hear about Nardo?"

"What?"

"He's worried about you. He dropped by, wanted to talk, very concerned. Says you should call him."

"Fine. You can reach me on my cell."

"Where are you?"

I hung up. Then I reread the salmon-colored flyer. Citizens for Good Cape Government were concerned that gambling would usher in a host of social ills. Drinking, drug abuse, street fights, gangs. Their logo featured their initials: CGCG.

Did the Consortium Guidance Consulting Group also use initials? CGCG?

If I'd had a car, I'd have sped off to investigate, without breakfast, without explanation. I might have left a note.

The thought of a note on the kitchen table gave me pause. God, I wouldn't leave Mooney a note. How could I even think of it, a note like the notes I'd left men who meant nothing to me? Thanks for a great evening. See you never.

I was having a hard time putting a label on how I felt. Up until last night I'd had one good male friend in my life and now what did I have?

I guess I have always believed that friendship precludes love, that the bond of friendship takes the fizz out of the sizzling messy chemistry of sex. Up until last night, up until this morning, I'd have insisted on it.

CHAPTER 36

I tucked the cab into a slot in front of 843 First Street. It wasn't a cab stand, but it wasn't a tow zone either. No meter, which was fine. I didn't want to attract the attention of a meter maid or a patrol car.

It was almost noon, the high, bright sun contrasting sharply with the chilly temperature. Members of the Consortium Guidance Consulting Group should be hunched over their desks, crunching numbers from last week's polls, inventing questions to trip up potential voters, polling citizens who'd rather be eating lunch than talking on the phone to a stranger.

Worker bees take lunch breaks between noon and one. That's when I would go in. Maybe the gate would be temporarily unguarded. I might have hashed out the plusses and minuses of a variety of approaches with Mooney, if he'd been there, sharing the front seat.

He'd returned triumphant to the Marshfield shack, bearing a dozen eggs, bacon, a half gallon of Tropicana, four grapefruits, a loaf of sliced Italian bread, salt, and two cups of steaming coffee encased in Styrofoam. The toaster was dead, so I grilled bread on the stove while Mooney peeled bacon slices and broke eggs into a cast-iron skillet the size of a wagon wheel.

While he cooked, I explained about the two CGCGs. "Up or over?"

I said "over" just to watch him flip the eggs with a warped spatula.

He caught me looking. "Something wrong with the eggs?"

"No."

"Something wrong with the big picture? You and me doing breakfast together?"

"I don't know, Moon. Maybe it's because you're the same as always, because here we are talking work."

"And you thought once we slept together, I'd treat you differently?"

"Maybe."

"That I'd be a different person? You?"

There was no knife sharp enough to penetrate grapefruit skin. I started peeling a yellow sphere, but Mooney insisted on using a hacksaw. The eggs were excellent.

After getting an encouraging medical update from Thurlow, Mooney felt the need to be at the hospital when Mitch Farmer woke. I was keen to check out the Cambridge consulting group as soon as possible. Mooney thought it a long shot. So we split, Mooney dropping me at the T station in Braintree so I wouldn't have to wait forever at a commuter stop farther south. En route, I connected via cell phone with Leroy, who agreed to bring a cab to South Station, which was terrific because I didn't have the time or the nerve to face down Gloria in Allston. It wasn't so much that I thought there'd be cops watching her building; it's that Gloria has six senses and then some. I was sure my old friend, who could sniff sex in the air from afar, would take one look at me and say, "Girl, what the hell have you been doing?"

I leaned back in the cab, recalling, picturing the night I'd followed "Ken," the pseudo-bridegroom, watched him leave the silver Volvo with the tote bag clutched in his hand. He'd still been carrying it when he came out, but who knew what he might have removed from its interior, what he might have left inside?

I couldn't prove it yet, but I was sure he'd been driving Danielle Wilder's car. I was convinced that "Ken" was the key, that "Ken" was Kyle, connected to Danielle Wilder by Amy's sighting at Radio Shack.

How did he connect to Julie Farmer?

They had eaten dinner at the same table. The waiter claimed he hadn't overheard the conversation, but he branded it unpleasant, argumentative.

"Ken" had to be the key.

The image of a key made me think of a car key. That made me think of Jonno, who'd brought me the box containing Sam's car key, and in turn, I thought about Eddie Nardo. I wondered whether Eddie had heard from Sam, whether he'd dropped by the house to give me a message from Sam. I checked my cell phone, just in case. Sam hadn't called and I was relieved.

Julie Farmer had hired me to follow the man in the Volvo. The case had taken a few odd twists and turns, but now I was back on the initial job. I glanced at my watch and decided it was time. As to an approach, I'd wing it, go with whatever hit me once I saw the setup at CGCG.

The Consortium Guidance Consulting Group was closed.

The door was locked and no one answered my knock. It was a business day, no holiday. The firms next door and down the hall were open. Their respective receptionists had no idea why CGCG's door was still locked.

It took some time to locate the building super, a skinny, surly man wearing cut-fingered gloves and eating a brown bag lunch in the furnace room of an adjoining building. It took some cash to convince him to talk.

"Huh, those guys," he said, with a jerk of his chin and a sniff, once bills had slipped into the pocket of his oversized jeans.

"CGCG. Who are they?"

"They pay the rent." Another sniff. Twitchy, too, probably a cokehead.

"Cash or check?"

"Huh, I'd have to look."

"Why don't you do that?"

There was a four-drawer metal file cabinet in one corner. The super gave me the eye, like he thought I might be planning to steal it. We glared at each other while the furnace clanked. I was getting ready to ask for a refund when he finally rambled over to the corner, yanked the second drawer from the bottom, and thumbed through a manila file folder.

"Check."

"Company check? Personal check?"

"Company."

"Sovereign? Bank of America?"

"Citibank."

Checks can be traced. I'd put Roz on it and maybe Mooney would help. Mooney. Oh, my God, he and I had finally done it. We'd had sex. We were lovers. . . . I almost had to shake myself physically to get back to the sunken room and the clanking furnace and Mr. Big Jeans.

"Do you have an emergency number for Guidance Consulting?"

"What do you mean, emergency?"

"Fire alarm goes off in the middle of the night, sprinkler system comes on, who you gonna call?"

He searched the file, ran a grubby finger down a page, gave me a number with a 508 area code. That's central Massachusetts. It also covers the Cape.

"Why is the company closed today?"

"Huh, you sure? Nobody there?"

"Not answering the door."

"Well, how about that?"

"You know about it?"

"Who says I know anything?" He was almost crowing with secret glee.

"You do, right? Smart guy like you?"

"I just figure they might be closed for good, that's all," he said smugly.

"Why?"

"Huh. Having trouble with the equipment, man says to me yesterday. Shredder on the fritz, cleaning out a ton of paper. Says he's waiting on one of those trucks."

"What did the man look like?"

"Some man. I don't pay him no mind."

"But he's waiting for a truck?"

"You know, like a shredder on wheels. Porta-shredder, yeah." He stepped aside to display six well-filled thirty-gallon trash bags stuffed into an alcove beside the furnace.

"I told 'em I'll burn it for half the price," the super said with a wide grin. "I did some of the bags, but I'm not finished yet. Been real busy."

"Can I see what you've got left?"

We dickered. I explained that I didn't intend to pay for bags he might have collected from some other office, some other building, for all I knew. He rolled his wily eyes and professed himself shocked, shocked, that I'd consider the possibility that he might be planning to deceive me.

I peeked into one bag, then another. There was left-over food as well as paper, but the paper belonged to Consortium Guidance.

We held a second round of negotiations, then the super helped me wedge the Hefty bags into the trunk and backseat of Gloria's Ford. As I drove around the corner, I saw him scurry into the building that housed CGCG, probably rushing to search for a warm body who might make him an offer for information about me.

CHAPTER 37

Mooney found me down by the beach, on a long flat stretch of sand bounded by strategic trash barrels. He cupped his hands and hollered down from the top of the dunes. "Aunt Pat flagged me as I drove in, told me a crazy woman was garbage-barreling down Burke's Beach."

I'd hauled a tarp, a rake, and the trash bags from the Marshfield house. "Aunt Pat?"

"All the ladies on the road are my aunts. It's a neighborhood thing. I feel about five years old here. Having fun?"

"If you can find another rake, I'll let you help."

"What a tempting offer. You lose something?"

"Found it." I jerked my chin to the left.

Mooney followed the gesture, knelt near the place I'd secured a pile of salmon-colored flyers under a hefty stack of stones. "Where'd the trash come from?"

"Consortium Guidance."

The salmon-colored flyers were identical to the one from Mooney's pocket. The headline read STOP PROPOSITION 6!

Mooney said, "I'll be right back."

There is no dainty way to sift through thirty-gallon Hefty bags. Primarily office waste, this stuff wasn't as bad as some I've encountered. No used needles or condoms, but the political consultants ate a lot of

295

pizza, and week-old pepperoni-and-cheese smells none too grand. It was almost enough to make me grateful for the wind that froze my ears. It dissipated the stink.

I had a method: outright garbage to the left, paper and objects of potential interest to the right. The Consortium Guidance Consulting Group read both *The Wall Street Journal* and the *Boston Herald*. They tossed their printer manuals. They did Chinese and sub-shop take-out as well as pizza. Somebody in the office suffered from a bad cold. The wind blew used Kleenex far and wide in spite of my efforts to contain it.

Mooney came over the rise, carrying a broom and a carton of disposable plastic gloves. The gloves would have been in the Buick's glove compartment, standard-issue cop gear.

"This is so romantic," he said, gazing at the trash heaps.

I tried to keep a straight face. "No luck with your old Indian?"

"Good chance he'll recover, but he may never remember what he wanted to tell Thurlow. His daughter's not sure he remembers his granddaughter's dead."

Small mercies, I thought.

"Didn't attract any followers?" That was Moon's way of saying he'd taken note of the cab.

"Didn't go home, didn't go to Gloria's." I hadn't gone to see Paolina either. The omission troubled me while I told Mooney about the abrupt closure of Consortium Guidance, the encounter with the building super.

"You got a phone number?"

"Roz already tried running it. It's a phony."

"Makes it harder to track."

"Did you have to wait long at the hospital?" I figured we might as well have a little conversation while we sorted and shifted the foul mounds.

"Thurlow wanted to chat."

"About?"

"Job stuff."

"You don't want to talk about it." The wind spiraled more Kleenex through the air. We'd probably get arrested for littering.

"You made the Boston papers. That's one thing Thurlow wanted to talk about."

"The other?"

"Dailey, the Boston fed who's after my ass."

"The red-faced guy? He was hanging around Charles River Park. And he stopped me on the road, almost like he wanted me to know he was following me. What's his game?"

"Wants my badge, wants Gianelli in the joint. Bastard's loaded for bear. He wasn't indicted in the Whitey Bulger business, but feeling in the bureau is that he's dirty."

"So he's trying to prove them wrong."

"Mr. Clean. Gonna put away the dirty copper."

"Nobody would believe that about you, Moon."

"Hey, it's true. I told Gianelli about the indictment, didn't I? And I know where you are, but I told Thurlow I didn't."

I stopped raking garbage. "You did not let Wilder's murderer walk."

He met my eyes. "Let's agree to disagree."

"But you're working—"

"I'm working this because you did not run over that girl. I don't even know for sure the hit and run reaches back to Nausett."

"It has to. Julie Farmer links Nausett and Boston. You can't get away from it. She was Danielle Wilder's closest friend. She contacted the BIA—"

"Yeah," Mooney said. "Okay."

We sorted trash awhile. I batted the rake at an aggressively curious seagull and he squawked off down the beach.

Mooney said, "How long have you had the key to Gianelli's car?"

"It was in a purse. In one of the boxes that Jonno brought by when he cleared out Sam's apartment."

"A mob errand boy."

"Jonno's not mob as far as I know. He's family. His mother married Tony G, but I don't know that he's mob. Nardo was angry when Jonno dumped the boxes on me. Like Jonno had overstepped his authority."

"Nardo's a stone killer. If they'd found his DNA in the graveyard with the girl's body—"

I said, "I'd buy it."

"But you still don't believe that Gianelli—"

"No."

The pesky gull started creeping back. When he encroached on the tarp, Mooney took a swing at him this time.

I barely paid attention. I was kneeling in the trash. "Hey, this could be a spreadsheet. Money in, money out." I held it up for Mooney's approval.

"Could be polling numbers," he said.

There was no way to tell. All the numbers were in neat columns. The rest was groups of initials.

"Code?" I said.

"Everybody's got their own shorthand," Mooney said.

"Like you're still officially AWOL with BPD?"

"I'll work it out."

A glint of silver caught my eye. Normally I don't mind getting my hands grimy, since crud washes off, but I was increasingly grateful for Mooney's plastic gloves. The CD was half-hidden by a rotting banana and too close to a dead mouse.

I held the disc aloft. "Keys to the kingdom?"

"Or a bootleg Michael Jackson concert." Mooney picked up a filter filled with damp coffee grounds and tossed it aside.

"You're just jealous 'cause you didn't see it first."

Bag Four was the jackpot, but I didn't realize it at first. There was more paper, a blend of lined notebook stuff and twenty-weight bond, hand-ripped into larger-than-confetti-sized chunks. When I noticed the first matchbook, I swept it into the discard pile. The second one, too, without bothering to read it. When I spotted the third, I noted its similarity to the rest. Then I bent and extracted all of them from the remains of a moldy bag lunch.

"Smoking while in the People's Republic of Cambridge," Moon said. "Great. We'll nail 'em for that."

The matchbook was glossy green with FOX-WOODS printed on the front and a sketch of a castle-like tower outlined in deep brown.

I said, "Jessica Franklin had matches just like this in her purse. Along with a deck of cards."

"Julie Farmer. When did you go through her bag?"

"She spilled it." I remembered her hands, the assured shuffle so at odds with the tearful eyes. "She knew how to handle cards."

"Like a pro? Thurlow told me the Nausett Council arranged to apprentice some of their young people at Connecticut casinos." Mooney peeled off his gloves, stepped downwind, and extracted his cell from his pocket. He punched buttons, waited till someone—I assumed Thurlow—picked up. "Hey, you know if Julie Farmer ever worked over at a casino? Call back on this line? ASAP. Great."

There were eight more matchbooks, but no empty cigarette packs or cigarette stubs. There were broken Bic pens, Styrofoam cups, brown paper bags, more rotten fruit with semi-frozen bugs to keep it company.

When the sun started sinking, we repacked the refuse, flattening and consolidating, since one bag had ripped when we had opened it. The wind made the cleanup a tricky, messy job.

"Some date, huh?" Mooney said as we trudged back to the house. He carried the bag of stinking prizes over his shoulder: the mutilated paper, the disc, the matchbooks.

We showered in icy water. The soap, which I hadn't even noticed before, now smelled terrific. We ate more eggs.

Often I found myself darting glances at Moon when he wasn't looking, gratified to find that his neck was exactly as I remembered it under the blue shirt collar, his hands strong, the fingernails short and blunt-cut. The confines of the house forced us together. Brushing against each other, even in passing, felt electric.

After we'd eaten, I suggested jigsaw puzzles.

"Sounds like a hot second date."

We separated scraps of paper, lined and unlined. I'm good at jigsaws. Paolina and I once put together a Monet water lily, the background blue on deeper blue, fading to purple and gray, the pieces positively minute. This was harder. We might not have been able to reassemble a single page if it hadn't been for a strategic ketchup stain.

The page had the bullet format of a PowerPoint presentation. Someone had scrawled the word *Strategy* across the top margin in pencil. Underneath: *25 CFR 83.7.*

Mooney said, "CFR is Code of Federal Regulations."

A laptop computer would have come in handy. The document, held together with aged Scotch tape from a kitchen junk drawer, read:

- The Petitioner has been identified as an American Indian Entity on a substantially continuous basis since 1900.
  recommend countering this based on 1900–1910 special Indian Schedules of federal census, newspapers, scholarly texts.
- A predominant portion of the petitioning group comprises a distinct community and has existed as a distinct community from historical times to the present.
  recommend countering this based on close Nausett links with Mashpee Wampanoag.
- The Petitioner has maintained political influence or authority over its members as an autonomous entity from historical times to the present.
  recommend countering this based on lack of tribal records from 1870–1872, 1910–1912. Also cite joint 1937 venture with Mashpee Wamps.
- A copy of the group's present governing document including its membership criteria must be submitted.
  reworded document ambiguously to cause further delay.
- The Petitioner's membership consists of individuals who descend from a historical Indian tribe.
  recommend hiring fraudulent signatories?

Mooney gave a low whistle. "It's a list of the federal criteria for recognition of Indian tribes." He had been reading over my shoulder. "Complete with suggestions and instructions on ways to screw the tribe."

Here's the kicker: The letterhead was the firm of Hastings, Muir, 158 Downe Street, Nausett, Massachusetts. The Nausett tribe's own attorney, their strongest advocate.

CHAPTER 38

"Refresh my memory," I said. "Danielle Wilder worked for Hastings how long?"

Traffic was light, and moving briskly. We were encountering more cars now, after crossing the Connecticut border.

Mooney's hands were easy on the steering wheel. "Years. More than three, almost four. She was going to go to law school and they were going to pay her way."

I bit my lip and tugged a strand of hair. Under what pressure? What compulsion?

Moon said, "I met him at Mitch Farmer's, in the upstairs hall, when I was trying to find Julie's room. Which I never did get to search, by the way."

"What was he doing upstairs?"

"Hastings? Cold pills, cough drops. The old man sent him up to—"

"But you said the old man's bedroom was downstairs. You said you looked into the downstairs rooms and—"

"Should have cuffed him then, for lying to me. Damn."

"What?"

"Hastings used the word *consortium*. Really. He was yapping about how the community and the banks, 'a wide consortium of interests,' all supported the Indians."

Some support. "And he came to Falmouth Hospital just to hold Alma's hand," I said slowly.

"You think Julie's grandfather caught on?"

"Or maybe Julie's grandfather knew Hastings was screwing the tribe all along."

We rounded a curve and the matchbook castle was visible, sparkling against the night sky. As we drove closer, it resolved itself into a skyscraper gilded by powerful lights. In TV commercials, Foxwoods rises like a lone sequoia in the middle of nowhere. Now I was surprised to see smaller buildings all around it, not on a strip, but in a cluster. The gaudy brightly lit signs reminded me of Vegas.

Mooney's dark suit looked like he'd spent the day working in it. I won't say he no longer looked like a cop, but by the time I'd finished, he didn't look as much like a cop as he usually did. He'd complained about the hair gel, hadn't said much about leaving his shirt untucked or the heavy gold chain I'd looped around his neck. His shoes, alas, were a giveaway. Nobody wears black laceup shoes but cops.

I was wearing stuff I'd acquired in Vegas, low-cut, tight, and black.

"We could spend the night," Mooney said. "They've got three hotels."

"I like your shack."

"You ever stay here?"

I read between the lines: Had I ever spent the night at Foxwoods with Sam Gianelli? "No." When Sam wanted to gamble, he went to Vegas. My jaw tightened.

Mooney said, "I don't see why I'm pretending. When we get inside, most likely I'm just gonna badge somebody."

"If it comes to that, fine. I just want to be able to go with the moment."

"Play with the rules, you mean."

"Isn't that what they're there for?"

"Christ, I'm glad you don't work for me anymore."

We held hands walking into the casino. I told myself it was part of my cover, but I liked the way it felt. I liked the way I felt, warm as burner-grilled bread in the chilly air. Contented. The feeling had been growing since last night, starting not with the love-making, but before, when I'd broken my vow of silence and told Mooney my secret.

My Catholic father would have looked me sternly in the eye, said, "Confession, girl, it's good for the soul." My mother would have warned me to tread carefully. She never trusted anything, my mother. I don't know if it was the Depression or the fate of European Jewry, but she considered every pleasure a warning that life was about to rip your heart out. I wondered what Paolina's shrink, Aaron Eisner, would say about that.

I felt like I'd stood upright through a force-five hurricane. I didn't have to pretend with Mooney. He knew exactly who I was, that terrified fourteen-year-old, the good cop, the bad cop, the good mother, the bad mother. And he was still here.

"It's coming together," I said. "I can feel it." Moon used to tease me about my "instincts," but often, near the end of a case, I swear I can feel a charge in the air, like static electricity, raising the fine hairs on my arms.

We could have, should have, waited till morning, started at the law firm, started slowly. But it was night and there had been casino matchbooks and playing cards in Jessie/Julie's bag and Thurlow had confirmed it: She had interned at Foxwoods. The casino sat at one end of the equation, with the Consortium Guidance Consulting Group in the middle, and Hastings at the other end.

The walkway to the front door of the tower was edged in sparkling lights. Colored lights overhead focused on the path, turning it into a runway, a catwalk, a place to be, a place to be seen. Music spilled from invisible speakers.

"Now this feels like a date." Mooney squeezed my fingers. "Feels like I won the lottery. I don't need to get lucky tonight. I already got lucky."

Casino designers are paid to pull you in the front

door. Once you're in, they urge you in deeper, with visual delights both obvious and subtle. In the depths, the lighting is soothing, indirect, and flattering. No clocks or windows give a hint as to the time. There is no time in casinos, only noise, chatter and pings and rumbles and rustles overlaid with cheery, upbeat music.

In one large room, roulette wheels shared the floor with green-felted craps tables while variegated lights shaded fabric-draped walls. In another room, the yellow-gold walls were dotted with flaring sconces. Chandeliers flooded a third with artificial sunshine and warmth. The occasional laughter might have been live or canned.

I grabbed Mooney's elbow.

"It's something, huh?" he said.

But I wasn't impressed with the colored lights shifting through the synthetic waterfall or the stained glass or the mile of deep red carpeting that invited suckers to the green-covered gaming tables.

"That bag." I pressed against Mooney's arm, turning him to follow the man in the blazer who carried the same type of bag "Ken" had hefted from the silver Volvo to the Cambridge building and back again, replacing it carefully in the trunk. This wasn't Ken. He was an average-sized man, fifteen years older than the man I'd shadowed through the night. But the bag was the same size and shape and we stayed on him, watching as he used a card key to enter a grilled enclosure at the far end of the vast casino.

"Ken carried one of those tote things."

"That's a courier bag," Mooney said. "Ballistic nylon, locktop. You need a key to open it."

"Money?"

"Money. Time to use the badge now?"

"Let's wait a little."

"You think Kyle's here?"

I shrugged. The man with the tote wore a maroon blazer with a gold logo on the breast pocket. There were other men wearing the same blazer. I thought it was worth a shot.

We passed through hallways lined with slot machines, neon arched and brightly lit. Men and women, the women outnumbering the men, yanked and laughed and swore and gasped, machinelike themselves, intense, focused. One woman, dazed, wiped her sweaty forehead with a white silk scarf, then stared at the makeup stain in disbelief.

It was a vast complex with multiple rooms for slots, table games, keno, and poker. The bingo hall was bigger than a concert hall.

"Bet you won't find him," Moon said.

Betting is an old custom with us.

"Bet I will."

Moon said, "If I win, we stay the night. I choose the hotel."

"And I pay?"

"Hey, they have heat and hot water. Big beds. Big bathtubs. Whirlpool spas."

"And I bet they get lots of check-ins with no luggage, too."

"What's old Ken-Kyle look like again?" Mooney asked.

"Six feet, white, blond, one-ninety. Blue eyes. Nice ass."

"You eat with that mouth?"

"Oh, Mooney, my dad used to say that all the time."

"I don't want to remind you of your dad."

"Do you gamble?"

"All cops play cards."

"Poker takes too much concentration."

"Blackjack, then."

We played small stakes, sat at slot machines. Eleven not-Kyles in maroon jackets strolled by. We had drinks at a narrow bar, moved from beer to Jack Daniel's, won and lost twenty-two dollars and change.

"Are you happy?"

The directness of Mooney's query stopped me cold. Happiness, my mother taught, was the precursor to disaster.

"Yes," I said. "You?"

"Yes. You're not sorry?"

"No." I found that my voice sounded stronger on the negative.

"We're gonna badge," Mooney said. "And I think I want to stay in a suite."

"Oh, yeah? Sit and watch."

Earlier I'd noticed a freckled man in a maroon blazer, fresh-faced and twenty-five. He seemed the closest in age and body type to Kyle. Sometimes people are drawn, like to like, I thought, with what I now recognize as alcohol-inspired clarity.

I put a glaze of hard liquor in my voice and eyes. "Hey, hon, where's Kyle tonight?"

"Kyle?"

"I shouldn't call you hon, not with the badge on your blazer, Roger. Or Rog. Is it Rog? You gotta know Kyle. Kinda looks like you a little? Kyle the cutie, you know? Blond guy, little bit taller than you, year or two older. Last name is something with an *H*." I knew that suddenly, too. Alcohol-inspired clarity again. Julie kept the same initials: Ken Harrison equaled Kyle H.

"Kyle Hudson, Kyle Harris, Kyle Hendricks, I could go on all night, but you just feel free to stop me when I get close."

The man's mouth twitched. "Haber. You want to see him?"

"Uh, actually, no. I just don't want him to see me." I lifted my fingers to my lips and whispered. "With my husband."

"Like that, huh?"

"You a friend of his?"

"Not that good a friend."

"But maybe you could just tell me if he's working?" I was playing with the gold hankie in his breast pocket, touching his tie, invading his space.

"He's up in Stargazer tonight."

The Stargazer Casino was on the twenty-fifth floor of the tower. I chatted with Roger a bit more, about the neat crowd and the great food and which games were best to play stoned and which to play sober. And in between I managed to learn that Kyle's shift would be over at two, in case I could manage to lose my husband for a little while.

Mooney didn't need to badge anybody to find out where the employee lot was. He simply circled the building, located the rear exit closest to the tower lounge, watched employees punch out and head to their cars. It was a fairly big lot. The silver Volvo had a Connecticut plate tonight. It still had a broken taillight.

Instead of sharing a room with a whirlpool, we sat in the Buick and waited.

CHAPTER 39

At 2:38 the man who was not Ken and not engaged to marry a now-dead girl who was not named Jessica Franklin hurried out of the building wearing his camel-hair coat. At 2:40 he entered the Volvo and revved the engine. We followed, well behind, minus headlights. I had previously warned Mooney to keep back, alerting him to Ken's erratic driving style and possible use of tacks.

I would have preferred the driver's seat, but the Buick has tricks of its own, so Mooney stayed behind the wheel.

"He should get that taillight fixed," Moon said.

"Bet he doesn't have the registration."

We took a right, then a left, onto a curvy tree-lined

two-lane country road. Hard going without lights, but Moon's a veteran Boston driver, a pro. I trusted him.

He didn't speak until we hit a straightaway. "At that restaurant, Mamma Vincenza's?"

"Yeah? Did you see him turn? Take the next left."

"I got him. You said they didn't come in together, this guy and your client?"

"Right. According to the waiter, he was already there. She joined him."

"She was running late?"

"My theory: He barely knew her. Maybe he'd met her once or twice with Danielle. Maybe he'd seen her at Foxwoods. She barged in on him, plunked herself down at his table."

Mooney and the Buick were losing ground. "Why?"

I was afraid the Volvo would fade entirely out of sight. "Maybe she wanted him to go to the police with what he knew about Danielle's death, what he knew about the link between Hastings and Consortium Guidance."

The Volvo's damaged lights were barely visible over a rise. Mooney's foot hit the gas and the Buick responded.

"He's getting on the highway," Moon said. "Thank God for that."

"She could have been using me to scare him," I said. "I know it sounds like I'm trying to make excuses, wriggle out of losing him, but I think she told him somebody was on his tail."

"That's why she hired you?"

Julie Farmer would have known my name if Sam had mentioned his ex-girlfriend, the former cop, to Danielle Wilder, if Danielle had mentioned me in turn to her best friend, Julie, maybe complaining that Sam talked too much about his ex. I wondered what Sam had said. *I know an investigator who never gives up, who doesn't know when or how to quit.* I wondered what Danielle had said to Julie. *If anything should happen to me, don't accept it at face value. Hey, maybe you can hire that bulldog ex-cop girlfriend Sam always used to go on about. Pass the headache on to her.*

I said, "Julie lied to me, gave me all that wedding hoopla, printed up her own invitation."

"Which wouldn't have been hard," Moon said, "considering the machine at her grandfather's house, the one that printed up all those flyers."

"But why lie to me?" I said.

"Out of habit?" Moon suggested.

Her mother had called her a good little actress. Not, perhaps, someone who believed honesty was the right policy always. The impersonation could have been triggered by a small thing, like finding the real Jessica Franklin's lost purse at Foxwoods.

The Volvo slowed and Mooney did, too. My right foot was pressed into the floorboards, as though I were operating an imaginary gas pedal.

Moon said, "So she wanted you to throw a scare into him."

"The scare thing was probably a last-minute inspiration, while she was having dinner with him. She wanted to know exactly where he went and who he saw." I was pretty sure she'd wanted it so much, she had broken the Volvo's taillight.

"Why didn't she go to the cops with what she knew?"

"What she suspected. She started to. She contacted the feds, right, Moon?"

"That's what the BIA guy said."

"But then, when she told her grandfather, he begged her to wait till after the election. Alma Montero overheard them arguing. It makes sense, Moon. Let's say the girl gets worried that her grandfather might be involved. He and Hastings are close; the grandfather could be making money off the tribe as well as the lawyer, taking kickbacks. So before she talks to the feds, she decides on an end run. Instead of going to the police, she comes to me. Instead of telling me the truth, she lies, to shield the old man. If I'd followed Ken/Kyle and he'd gone from CGCG to her grandfather's house, she might have decided to drop the whole mess, forget about the feds, let Sam go down for Danielle's death."

Mooney nodded. "She'd have had to weigh it out: her grandfather's disgrace against her best friend's murder."

"Right," I said, amazed that we were tossing around the possibilities, just as we used to when we'd partnered on a case. Amazed that nothing had changed. I checked his profile in the dim reflected light from the instrument panel. Oncoming headlamps glinted off the deep brown iris of his right eye.

Everything had changed.

We followed 95 North, a well-lit major highway, toward Providence, and most of the time we kept the lights on, one more pair of round bright eyes on a well-traveled road. Even this late, traffic hummed, long-haul trucks and passenger cars, campers and tankers. Mooney started talking about taking the Marshfield exit instead of following Kyle all the way to Boston, letting things rest for the night. But near Providence, the Volvo veered off 95 onto 195, the quickest route to the Cape.

"Maybe he's headed to Nausett," I said. "Might be good to see where."

Mooney's lips tightened.

"Let's just see where he goes," I said. "We get an address on him, we can learn a lot more by the time we brace him. Want me to drive? You can pull into the—"

"No."

"Sleepy?"

"No."

I know now I was pushing it, pushing him, and I'm not sure why. Maybe I was trying to stick pins in the balloon of my contentment. Maybe I was wary of being alone with Mooney at the Marshfield house.

I've had trouble with men. I'm independent and proud of it, maybe overly proud of it; I know that. Maybe I choose men I can't stay with because I'm afraid that if I find one I love, one I want to make a life with, one my long-dead mother might approve of, I'll flip, change, turn into the ghostly twin of my devoted, worried, beleaguered mom. Become part of something that might start with sharing, start as partnership, but end in tyranny, like my parents' marriage did. Lose my independence. Lose myself. Live every day with grinding soul-wearing compromise.

Dr. Eisner would have had a field day.

The miles hissed by: place names on green signs, side roads, glistening lights. 195 to 25 to Route 6, but only as far as the second exit.

Mooney spoke for the first time in twenty-five minutes. "You think he made us?"

I shrugged, then realized he couldn't see me. "No."

"What's down 130?"

"Mashpee, I think. Eventually."

With the headlights off and few if any streetlamps to guide us, Moon slowed the Buick to stay on a road bordered by low flat countryside, shrubs and bogs. He sat bolt upright, head jutting forward, eyes searching beyond the windshield.

"Did he turn in?" he asked.

"Yeah, there on the right. It's narrow."

"Carlotta, I don't like this."

"Moon, hang a left. Turn around—"

There was suddenly plenty not to like. As we passed a crossroad, a car pulled out behind us, engine roaring, lights flaring. Skewed sideways, blocking the road in front, the Volvo. No choice but to hit the brakes. Hard.

Moon's door fell open and the beam from a high-intensity flash blinded me. I fumbled for the door handle, remembered too late that the passenger door was stuck. A thud and Mooney grunted. His head fell forward, hit the steering wheel. The horn blared, then stopped as someone shoved Mooney back in the seat. I was still light-blind. I raised my hands to shield my eyes, and then hands closed around my wrists, yanking my arms.

Before the night went dark, I remember thinking I knew those voices, those familiar shadows.

CHAPTER 40

Someone made a sound like a hurt animal. After a two-second lapse, I realized it was me and I was being hauled to my feet, frog-marched down a corridor and into a room with dim and spotty light. Around me, an elongated space echoed, filled with empty shelves and narrow iron cots. Round metal lighting fixtures dangled from high wooden rafters. What was this place? A hangar, a warehouse, a prison?

My inspection of the narrow chamber came to an abrupt halt, my eyes caught by the tableau at the far end. Mooney was tied to a chair by thick rope that looped around his chest and his legs. Eddie Nardo, small and precise, cashmere overcoat draped over his shoulders, was seated nearby in a folding chair. Nardo's tie was patterned, red and gold. His fedora belonged in a black-and-white movie from the forties.

Jonno San Giordino was more casually dressed. No tie on his open-collared shirt. Boots, not shoes. Sap in hand, he loomed over Mooney.

Blood welled and dribbled from Mooney's nose. A dark stain crept down the left side of his neck.

The walls were painted a dull army green. My brain sputtered like a misfiring engine and emitted the words "Camp Edwards." Hurricane Katrina victims had been housed in temporary quarters at Camp Edwards, which, along with the Otis Air National Guard Base, made up the vast Massachusetts Military Reservation. The smell of sweat and cigarettes lingered. Barracks, I thought, iron cots for soldiers, a deserted barracks.

There are constant rumors that Otis will close. Maybe we were there, at Otis not Edwards, in some abandoned corner of the air base. I was missing a chunk of time. I remembered a seamless midnight car trunk, the deep panic of darkness.

Nardo, still seated, jerked his head in my direction. "Maybe you want to tell us why you're so keen to talk to Haber? Your boyfriend doesn't seem to enjoy conversation."

The name Haber threw me, and then I thought *Kyle,* and it came flooding back. I moved my eyes left and right because it hurt less than moving my head. Kyle was nowhere to be seen. Unless he was behind me. Someone was back there, out of sight, gripping both my elbows hard and tight.

They used to test-fire ammunition on the military

reservation. It was so remote, so isolated that no one complained about the noise.

I swallowed the sharp taste of vomit. "He doesn't know."

"Outside."

A breath, then I realized Jonno was speaking to the unseen man behind me. I tried to will my legs to move, but before I could gather myself, the instant the unseen man let go, Jonno lunged, grabbing my hair at the nape. He yanked it, forcing me to my knees.

My hands wouldn't move. Jonno's knee was sharp against my back. Between his fingers and thumb, a silver cigarette lighter. His fingers moved. The flame hissed as he dragged me across the floor, half-shoving me with that knee in my back, moving me closer to Mooney.

"Hey, cop," Jonno said. "You like to watch women burn?"

Mooney said, "Kyle's just the courier."

"Moon—," I said.

"Shut up," Mooney said.

"Go on. Courier between who?" Jonno's voice was less important than the snick of the lighter, the disappearance of the flame. I tried to gather saliva in my mouth, enough to swallow.

"The tribe's lawyer," Moon said. "He's playing both sides, taking the Nausett's money, funneling it to the opposition. Taking money from other tribes, too, so the Nausett are paying their lawyer to work against them."

"Sweet deal, some lawyers have," Nardo said.

My hands were loose; it wasn't my wrists that were tied. It was higher up. I wasn't bound with rope or wire, but I couldn't move.

"Tell me more, cop," Jonno said.

"That's all I—"

The lighter flared again. I felt the flame hit my right ear, the hiss combining with a sharp intake of breath. I clamped my lips, my jaw, and then Mooney was talking, words pouring out, and the flame went away. The searing torment stopped. Sweat beaded my forehead. I tried to slow my breathing, figure out what pinned my useless arms behind me.

"Wilder finds out what's going on," Mooney said. "She arranges a little blackmail on her own, small stuff, but then she starts sleeping with Gianelli— match made in heaven—and one night she tells him her little story. He puts the real heat on Hastings: Give the mob a piece of the tribe or else. I don't know, maybe the Boston mob is putting up the money for the land deal?"

"Don't stop now. You're hot."

"Wilder doesn't like Gianelli horning in. Maybe she got moral, decided to be a friend of the tribe."

Jonno snorted. "That bitch? Hell, no, she wanted to make a splash, get her fucking name in lights. Thought she'd be the star of Washington, wouldn't have to go to law school, work her tail off. She'd go straight to fame-and-fortune-tabloid-heaven, the fucking bitch."

Mooney raised his head, met my eyes for the first time. "Gianelli killed her."

I was wearing a black tank, a transparent black overblouse. The blouse, still buttoned, had been yanked down past my shoulders. It bit into my arms at the elbow.

"No cigar for you, cop," Nardo said. "Not Gianelli. Not this time."

Jonno said, "Would you believe the old goat, Hastings? You wouldn't think he had it in him, would you, but the bitch pushed the old goat too far. Goes to show you. He throttles her right there in the office, and then he calls us, his brand-new partners, to ask for help. Just like now, when Haber calls us to say you guys are looking for him in the fucking casino. Smart play."

"The lawyer called *me*, kid, not *us*. Not you." Nardo's eyes sought mine. As though he were talking not to Jonno, but to me.

"Yeah," Jonno agreed, sounding puzzled.

"When Hastings called the first time, I made a mistake. Jonno, you know you talk too much? See, I asked Jonno to handle it and then we had this big fucking mess."

I couldn't turn my head to see whether Kyle was in the room. I didn't know if there were other men. I couldn't see the far wall of the shadowy space. Nardo had to be carrying. He always did. Jonno probably had a piece. Somebody had Mooney's Glock. Three guns in the room. At least.

Nardo kept talking, his voice even and low. "See, Jonno's got this problem. Jonno's got a hair up his ass about Sam. Has had, ever since the old man bought his mother, cash on the barrelhead."

"Don't mention my mother. Don't say her fucking name."

"I'll think about it. In the meantime, why don't you let go of Sam's woman, Jonno?"

"Why don't you try and make me?"

"I'm an old-fashioned guy. I don't like this bullshit, bringing in women, kids."

"Old-fashioned, Nardo. Yeah, that's what you are." Jonno's grip on my hair tightened.

The fabric of the blouse was strong, cheap stuff, but the buttons were weak, tiny fake mother-of-pearl things. They would break under pressure. I was sure they would break.

Nardo said, "I tell him, take care of Wilder's body, a task a moron could do blindfolded, so what does he do? Does he haul it out, dump it in the ocean? Does he bury it where the sun won't shine? Does he do any kind of reasonable job hiding a corpse nobody's even gonna ask about? I mean a girl like that disappears, who gives a shit? The cops don't even make a report. And Hastings would have told them, yeah, she took a vacation to one of those islands where girls disappear and nobody ever finds them. Or maybe Mexico. Who fucking cares?"

Hastings killed Wilder.
Jonno framed Sam.

The lighter flared near my eyes and I thought: *If my hair catches fire, if my hair catches fire . . .*

I didn't see Nardo's gun until it was in his hand, as smooth a piece of sleight-of-hand as any magician. I thought it was over.

He was pointing the barrel high. He was aiming at Jonno. "Drop the lighter."

When it hit the ground, it barely made a sound.

"You got us in a whole fucking mess, Jonno."

"Which is gonna work out fine for you. What the fuck are you—?"

"Shut up," Nardo said.

"You've been holding back money on Sam, cooking the books, cheating him—"

"Shut up! Cop, listen to me. I want to deal. I'll give you Jonno, understand? You can have him for Danielle Wilder. Sam's out of trouble. He comes back and we go on the way we were."

"Hastings," I said.

"The lawyer's too valuable. He's untouchable, okay? Listen, just think about it like it's the government. You can't touch the big guys, you know? So the little ones take the fall. Jonno's a small fish. You get him for the girl, one for one."

I said, "What about the other girl? Julie Farmer?"

"See? Her, Jonno did kill. To keep her from going to the cops, and to put you in the frame with that key. That one's a slam-dunk. You know how dumb he is? I'll tell you. He gets boxes to pack your stuff from Sam's place; where does he get them from? I tried to take them back. Each and every one, on the bottom, it's got a logo: CGCG. You ever unpack them, fold 'em up to toss away, and bingo. He's an out-of-control dumb-as-shit punk and you, cop, can take him off the street, do us all a fucking favor. Do you go for it? I can kill one of you or two or all three. Doesn't matter to me."

It must have mattered to Jonno.

He shoved me to the floor, but I was diving already. It took him too long to snatch the gun from his coat pocket. He never even got to fire it. Nardo took him in the throat with a bullet and Jonno sat down hard before the next one hit him under his left eye.

I strained against the fabric of the shirt, stretching, reaching, stretching.

"It was him or you, huh, cop?" Nardo's voice stayed relaxed and conversational. "Guess you had to shoot the bastard. But, oops, the both of you musta fired at the same time. It'll play. You know it will."

Mooney didn't speak.

Nardo raised the gun barrel, moved it to the right. I tensed every muscle in my chest and arms, felt black despair descend like a curtain. I knew I couldn't stop the bullet.

The sound was deafening, like a cannon. Nardo's gun arm exploded and he screamed, a high-pitched sound like a child in pain. Nardo's jacket blossomed blood. The red-faced federal agent moved in from the left, shooting round after round, emptying the clip like on a firing range, and I watched Nardo's flesh jerk with the shots. I don't remember moving, but I was next to Mooney, bending over him, fumbling at the thick ropes. The knots resisted.

It seemed like I heard the agent's voice from far away, from underwater.

"Move aside," he said.

"What?"

"Jesus, you make trouble. Move it! Sam told me you wouldn't let it go. Step aside, so I can gun the cop and then we'll fix it up as best we can. We don't got a lot of time here."

My left hand froze on the rope. "You work for Sam."

"Well, hello, sunshine," Dailey said. "Dawn breaks over Marblehead. Yeah, I fucking work for Gianelli. Years I've been working for Gianelli, and he says you should fucking listen for once in your life, do what he says, and get out of the fucking way."

I lowered my eyes to meet Mooney's. They were as dark as stagnant water. Empty.

"I'm sorry," I said.

"She's a cupcake, huh?" Dailey said. "A real sweet one."

It was the last thing he said. His eyes widened when I shot him with Nardo's Beretta. He went down fast. I didn't need the whole clip.

CHAPTER 41

They buried Big Tony Gianelli when the soil under the first layer of mush was still hard with late frost. Some said Katharine's abrupt departure killed him; some said he never noticed she was gone. I didn't make the funeral. I'd had enough of death. I didn't need to hear the old words intoned over the inert body of the old crook.

Forsythia burst into yellow bloom with the ground still snowmelt damp, and suddenly the long Boston winter was over. With it, the Wilder/Farmer case came, if not to the end, to a pause.

Kyle Haber, who had been the third of the bad guys, relegated to guard duty till Dailey smacked him down with a Maglite, sang freely. Old Mitch Farmer talked as well as he could, given the aftermath of the stroke, given his terrible burden of guilt. Not criminal guilt. He had believed Hastings when the man insisted he could explain. He hadn't believed his granddaughter when she said the lawyer was two-timing the tribe.

Brad Hastings, pillar of the community, tried the easy way out, an overdose of Ambien, swallowed with most of a bottle of Jim Beam. Either he didn't take enough or the housekeeper found him too soon.

Truth is such a slippery devil, hard to recognize when he enters the room. Hastings, who denies killing Danielle, has adopted a civic stance. Well, yes, he may have betrayed his clients, but he was morally opposed to gambling, he says. Now.

But it was always about the money. The Nausett tribal leaders were willing to throw money at Hastings to help him grease the K Street wheels. How easy it must have been for Hastings to inflate his demands, tell the tribe he needed more and more money, what with opposition to Proposition 6 strong and growing. He must have started small, building up Consortium Guidance, which Roz traced back though a series of straw men to a dummy holding company fully owned by Hastings. Through Consortium, Hastings started accepting money from other tribes, other gaming empires, who had their own vested interest in keeping gambling out of the Commonwealth.

He had a profitable fiddle going till Danielle Wilder, clever girl, figured it out. And if Wilder hadn't told Sam, it might have stayed small, the mob might have stayed out. And if Wilder hadn't told a dear friend, Julie would still be alive.

Hastings's murder trial is scheduled for the fall.

I still dream about the night at the barracks. I can't untie Mooney. I fumble at the ropes and the sweat pours down my face and trickles down my back and I wake in a tangle of sheets, a knot of panic in my chest, pain searing my ear, until Mooney murmurs something soothing and I know it's okay. I know I have not become one of the monsters I lived with, one of the devils I pursued.

That night, we extinguished the lights, not knowing

who might have heard the shots, who might open fire next. I felt the need to laugh, knew it would come out high and shrill, realized I had clamped my hand over my mouth. Mooney found a small flashlight. By its weak and wavering beam, we searched for a cell phone, rifling the pockets of dead men, violating the rules.

Mooney didn't call 911. He called Thurlow's personal number. Thurlow helped us pick up the pieces. And Eddie Nardo was right.

The little fish got caught. The big ones swam leisurely away. The feds are still trying to decode the evidence I took from Consortium Guidance. Kyle Haber couldn't or wouldn't say who, besides Hastings, was providing the cash to defeat the Nausett tribe's land purchase. Cash is cash, cold and hard to trace, and Haber says he was just a courier, just a guy who muled money from here to there. Sometimes a little muscle, sometimes a guard.

I'm grateful he wasn't a better one. He never heard Dailey coming, never saw what hit him.

Dailey had placed a homing device under the rear bumper of Mooney's Buick. Otherwise I wouldn't be here at McLean, walking the grounds with Paolina and Mooney, exclaiming over a raft of purple crocuses.

We're very careful with each other, keeping our voices low, our eyes wide, experimenting with the idea of it, the idea of the three of us. I don't know if Mooney feels this way, but I feel like I have a new window on the anxiety that led Paolina to cut herself.

I'd been thrown into the trunk of the Buick; Mooney had traveled in the trunk of the Volvo. Both of us knew the taste of that terrifying darkness, a shadow of the velvet horror Paolina had faced in Colombia. It's turned into part of my nightmare. And I was older, and I'd been a cop.

Mooney still was.

You go AWOL, you're in trouble. You walk in with two solved murders, dead mobsters, and a renegade federal agent, you get welcomed back more warmly than you might have been greeted otherwise.

Of course, Dailey had warned Sam to leave town long before Mooney ever got the idea to do the same in order to save me the humiliation and grief of having my lover charged with murder. I'm sure Sam, now firmly the Boston mob's heir apparent, attended his father's funeral. Every federal agent in town must have been there, too, snapping photos of faces shaded by wide-brimmed hats, writing down license plates.

Sam and I have spoken. Twice.

The first time, he told me exactly what "happened in Las Vegas." Solange had skipped one key detail, for all her seeming frankness. I can only imagine she found the discussion of bodily fluids distasteful.

Prior to Sam's December visit, she had gotten a visit from a young man with a strange request. A used condom, one of Gianelli's, would she save one? Sell the young man one? Name her price. Solange had sent him packing; a weirdo, she'd thought, some wacko pervert. But she had mentioned it to Sam, that last time in Vegas. So Sam had suspected that someone was out to get him, to topple the Gianelli empire. He didn't know it was Jonno, his father's wife's son.

The DNA submitted in the Wilder case was Sam's hair, root ball still attached. Jonno hadn't succeeded in Vegas, but he must have broken into Charles River Park, carefully stolen hair from Sam's silver-backed hairbrush. The DNA made the district attorney think long and hard before charging Hastings with murder. The trial attorneys are afraid it will muddy the case so badly that a jury will never convict.

The second time, I saw Sam in person. I needed to do it that way. I'm still not sure why.

I never meet a flight at Logan. You fly in to visit me, you take the T or you take a cab because I know the traffic at Boston's airport. I know the Sumner and the Williams tunnels and I know the Dig, so I don't drive to Logan unless I'm piloting a hack and getting paid by the half mile; it's as simple as that.

This once, I made an exception, parking my rental in the Central Lot, a gazillion miles from Terminal E, where the international arrivals land, striding purposefully over the new tile, noting the public art, the New Englandy lobsters and horseshoe crabs that studded the flooring, listening to New Age music piped in to fill the interminably long corridors. I got to the reception area early, perhaps as penance, and sat in a molded plastic seat that had been molded for someone else's bottom. Public service announcements bombarded me: Do not leave your luggage unattended; do not accept packages from strangers. Twice, I went to the ladies' room and washed my hands.

Sam's eyes had lit when he saw me, but then there was a subtle change, a darkening that made me wonder what he'd heard, what he knew. For a guilty moment, I'd felt like running away, sprinting for the escalator, and disappearing into the night.

"Hey," he'd said. "I wasn't expecting you. There's guys here to pick me up."

I'd stared at the two dark-haired men in suits. "I know."

"Pretty obvious?"

"They look uncomfortable unarmed."

"I'll tell them to get lost."

I'd said, "No. I'm not staying."

"Me, neither. Let's go someplace."

"No," I'd repeated. "That's not what I mean. It's better if we do it here."

"Do what?"

"Say good-bye, Sam."

The two bodyguards had approached tentatively. One had nodded briefly, wordlessly accepting Sam's attaché case. The other had stood, hands loosely at his sides, knees slightly bent, ready in case a fight broke out.

"There's food in Terminal C if you don't want to go far," Sam had sounded puzzled. "There's nothing here in E."

I'd suggested that we take a walk, asked him to

leave the goons behind. While he conferred with them, I'd concentrated on breathing, in and out, on not looking at Sam Gianelli. I confess, he exerted a powerful physical pull as we'd strolled down the corridor toward the duty-free shop.

"So," he'd said, "things went big-time wrong and you got stuck in the middle. You probably think I owe you an apology, but I tried to—"

"No."

"So? You don't like the danger level inherent in being with me? Carlotta, listen, Italy was terrific, better than terrific. Incredible. Sicily. Palermo. You could come with me for a little while, test it out. Bring Paolina, see how she adjusts. She'll love it. You'll see. Spanish and Italian are so close, she won't have any trouble."

"I'm not afraid to be with you, Sam," I'd said slowly, watching my shoes as they met the tiles. "That's not it."

"What?"

"Danielle Wilder."

"I didn't kill her."

"You might as well have killed her, Sam."

"Oh. I see. The jury's in."

A man and a woman rushed down the corridor, late for a flight, holding hands and swinging their arms as they ran. The matching grins on their eager faces caught my eye and held it. I'd run like that once, holding tightly to Sam's hand.

I shook the memory off and said, "You wanted an in

with the Nausett tribe, so you went after the para-legal—"

"Oh, no. Forget that. I did not seduce her and turn her and abandon her. Danielle Wilder was no innocent. She was a gift for the taking. We hit it off in a bar and, believe me, she was out for the main chance. She couldn't tell me about her crooked boss fast enough."

"She deserved what she got?"

"I'm not saying that."

"You use people, Sam."

"Not people I love."

"Are you sure who they are, Sam?"

I turned my head. The man and woman had made it as far as the security line. The man struggled, laughing and wrestling with backpack and jacket, hopping on one foot, then the other, to remove his shoes. The woman slipped hers off quickly.

Sam said, "What's going on here? You said you loved me."

"I do, Sam. I love you, but I don't like you. I don't admire you and I can't live with you. I can't marry you. I won't."

"So good-bye?" he said.

"Yes."

"The good cop wins."

For a moment I'd thought he was talking about Mooney, that Sam knew about Mooney, and while I'd never meant to hide that from him, I hadn't exactly spelled it out yet. I may have been fooling myself, but I'd convinced myself that I'd made the decision to split with Sam before that night in Marshfield, that the night in Marshfield would never have happened otherwise. Then I'd realized that Sam hadn't been talking about Mooney at all. That he'd been talking about me, that I was the good cop. Which meant I was the bad cop, too.

"Don't call me," I said. "Don't call Paolina."

"Carlotta, we can work something out. Come on—"

"No, Sam, we can't work it out. Look what's just happened. You knew you were being framed, but did you talk to me? You kept me in the dark; you told your hired goons to keep me out of it. And, no, I'm not saying it's your fault. Fault has nothing to do with it. It's just who you are, how you were brought up, how you think. Clap the women and the children in the safe house. Do the dirty work; don't talk about it. If there is fault, it's mine. I let myself get blinded by you. I didn't want to hear, so I didn't listen. I didn't want to know. But it won't work for the long run; I'm not that kind of person. I have to love all of you, not just the part you let me in on."

The recorded announcement warned me not to lose sight of my personal belongings, and a distant cash register beeped. I could hear people chatting as they queued to buy candy bars and newspapers before boarding flights to distant places. Sam opened his mouth, but I no longer wanted to hear what he had to say.

"I'm not done," I told him. "Even if you walked out on the mob today, there's too much I've ignored in the

334

past, and I can't forget about it. I won't. And there's Solange, and I can't work that out. We play by different rules, Sam, that's all it is. The game is the same, but the rules are different for me and you, and I'm not going to change and neither are you."

The corridors seemed twice as long and twice as empty after I'd turned and walked away, as though I'd had to march for hours through a twisting labyrinth before making it back to the distant parking garage and the car. Three-quarters of the way there, I'd straightened my shoulders and lifted my head, already starting to feel lighter, as if I'd cast off a weight I'd been carrying for too long.

I never had a ring, so I didn't have to send it back.

I passed a stand of lilac bushes and stopped to inspect the hard, intact buds. There were fat buds on a nearby stand of rhododendrons, too. Aphids on the undersides of evergreens. When I looked for Paolina, I couldn't find her, but after a while, I heard the low murmur of the Andean pipes.

She was sitting under a yew tree, and my impulse was to reprove her for sitting on the damp ground. I let it go. Mooney sat there, too, legs stretched, brown hair tousled, listening and chewing a blade of grass. I joined them, and Paolina played a tune that sounded as old as the earth beneath our feet.

I'm okay, getting through tomorrow, then the day after that, looking forward to Paolina going back to school whenever she's ready, or taking the GED, if she'd rather. Who says we all need to march through life in lockstep, graduating high school at the same time, starting college at the same time? I'm working; I've got a couple of new cases that will keep groceries on the table. Oh, and Proposition 6 passed. The Nausett can buy the land, but they'll have to look for a new lawyer and a legitimate source of funds.

Casino gambling is headed to the land of the Puritans and the Pilgrims.

Me, I'm gambling on Mooney. It feels like a sure thing, but who knows?

Center Point Publishing
600 Brooks Road • PO Box 1
Thorndike ME 04986-0001 USA

(207) 568-3717

US & Canada:
1 800 929-9108
www.centerpointlargeprint.com